"You didn't raise a fool, Caleb DeBoer." Gen smiled.

"I hope not," he said. Gen wasn't raising any fools, either. Today Gen had exhibited just the right balance of concern and calm, and the girls had picked up on it right away. He was impressed.

"Oh, look." Gen pointed. A cinnamon-colored hummingbird darted to one of the columbine flowers and hovered there. "It's the first one I've seen."

"It's a rufous hummingbird," said Caleb. "They're not common this far north."

"Then we're lucky to be able to see them. Oh, look, there's another one. His mate, I'll bet." Delight transformed her face to beautiful.

"I'll bet you're right." Caleb watched the hummingbirds for a moment, but he couldn't help turning to watch Gen instead.

Sunlight picked up the subtle colors in her hair, making the golden strands shimmer. That faint citrus scent he'd noticed the first time he met her mingled with the floral aromas of the garden.

"Beautiful," Gen breathed.

And she turned to look at him...and their eyes locked.

Dear Reader,

People sometimes ask me where my ideas come from, and often the answer is that I haven't a clue. But the seed from this book came from a newspaper article I read a couple of years ago that talked about how peony farming has taken off in Alaska in the past twenty years. Peonies used to be reserved for spring weddings, but peonies bloom much later in Alaska than in warmer parts of the country. Now that Alaskan farmers have begun commercial production, summer brides in North America can carry beautiful peonies in their bouquets, too.

As soon as I read about the peony farms, I knew I wanted to write a story that took place on one, and so I needed a farmer. Caleb is a divorced father and is struggling to stay close to his teenage daughter. And I had a character, Gen from *An Alaska Family Christmas*, Tanner's sister and mother of two energetic girls, who really deserved a happily-ever-after. That was the beginning.

There's a lot more to the story, of course—family secrets, friendship, trust issues, romance, a pair of mischievous rescue kittens, an unexpected encounter with Alaska wildlife and much more. I hope you enjoy Caleb and Gen's story. If you'd like to contact me or find out more about my books, you can visit bethcarpenterbooks.blogspot.com, where you can find links to my email, Facebook, Twitter and Instagram, or sign up for my newsletter. I'd love to hear from you!

Beth Carpenter

HEARTWARMING

An Alaskan Family Found

—

Beth Carpenter

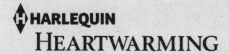

HARLEQUIN®
HEARTWARMING™

Recycling programs
for this product may
not exist in your area.

ISBN-13: 978-1-335-42680-2

An Alaskan Family Found

Harlequin Enterprises ULC
22 Adelaide St. West, 41st Floor
Toronto, Ontario M5H 4E3, Canada
www.Harlequin.com

Printed in U.S.A.

Beth Carpenter is thankful for good books, a good dog, a good man and a dream job creating happily-ever-afters. She and her husband now split their time between Alaska and Arizona, where she occasionally encounters a moose in the yard or a scorpion in the basement. She prefers the moose.

Books by Beth Carpenter

Harlequin Heartwarming

A Northern Lights Novel

The Alaskan Catch
A Gift for Santa
Alaskan Hideaway
An Alaskan Proposal
Sweet Home Alaska
Alaskan Dreams
An Alaskan Family Christmas
An Alaskan Homecoming

Visit the Author Profile page at Harlequin.com.

Dedicated to all the farmers out there who grow the food we eat, the fibers we wear, and the flowers that bring so much beauty and pleasure into our lives.

Special thanks to peony farmer Barbara Henjum for the tour of your wonderful farm and gardens, and for your patient answers to all my questions about growing peonies in Alaska. Also, thanks to Rita Jo at Alaska Perfect Peonies.

And always, I'm grateful to my editor, Kathryn Lye; my agent, Barbara Rosenberg; and the staff at Harlequin for making this book the best it can be.

The peony varieties in this story are fictional. Many are named in honor and memory of some very special women I've known.

CHAPTER ONE

"I'M GETTING MARRIED!"

"Uh, congratulations." Caleb DeBoer shifted his cell phone to his left ear while he reached down to pull a hawkweed springing up at the base of the Peggy's Pink peony crown. He wasn't sure why Christabel Adams, sales and marketing manager for the Susitna Peony Co-operative, would be calling him before eight in the morning to share this news. As newly elected chair of the co-op board, he'd developed a cordial enough professional relationship with Christabel, but they weren't exactly friends.

Thor pushed his head under Caleb's hand, and he scratched behind the dog's floppy ear while he waited to hear more. Maybe this was a segue to a discussion about a professional discount for Christabel's wedding flowers.

"Thanks! We're flying to Vegas this weekend."

"Oh." So that was a *no* on the flowers. Now, in mid-May, the earliest peonies in the lower forty-eight might be starting to bloom, but here on Jade Farm near Willow, Alaska, the leaves were just unfurling from the peony crowns. The first blooms wouldn't be budded until July, well after their more southern relatives were done. That was the co-op's niche, providing peonies for late-summer weddings and other special events. But apparently not for Christabel's nuptials. "Well, best wishes on your marriage."

Thor, spotting movement in among the lilac hedge on the north edge of the field, went to investigate.

"Thanks. But..." She paused, and he got the sense she was about to get into the real reason for her call. "We won't be coming back for a while."

Of course, they would be taking a honeymoon. Someone would need to cover Christabel's responsibilities while she was gone, a duty that traditionally fell to—oh, shoot—the chair of the co-op board. Did Vickie Faramund, his neighbor to the north, know this was coming when she'd insisted she'd held the position long enough and it was Caleb's turn? He wouldn't put it past her.

He stifled a sigh. "I understand. Could you come by this afternoon or tomorrow to show me the system and catch me up on anything pending?" Vickie had trained Christabel on the website and ordering system when they hired her. Caleb was only marginally familiar with how it all ran.

"Sure." Christabel sounded relieved. "Today at two, okay?"

"That will work." It would shoot a hole in the middle of his afternoon, but at least he had the full morning to devote to repotting his basil seedlings and applying the spring dose of fertilizer to his peony fields. He wanted to get the most time-consuming chores out of the way so that he'd have more time next week when he picked up his daughter in Anchorage and brought her to the farm for the summer. Oh, and he needed to remember to pick up a new greenhouse thermostat while he was there.

"Thanks! I'll be sure and spread around our brochures to the wedding venues while I'm there. You know, talk it up. Let everybody know what fantastic flowers we have. Alaska peonies are the best!" He could almost imagine the pom poms waving Christabel's enthusiasm made her ideal for her job marketing their flowers, but she had a tendency to stray off topic.

"How long will you be gone?"

"Well, that's another thing." She cleared her

throat. "Um, Justin's uncle—not the teacher but the one who had the pipe company—he retired and sold his company for like a bazillion dollars. You should see his house on the hillside. It's incredible. Anyway, he just bought a sailing yacht. He's naming it the Scottish Piper, because their name is Scott, and he made his money from pipes. Isn't that cute?"

"Yeah. Cute." What did her fiancé's uncle's boat have to do with anything? Caleb pulled another weed. Sounds of a scuffle drew his attention to the lilac hedge. A mottled snowshoe hare, in the process of turning from winter white to summer brown, darted from between the shrubs across the gravel drive and toward the peony field. Spotting Caleb, the hare changed direction to dash alongside the ditch, which, thanks to last night's rain, was running with water. Thor, five paces behind, tried to cut off the angle by running directly toward the ditch. Caleb covered the phone with his hand and hollered at the dog to stop, but Thor ignored him and plunged through the muddy water, only to lose sight of the hare, who had slipped away between the rows. Great. Now Caleb could add washing the dog to his list of chores. He turned his attention back to the phone call.

"—and then sailing from Hawaii to Alaska,

planning to be back in late August or early September."

September? He'd assumed he would need to cover for a week or so while they had a honeymoon in Vegas. "I—I'm sorry. I didn't get all that. What about sailing from Hawaii?"

Christabel huffed. "I said we're crewing on Justin's uncle's yacht for the summer. I know it's kinda leaving you in the lurch, but this is just too good an opportunity to pass up. Justin loves sailing, so this is like a dream come true for him, you know?"

"Huh." Caleb had nothing against Christabel's fiancé chasing his dreams, but did he have to drag their marketing manager along with him in the middle of their busiest season? "So this is your two-week notice?"

"Oh, uh, well, no. Because we're flying to Vegas in four days, so I can't give you two weeks. And I'm not resigning. I mean, I love this job so I'd like to come back in the fall if I can. I realize you'll have to hire someone else in the meantime, but you know, if you could get somebody to cover like you would for maternity leave or something, that would be great."

"I see." He supposed working remotely was out of the question, as well, since she would be in the middle of the ocean. Besides, she needed to be available to visit the co-op farms. "I'll have to talk with the rest of the board before we make a decision."

"Sure, of course. We can talk more when I see you this afternoon."

"Okay. Thanks for the call, Christabel." Now what? As chair, it was his job to recommend a course of action to the board, which consisted of representatives from the seven peony farms in the co-op. Obviously, they would need someone to take over Christabel's position, but should they hire someone temporary or permanent? On one hand, Christabel had done a good job dealing with customers and keeping up with social media. On the other, she was taking off with only four days' notice. Vickie had worked closely with Christabel. He'd call and get her advice.

But before he could pull up Vickie's number, his phone rang again. According to caller ID, the call was from his daughter's school in Anchorage. Chances were they weren't calling him first thing in the morning to tell him everything was fine. He braced himself and answered. "Caleb DeBoer."

"Hi. This is Gen Rockford. I'm interning with Doreen Holman, your daughter's counselor at Goldenview Middle School."

"Yes, Ms. Rockford. What can I do for you?"

"I was calling to verify that you still plan to attend the meeting today."

"What meeting?"

"The meeting to discuss Fleur's— Oh, wait. I see here that Doreen had set up the meeting with Mallory DeBoer only. I'm sorry. Your name was listed in Fleur's record and—"

"Mallory is my ex-wife, but I'm supposed to be informed about this sort of thing."

"Oh, I apologize, then. I'm sure Doreen didn't deliberately leave you out."

Maybe the counselor hadn't, but he couldn't say the same for Mallory. Or Fleur. "What time is the meeting?"

"It's at ten thirty."

According to his phone, it was eight thirty now, and it was almost a two-hour drive from his farm to the south side of Anchorage. "I'll be there."

"Oh, excellent. I'll call Mallory to verify as well. We've found that in-person parental involvement can make all the difference in a situation like this."

A situation like what? With only five days left in the school year, it wouldn't be about something minor. He almost asked, but if he was going to make that meeting, he needed to get on the road now. "Good. Do that. You'll let me know if she reschedules?"

"Of course. In fact, I'll text to verify the time once I speak to Mallory. Okay?"

"That would be great. Thank you."

"You're welcome, and I'll plan to see you at ten thirty, Mr. DeBoer."

Caleb pocketed his phone and pinched the bridge of his nose, trying to stave off the headache threatening to form. Obviously, Fleur and her mother hadn't been keeping him in the loop. Fleur was in some sort of trouble, but he had no idea if it was behavioral, grades, or what. He could call Mallory, but most likely he'd get her voice mail and anyway he needed to get on the road. No doubt once he arrived at the school, he'd find out exactly what was going on and what the counselor thought they should do about it. And then he'd need to hurry back to meet up with Christabel and figure out how to handle that.

His farm chores would have to wait.

CALEB PULLED INTO the Goldenview parking lot. Thanks to fifteen minutes spent waiting while a moose coaxed her twins across the Parks Highway, he was already two minutes late to the meeting. The counselor or intern or whoever she was had texted as promised to verify the time. He parked and hurried to the front door, where he had to press a button and wait to be buzzed inside.

Once he'd shown his identification and signed in, a student helper escorted him down the hallway to a glass door marked Counseling Office. Behind the door was a waiting room with clusters of chairs outside a row of doors marked with individual counselors' names.

He stepped through the doorway and spotted Mallory flipping through a magazine. As usual, his ex-wife looked unruffled and professional, wearing a tailored beige jacket over a green blouse, with a matching skirt, her hair caught back neatly in a twist. He ran his fingers through his own hair, wishing he'd taken ten minutes to change out of the faded jeans and sweatshirt he'd worn to work in the fields, but then he would have arrived even later. All of this could have been avoided if Fleur had told him about the meeting when they'd talked on the phone yesterday.

Speaking of Fleur, she came shuffling into the waiting room, looking down at the note in her hand. His daughter no doubt thought the thick lines she'd painted around her eyes made her look older and more sophisticated, but in Caleb's opinion, the heavy makeup just transformed her face from beautiful to generic, like one of those yellow emojis on his phone.

When she looked up, she embodied the big-eyed, startled emoji. "Dad?"

"Hi, Fleur."

Mallory looked over. "Oh, Caleb. I didn't see you come in. They're waiting on us. I said I'd let them know when you arrived." She led the way into the office, moving past Fleur to take one of the chairs surrounding a low table near the window as though she knew the drill. Two women, one with gray streaks in her hair and the other younger, talked quietly over some papers at the desk on the far side of the room.

When Caleb passed Fleur she hissed, "What are you doing here?"

"Attending a conference with your counselor, apparently," he whispered back. "Although it would have been nice to know about it before this morning. I barely had time to get here."

Fleur licked her lips. "We, uh—"

"Fleur, is this your father?" the younger woman at the desk asked in a pleasant voice.

"Yes," Fleur admitted, shuffling her feet as though having a father was something to be embarrassed about.

The woman crossed the room to shake his hand. "I'm Genevieve Rockford. Call me Gen. I'm so glad you could make it." Her grip was firm, and her smile looked genuine. He detected a faint whiff of citrus, clean and fresh.

"Hello, Gen. I appreciate the heads-up. Sorry if I kept you waiting. There was a holdup on the Parks Highway." When he'd heard the word *intern* this morning, he'd pictured someone in her early twenties, but he'd guess this woman to be more than a decade past that, almost his age. Attractive, with golden-brown hair. Her gray eyes had little lines at the corners, as though she smiled often.

"Not at all. I didn't realize you were driving in all the way from the Parks Highway. This is Doreen Holman, Fleur's counselor."

"Caleb." Caleb shook hands with the other woman, and at her direction, they all moved to the area where Mallory was already settled. Fleur flopped into the chair beside Mallory, and Caleb took the next one, placing him between Fleur and Gen.

Doreen spoke first. "Thank you both for coming in today. Fleur, I'm sure you know why we're back here." She aimed a chiding but friendly smile at Fleur, who acknowledged it with an almost undetectable eye roll. Mallory nodded. Caleb felt like he'd been dropped in the middle of a movie with no clue about the plot, but before he could ask what was going on, the counselor continued, "Gen has been interning with me this semester while she finishes her master's degree, doing a fantastic job, by the way." She turned her smile toward Gen. "She's been working with Fleur, and so she'll be running the meeting."

"Thanks, Doreen. Just to catch us up," Gen said, nodding toward Mallory but then turning to Caleb, "six weeks ago when we met, Fleur was in danger of failing four of her classes."

Caleb blinked. Fleur failing? The kid was reading before she turned five. Her grades throughout elementary school had been mediocre, but she'd certainly never been in danger of failing. What was going on?

"I'm happy to say that since that time," Gen continued, still looking at Caleb, "she has brought her grades up in two of those classes, to a D in general science and a C in English." She turned to Fleur. "So good job on that, Fleur."

Fleur grunted an acknowledgment and Gen continued. "However, you're still failing history and algebra."

Fleur didn't look surprised, but Caleb sure was. When Fleur was at the farm the weekend before last, he'd proofread a history research paper that she'd said was worth 20 percent of her grade. And it was good. They'd gone over the rubrics together, so he was sure it was complete, and Fleur had even added in some extra illustrations she'd done herself. So how was she failing? Come to think of it, the last report card he'd seen was from the end of the first semester, with mostly Bs and Cs. How could he have forgotten to ask Fleur about her grades at midterm? And what were they going to do about them now, with only a week left in the school year?

Caleb looked to his daughter for an explanation, but she wouldn't meet his eyes. He turned to Gen. "I'm sorry. This is all news to me. Can someone fill me in on this improvement plan from six weeks ago?"

"Of course. Fleur, do you want to explain?" Gen asked.

"It was no big deal," Fleur mumbled. "I just missed some assignments."

"And…" Gen prodded.

"And I had to make them up and do some extra credit." Fleur finally looked up. "And I did."

"Yes, you did all the extra credit work assigned and you made up most of the assignments you'd missed up to that point, and that's quite an accomplishment." Gen pulled out a stack of papers and leafed through them. "But your teachers are saying in the last four weeks, you've missed several more."

Fleur shrugged.

Caleb leaned forward. "May I see those?"

Gen handed him the stack, printouts of assignments and grades from each class. Caleb looked over the first sheet, history. Five assignments were marked as zeroes, including the research paper. He pointed it out to Fleur. "Okay, I know you did this paper because I read it ten days ago. Why is it missing?"

Fleur shrugged. "I guess I didn't turn it in."

After all that work? "Well, can you turn it in late?"

"I guess so."

"Yes, Mr. Jackson has a policy of accepting assignments late, for partial credit," Gen clarified.

"Where is the paper now?" Caleb asked Fleur.

"In my locker."

Which begged a whole different set of questions, but he tried not to get sidetracked. The rest of her grades were mostly As and Bs. "So if my math is right, if you turn in this paper and net at least a C after getting partial credit, you're within two points of passing. Correct?"

"I guess."

Gen looked over his shoulder. "Yes, that's exactly right. So, Fleur, if you've finished the paper, what kept you from turning it in?"

"My locker's stuck."

"Again?" Mallory raised her eyebrows. It was the first time she'd spoken.

"I'll contact maintenance." Gen pulled out her phone. "What's your locker number?"

Fleur told her and Gen texted something. "Ms. Kelly will get right on it."

"Wait, this has happened before?" Caleb asked.

"All the time," Fleur confirmed.

Gen sighed. "It's a design flaw. If students pack the lockers too full, stuff slides under the latch and the combination won't open the locker. Ms. Kelly, our custodian, has a tool that can get it open."

"How long has your locker been stuck closed?" Caleb asked.

"You mean this time?"

"Yes."

Fleur took a moment to think. "Since the day before the paper was due, I guess."

"And you didn't submit a request for help?" Gen asked.

"I was busy."

"Huh." Gen looked like she didn't buy it, but she moved on. "Okay, well, once your locker is accessible, you can turn in your history paper and get credit for that at least. What about these other missing assignments? Do you have them ready to turn in?" She didn't look surprised when Fleur shook her head. "I've talked with your teachers in the two classes you're failing. They've agreed to give you an incomplete and update your grade later if you turn in all the missing assignments before August first. Let me emphasize, that's *all* of your missing assignments, the five in history and fifteen in math. It's all or nothing—no partial credit this time."

"But that would ruin the whole summer!" Fleur frowned, but then her face brightened. "I can't. I won't be here this summer. I'll be out on the farm in Willow with my dad."

"Do you not have internet?" Gen asked Caleb. "We could work something out via mail if necessary."

"Of course we have internet," Caleb replied. "And rest assured Fleur will be completing the missing assignments." He gave his daughter a stern look. "All of them."

"Fleur, do you agree?" Gen asked.

She slumped back in her chair, looking defeated. "I guess."

"Because if you don't complete the assignments, you will be repeating these two classes next year."

"Okay, whatever. I will."

"Mallory, do you have anything to add?" Gen asked.

Mallory gave a bland smile. "No, this is Fleur's responsibility. I'll trust her to handle it."

Mentally, Caleb scoffed. Yeah, because Fleur had obviously been handling things so well up to this point. How could Mallory look so calm when their daughter was failing school? But he and Mallory had always had differing approaches to parenting. Yet another reason their marriage failed.

"All right, then. Caleb, here's my card. If you'll give me your email address, I'll cc you when I send Fleur a list of all the assignments she'll need to complete." Gen's phone vibrated on the table, and she picked it up. "Oh, good. Ms. Kelly has your locker open. You can pick up that history paper on your way back to class and turn it in today. Thanks for coming, Fleur."

Fleur left the room. Caleb expected a little more discussion among the adults, but once Gen had written down his email address, the two counselors thanked Mallory and him again and said their goodbyes. Mallory slipped into the hall and Caleb hurried after her. "Mallory. Wait."

"I need to get back to work," she answered without slowing her stride.

"I'll walk with you." He stepped up to keep pace. "Why didn't you tell me Fleur was having academic problems?" He tried to keep his voice low as they walked through the quiet hallways.

Mallory waved her hand. "It's just an organization problem she needs to work through. Nothing serious."

"Failing four classes sounds serious to me."

"She made up the work."

"You still should have told me about the meeting today."

They turned down the hall that led to the front door. "I was doing you a favor. It's silly for you to drive all the way to Anchorage to hear them say something they could have emailed in five minutes."

"But they didn't email, and neither did you. Fleur is my daughter, too. I need to know when she's having problems."

"Fine. I'll let you know if anything else comes up in the next five days. You're still picking Fleur up on Monday?"

"If that works for you."

She shrugged. "It's fine. I'll make sure Fleur is packed and ready to go for the summer."

"Thank you."

They reached the doors, but Mallory paused before going out and reached over to fiddle with a ring on her left hand, an unfamiliar diamond Caleb hadn't noticed until now. He knew Mallory had been seeing someone named Charles for several months, but he didn't realize it was serious. "Is that—"

"Yes." She smiled. "I'm getting married."

"Oh. Uh, congratulations." Why were the women around him suddenly deciding to get married? Was there something in the water? At least Mallory wasn't marrying the man who had broken up their marriage. It would have been hard to take, having his daughter living with him. Caleb managed an awkward hug. "I hope you're very happy together."

"Thank you, Caleb. I appreciate that."

"So when is the wedding?"

"August fifth." She smirked. "You're not invited."

"Ah, I assumed not."

"But I will need to take Fleur shopping for a dress and some other wedding-related activities during the summer."

"Of course." Technically, he had Fleur all summer except for every other weekend, but they'd always been flexible with one another's schedules. "Let me know, and I can bring her in, or you can pick her up."

"Okay. Well, I'll see you...whenever."

"Okay, then. Bye, Mallory." He watched her go out the door. Mallory was getting married, which meant Fleur would have a stepfather whom Caleb had never met. He only knew about the man because Fleur occasionally mentioned him in passing. She seemed okay with him, if not terribly enthusiastic. But then, Fleur's enthusiasms didn't tend to embrace the adults in her life right now.

Could this be why Fleur was suddenly having problems in school? Was she worried about this sudden change in her life? Once more, Caleb was completely out of the loop. He just wished he could fix the locker or Fleur's attitude or something—but to some degree, Mallory was right. The assignments were Fleur's responsibility, and ultimately, she had to be the one to do them. And she would have to be the one to forge a relationship with her stepfather. It wasn't as though Caleb didn't have enough on his plate. Between dealing with Christabel's upcoming absence and the farm chores—oh, speaking of chores, he should have time to pick up that thermostat before heading back home for the meeting with Christabel.

What time was it now? He patted his pockets. Shoot, his phone must have fallen out of his pocket when he was sitting in the counselor's office.

Of course it did. Because that was the sort of luck he was having today.

GEN CLOSED THE office door and turned to her mentor. "What do you think? Will Fleur do the work?"

Doreen made another note and closed the file. "I'm optimistic. She's shown before she can. Being at her father's house might make a difference. He sounds sincere about making sure she does the assignments. But then, some people are much better at making promises than keeping them."

Yes, Gen knew all about those people. She used to be married to one. Larry had been quite convincing when he'd promised to be faithful to her. And when he'd promised to be a hands-on, involved dad. And—after he'd broken both of those promises and Gen had divorced him and moved herself and her daughters home to Alaska—when he'd promised to stay in touch with his girls. And yet, the last time he'd initiated a call to them had been on Maya's birthday, seven months ago, and only because Gen had reminded him two weeks in advance.

But somehow, she got the idea Caleb De-

Boer might be different. After all, as soon as he'd learned of the meeting, he had dropped everything to drive from Willow to Anchorage this morning. Larry would never have done that. Still, "Why wasn't he involved for the past few months? You sent an email as soon as Fleur's grades dropped, and then we had that meeting six weeks ago. Why now?"

"Well, that might be my fault," Doreen admitted. "The email we had on file for him bounced, and when I contacted the mom to update it, she said he didn't live here and implied he wasn't involved in Fleur's life. So I let it go. We had his phone number. I should have called him directly."

"Well, anyway, he's involved now. Hopefully, it will make the difference."

"Fingers crossed." Doreen glanced at the clock and gathered up an armful of folders. "I'm due in the principal's office in five minutes to go over some things." She grinned. "Including the evaluation for your internship, which—spoiler alert—will be excellent. You're going to make a great school counselor."

"Thanks, Doreen. That means a lot, coming from you."

"So you're done with all your classes?"

"All but my last few papers for this internship. I have a job this summer with a gift shop downtown, but I'm hoping to start as counselor this fall."

"Have you applied for any jobs yet?"

"Sure. For every open position in the Anchorage School District."

"You want to stay in Anchorage?"

"I'd like to. I grew up here, and I have family."

Doreen tucked the folders into a tote bag. "Are you hoping to get something on the south side close to home?"

"Not necessarily. It's my brother's house, actually, and once I'm employed and independent, I'd like to find a new place for me and the girls."

"Yeah, I can see that. A friend of mine manages an apartment building on the east side, so if you want something in that area, I could set you up with her."

"I'll keep that in mind. Thanks, Doreen."

Doreen glanced at the clock. "Oops, gotta go."

As she slipped out the office door, Gen's cell phone vibrated. Speaking of summer jobs... She cleared her throat and answered in her most professional but friendly voice, "Hi. This is Gen."

"Gen, it's Marsha, manager of Arctic Heirlooms downtown."

"Yes, Marsha. I'm looking forward to working with you. Are we still on for training a week from Friday?"

"Um, that's why I'm calling. Turns out we're not going to be needing extra help this summer after all."

"Oh, but I thought—"

"I thought so, too, but it seems the owner had already hired someone to fill the position and neglected to let me know."

"Huh. That seems kind of, uh, counterproductive."

"Tell me about it."

"So you don't even need anyone part-time?"

"I'm afraid not. Sorry. I know you were counting on this summer job."

"I— Yeah. I don't suppose you know anyone else who's hiring?"

"Not off the top of my head. But if I hear of any openings, I'll let you know."

"Thanks."

"Okay. Well, goodbye."

"Bye." Gen almost thanked her again, and then realized there was no real reason to thank someone for firing you. What was it they said about the best-laid plans?

Now what? She'd been hoping to make enough money from this job to be able to move out of Tanner's house in a month or two.

Tanner's wife, Natalie, taught at a college in New Mexico and they lived there most of the year, but they usually came home for at least a few weeks in the summer. Tanner adored his nieces, and so did Natalie, but Gen couldn't help but feel that they should be able to enjoy their own home without having Maya and Evie underfoot all day long.

"Excuse me."

Gen jumped at the sound of a deep voice behind her.

Caleb DeBoer stood at the door. "Sorry, I didn't mean to startle you. The door was open. I believe I left my phone in here."

Gen crossed to the conversation area and spotted the phone wedged between the seat and the arm of the chair. "Here it is." She handed it over to Caleb.

"Thanks." He tucked it into his pocket. "And thanks again for calling me about Fleur and the meeting. I didn't realize she was in grade trouble, or I would have stepped in earlier."

"I gathered that. I'm sorry we didn't contact you before."

"I understand. So her mother just told me she's getting remarried. Could that have something to do with Fleur's problem? Is she rebelling?"

Gen had noticed the ring. "It's certainly possible, but I don't really think so. When I've talked with Fleur, she hasn't mentioned being upset about anything like that." If anything, Fleur was more caught up in the day-to-day drama that was life in middle school, but Fleur had mentioned that in confidence. "Honestly, I think she simply needs to develop better organization and motivation. Middle school is different than elementary. Believe me, Fleur isn't the first student to have difficulties adjusting to having several different teachers and classes to juggle. I believe, with your support, she'll be able to make up the work, and with a year of experience under her belt, she'll do better next year."

"I hope so." He started to turn away, but then he paused. "I'm sorry, but I couldn't help but overhear part of your telephone conversation. I gather you had a job fall through?"

"I did," Gen admitted, wondering why he cared. "I'm hoping for a position as a school counselor in the fall, but in the meantime, I'd planned to work in a gift shop downtown for the summer. But they changed their minds."

"Are you good with social media?"

"Average, I'd say. I know the basics. Why do you ask?"

"Well, as it happens, I know of a job opening you might want to consider."

"Oh?"

"The Susitna Peony Cooperative's sales and marketing manager is taking a leave of absence, and we need a temporary replacement."

"Sales and marketing manager?" Gen had a bachelor's in psychology and was about to finish her master's in counseling. Her only sales experience had been as a barista. "I don't know that I'm qualified. It sounds—"

He chuckled, and she was struck by how much more approachable he seemed with a smile on his face. Handsome, even, with strong features and dark hair with a tendency to curl. "Keep in mind that the manager is also the entire staff. Basically, the job is to keep track of the members' peony inventory, accept orders and promote the co-op by posting pictures, articles and things like that on social media. It's part-time—twenty hours a week."

"Is this something I could do from Anchorage?"

"In theory, but you'd be driving back and forth all the time to visit the farms, take pictures, things like that, so it would be better to live in the area. There are seven peony farms in our co-op, four around Willow, two around Wasilla and one near Big Lake."

"I don't know. I have two daughters and I doubt it would be easy to find a short-term lease." With several popular lakes in the Willow area, summer rentals would be in high demand.

He thought for a moment. "Maybe I could help with that. I have an empty cabin on my farm. It's nothing fancy—two bedrooms, one bath, kitchen and living room combination."

"Bathroom, as in running water?" Gen loved her family's off-the-grid cabin in the backcountry, but she wasn't too keen on spending an entire summer without plumbing. Especially with two little girls.

Caleb laughed. "Yes, hot running water. Electricity. Propane stove. Even internet and a dishwasher. All the modern conveniences."

"That sounds nice. How much would you want in rent? And do you know about how much this job pays?"

The figure he quoted was more than she would have made working at the gift shop. "I'd throw in the cabin for free."

"Free? Why?"

"Why not? It's just sitting there, empty."

"That's very generous. The job sounds intriguing. How do I apply?"

"You just did. I'm currently co-op board chair, so it's my job to find a replacement. Officially, I'll need board approval so if you'd shoot me a résumé or something to show them,

I'd appreciate it, but if I can give them a qualified applicant, they're not going to say no."

"Don't you want to know my qualifications, or work history or anything?"

"Well, you deal with middle school students all day, so you're obviously patient if not a bona fide saint. You just earned an advanced degree, so I'd imagine you pick up knowledge quickly. Your boss seems to like you, so I suspect you're dependable. I'm sure you had to pass a background check to work in the school district, so you're not a serial killer. You don't hate flowers, do you?"

"I love flowers."

"Well, then, consider this a job offer."

"Really?"

"Really."

Could she take the girls and move to the Mat-Su Valley for the summer to live on a farm with a man she just met? The job sounded interesting, and she did love flowers, peonies especially. "Let me give it some thought. When do you need my answer?"

"Sooner is better, but a week would be okay."

"All right, then. I'll email you a résumé and let you know, one way or the other, by next Wednesday." Or sooner, because if she wasn't going to take the job, she needed to get busy finding another one.

"Great. You've got my number. My place is called Jade Farm if you want to look it up. There's a link from the Susitna Peony Cooperative website. I'd give you a business card, but I ran out." He grinned. "If you take the job, you should probably order more."

She laughed. "I'll keep that in mind."

"All right, then. It was good meeting you, Gen, and I hope to see you again soon."

CHAPTER TWO

THE NEXT MORNING Gen sent the list of missing assignments to Fleur and her parents. Doreen was off-site, so Gen had the office to herself. Once she'd finished posting the notes, she sat back and took a moment to consider Caleb's job offer. Sleeping on it hadn't brought her any closer to a decision.

On one hand, after checking out all the amazing blooms on the Susitna Peony Co-op website, she was tempted. It sounded like a fun job, taking pictures, publishing interesting tidbits about peonies and working with planners and brides to make sure they got the wedding flowers they wanted. But it meant leaving Anchorage for the summer.

After her divorce, she'd moved her two girls from Florida to Alaska so that she would be near her family. Recently, her mother had begun snowbirding in New Mexico, where Tanner and Natalie lived, but she would be returning to Anchorage this weekend, and the girls could hardly wait to see their grandmother. Gen hated to move them out of town just when Mom was back, although with Willow only two hours away they could still visit frequently.

Then there was the matter of the cabin. Gen had done a little sleuthing, checking out the satellite view of Jade Farm, and was pleased to see the farm was only about two miles out of Willow, and while Willow was tiny, it would have the basics like groceries and gas. It appeared that the main house was on the southeast corner of the property near the road, with several smaller structures behind it. Another, smaller house, presumably the cabin Caleb had mentioned, was at the end of a long drive in the northwest part of the property, adjacent to a small lake. Which meant extra vigilance to make sure the girls stayed out of the water. In between the two were long rows of plants, which must be the peony fields, another place she'd need to make sure the girls stayed out of. But it appeared the cabin had a fenced backyard, which would help. Would it feel awkward, living on a farm with a stranger, or were the houses so far apart it wouldn't matter?

The bell rang and the halls outside filled with students changing classes. Someone knocked, and Gen looked up to see Fleur standing at the open door. "Hi, Fleur. I emailed your assignments. Did you get that history paper turned in?"

"Yes, but Mr. Jackson says because it's more than a week late, he'll take off two letter grades. So the best I can get is a C."

"Frustrating to work so hard on a project and lose all those points just for being late, isn't it?" Gen commented, trying to subtly mix a learning opportunity with sympathy.

"Yeah. Can you talk to him or something? My locker—"

Gen laughed. "Ms. Kelly told me about your locker. Did you really stuff three down coats plus snow boots, one shoe and all your books in there?"

Fleur offered an impish grin. "Well, when it started getting warm in the afternoon, I kept forgetting my jacket, then I'd wear another one the next day and I had to stuff it in with the others. Down is supposed to be packable."

"Maybe, but three in a locker is a little much. And why only one shoe?"

"I couldn't get the other one in there, so I carried it in my backpack."

"I see. And why didn't you ask Ms. Kelly to open your locker the first day you noticed it was stuck?"

"Well, uh, last time she did it she said to clean out my locker, but I hadn't gotten around to it yet. And I thought if I let the stuff sit there for a while, the coats would kind of deflate, like old balloons."

"Uh-huh." That almost made sense, in a seventh-grade-logic sort of way. "Have you cleaned it out yet?"

"Yeah, Ms. Kelly gave me a big garbage bag and I took everything home." The second bell rang. Fleur was going to be late for her next class.

Gen reached for her pad to write a hall pass. "That's good. Did you just come by to tell me about the history paper?"

"I guess." But Fleur didn't seem to be in any hurry to leave. "Sorry about my dad barging in on the meeting yesterday. I don't know how he found out about it."

"He found out because I called him," Gen explained. "And it's good that he was here, since you'll be living with him this summer while you're working on your makeup assignments. Don't you think so?"

"Maybe." Fleur sighed. "The farm's boring. Dad's always working and never has any fun. I don't think he's been to a movie in, like, years. And I have to spend the entire summer all by myself in the middle of nowhere just because he's my dad."

"If you show initiative toward getting those

assignments finished, he might agree to bring you to visit your friends in Anchorage now and then."

Fleur drifted over and flopped in a chair without any invitation from Gen. "It doesn't matter anyway. I don't have any friends. I found out Brooklyn and Owen have been sneaking around behind my back. Now everybody's taking their side. So I might as well be out in Siberia doing all my stupid schoolwork."

"I'm sorry to hear about your friends," Gen told her, although privately, she thought Fleur was better off without Brooklyn, who liked to toy with people for her own amusement. The other kids were okay. "You know, Jade Farm looks really nice in the pictures."

"Why were you looking at it?"

"Your father offered me a summer job with the peony co-op and said if I wanted, I could live in the cabin on the farm."

"Cool! Are you going to take it?"

"I haven't decided yet."

"You should! Then at least I'd have one person to talk to."

Gen laughed. "Your father seemed quite talkative to me. And if I came, I'd bring my two daughters with me."

Fleur's eyes widened. "You have kids?"

Gen smiled to herself. Students seemed to

think teachers and other school authorities were put away in closets at the end of the day rather than having real lives outside school. "Yes, Maya and Evie. They're six and seven."

"I bet they're cute. I like little kids. You should totally come."

"I'm considering it. Now, aren't you supposed to be in English?" Gen signed the hall pass and tore it off the pad.

"Thanks." Fleur accepted the pass and headed toward the door, looking more cheerful. "See you at the farm?"

"I'm not making any promises, but we'll see."

"Whatever." But Fleur was grinning. "See you, Ms. Rockford."

THOR TURNED REPROACHFUL eyes toward Caleb the moment he spotted the spray nozzle in Caleb's hand. Caleb laughed. "You're the one who had to run through the ditch yesterday. You know Francine can't take you into the nursing home today if you're covered with mud."

At the mention of Francine's name, Thor wagged his tail. He loved Francine even more than he loved his weekly job visiting nursing homes and hospitals with her. At Caleb's urging, the dog stepped onto the grate and allowed Caleb to wet him down and then rub dog shampoo through his curly coat. Thor closed his eyes in pleasure. Caleb wasn't sure why the dog always acted as though bathing was a punishment when he obviously loved it. Today's bath took a little longer than usual because Thor was overdue for a clip. Another thing to add to the list. Along with cleaning the cabin if Gen Rockford accepted the job offer.

Was it a mistake, offering up the cabin to someone he'd only met once? Since the divorce eight years ago, he'd been by himself on the farm except for every other weekend and summers, when Fleur came to stay. Mostly, he liked being alone, but he missed his daughter, and he always looked forward to his time with her. Up until the last year or so, Fleur had always looked forward to it, too, happy to spend time outdoors and swim in the lake. But since she'd started middle school, she'd had nothing good to say about the farm, and nothing Caleb did or said seemed to please her. According to his neighbor Vickie, it was typical teenage behavior, but he missed the little girl who always had a hug for her daddy.

Maybe he should have consulted Fleur before offering to let Gen use the cabin, especially since she was bringing her daughters. Fleur might resent having someone connected with the school so close during her summer break. Not that it would be much of a break, with all the work she'd be catching up on. How had Mallory let her get so far behind?

Mallory had always taken a laissez-faire attitude toward parenting. She'd seen some television program claiming letting children make mistakes and suffer the consequences was the best way for them to learn. Caleb could see her point, but in this situation the consequences for Fleur's failure to turn in her work and pass classes might not become apparent until years later, when she wanted to get into a particular college or program. Parents made the rules because they had more experience and better judgment than teenagers. That was why they called them parents. At least, that was what his mom and dad used to say.

Anyway, he had offered up the cabin and Fleur would just have to deal. And so would he. Assuming Gen did take the job.

He hoped she would, and not only because otherwise he would have to find someone else to fill the position. He'd been impressed with the way Gen had managed the meeting with Fleur, with a businesslike and yet friendly attitude. And that when she realized he hadn't been included in the first meeting, she'd apologized rather than making excuses. She didn't seem to be the type who would get flustered over calls from demanding brides, like the one Christabel had mentioned last summer, who called the day before they were due to ship, saying she wanted red instead of white flowers, and oh, by the way, not until December, as though they could wave a wand and make peonies bloom during the winter. Caleb was glad he wasn't involved in that conversation.

He turned on the warm water spigot and rinsed the suds from Thor's coat. As soon as he finished, he dropped the hose and jumped back, knowing from experience what happened next. Thor gave a vigorous shake, sending water flying in all directions. Once the dog stopped, Caleb grabbed an old towel, blotted as much water as he could and went over him with a brush. He patted Thor's shoulder. "Okay, we're done. Let's put you on the deck to lie in the sun and dry. Francine will pick you up in two hours, and she'll appreciate it if she doesn't have to smell wet dog all the way to the nursing home in Wasilla."

Once Thor was situated, Caleb headed into the main greenhouse to repot the basil seedlings. Another three weeks or so, and they'd be ready to take to the farmers' market in Wasilla. Herbs weren't his main business, but they kept him busy and brought in a little cash while he waited for the peonies. He'd just finished when he heard a car coming up his drive. He washed his hands and went to let Thor out.

Thor, who had no doubt heard Francine's car long before Caleb did, was waiting at the gate, quivering with excitement. When Caleb opened the latch, the dog all but bowled him over in his hurry to dash to the driveway, where Francine was getting out of her car.

"There's my beautiful boy." She bent over to rub his ears and kiss his head. "Smells like you had a bath. Were you rolling in something disgusting again?"

"Not this time," Caleb told her. "But he chased a rabbit through the mud."

"Well, dogs will be dogs." Francine gave Caleb a sly smile. "I hear you might be getting a new woman in your life."

"A woman? That's news to me."

"Oh? Maybe I got the story wrong. I heard you're hiring someone to take Christabel's place for the summer, and that she's moving into your cabin."

"Oh, that." It never ceased to amaze him how fast information spread through this community. Francine didn't even live in Willow, but in a senior apartment complex over in Palmer. But she and her husband had run the feed and farm store north of Wasilla for years and years, so of course she knew all the farmers in the area. "You must have been talking to someone on the co-op board."

Caleb had conducted an informal phone poll of the board regarding his plan to replace Christabel with a temporary employee. Everyone had indicated support for the plan except Clancy Latham, but then, you couldn't wish Clancy a good morning without getting an argument.

"Vickie told me. Said you sounded pretty taken with this Gen person."

Oh, he could see where this was going. Better head off those two matchmakers at the pass. "I was just happy to have found a potential job candidate. And it's not a done deal yet. She might still turn it down."

"Well, I hope she says yes. You could use some company around here. Speaking of company, when does Fleur arrive for the summer?"

"Next week."

"Oh, good. Maybe I can talk her into going on visits with me and Thor."

"That would be great. You'd better ask her, though. Anything I suggest is automatically a bad idea in Fleur's not-so-humble opinion."

"Ah, yes. I remember that stage. Don't take it personally. I hear Clancy gave you some trouble."

"Just Clancy being Clancy. He wanted to replace Christabel permanently instead of hiring someone for the summer. Kept muttering something about her generation not knowing the meaning of loyalty."

Francine laughed. "You'd think he was my age instead of in his thirties."

"It didn't matter anyway because the other members all agreed with my plan. Vickie said she'd train the temporary employee, which is good because I don't have a clue. Yesterday, Christabel tried to bring me up to speed, but all this social media stuff goes right over my head."

Francine patted his shoulder. "Well, we all have our strengths. Come on, Thor. We'd better get going. I'll see you this evening when I bring him home, Caleb."

"Have a good day." He watched her drive away and was headed for the small greenhouse to replace the thermostat when his cell phone rang with an area code he didn't recognize. He ignored it, assuming it was some bot offering to extend his car warranty, but then he remembered that Christabel had said she would be forwarding co-op calls to his phone and answered. "This is Caleb DeBoer."

"Oh, I was calling for, uh, Christabel at the Susitna Peony Cooperative."

"Yes. Sorry, Christabel is out of the office." Not that they had an office, but it sounded official. "How can I help you?"

"I had questions about these wedding packages. Can you explain the difference between the Deluxe Peony Extravaganza and the Peony Bridal Spectacular? And can I substitute pink peonies for the white ones?"

Where did they come up with these names? Christabel had shown him the order page with the various packages, but he didn't have them memorized. "Sure. Give me a few minutes to get to my computer and I'll take a look."

"Okay, but I don't have much time. Maybe I should call back tomorrow and talk to Christabel."

"No, Christabel will be out for a while. I should be able to sort this out for you. I'll hurry." Caleb muted his phone and dashed for the house. He hoped Gen called soon to let him know one way or the other. He needed to get this position filled or it was going to be an awfully long summer.

CHAPTER THREE

"IT'S YOUR TURN to load the dishwasher!"

"Nuh-uh! I did it yesterday!"

"Girls, please!" With effort, Gen kept her voice calm as she looked up from her laptop. The last thing she wanted was to escalate these tense negotiations. "Maya, I think it's your turn but check the chore chart."

Four little feet scurried to the calendar on the pantry door. "See!" Evie was triumphant.

Maya groaned. "I already wiped the table. Whoever wipes the table doesn't have to load the dishwasher."

"But it's your turn! If your name is on the chart you have to do it. That's the rule." Having almost completed the first grade, Evie considered herself an authority on rules. And on most everything else.

"But you're supposed to wipe the table and I already did it."

"That's not my fault." Evie sniffed. "You should have checked the chart first."

"Mommy!" the two girls cried in unison.

Gen, knowing she could have wiped the table, loaded the dishwasher and taken out the trash in the time they'd already spent arguing, took a calming breath. "Maya, you need to load the dishwasher because it's your assignment tonight. Evie, since your sister was kind enough to wipe the table for you, you should be kind enough to help her load. Now hurry. It's already past your bath times."

Both groaning at the unfairness, the two girls transferred the plates and plastic glasses from the counter to the dishwasher racks. Once they were done, Gen reached into a high cabinet for detergent and filled the cup. Evie closed the door and reached for the start button.

"No, I get to push the button." Maya shoved Evie's hand away and pressed Start.

"Mommy!" Evie wailed.

"Enough. Bath time. And then we'll read one of the new books Aunt Natalie sent you."

"Can we have bubbles?" Maya asked.

"Sure."

Evie pushed ahead. "I'm first."

"No, me!" Maya pushed back.

But Gen had already foreseen this scenario. "I looked at the chart. Maya gets the first bath. Evie chooses the book. Evie, I put the new books in the basket beside the couch. Go make your choice while I help Maya with her bath."

A few months ago Evie had decided she was too big to bathe with her sister, doubling Gen's time on bath patrol.

Gen poured in a generous capful of strawberry-scented bubble bath and ran the water. She considered fetching her laptop so that she could at least add a sentence or two to her final self-evaluation for the internship while she sat with Maya, but bringing a computer into a room where Maya was playing in water was just asking for trouble. Besides, she'd been putting in extra hours for the past few weeks getting all the requirements checked off for her degree, and she owed her girls her full attention for at least a little while.

Maya settled in among the mountains of suds and reached for a handful of plastic animals from the pail hanging beside the tub. With a tiger in one hand and a Holstein in the other, she bobbed them up and down among the bubbles. "Mommy, can we have a tiger?"

Gen laughed. "No, tigers are wild."

"Can we have a cow?"

"No. Cows live on farms and ranches."

"Can we have a dog?"

Ah, this was where this was heading. "No. We can't have any pets until we have a place of our own." They'd had this conversation many times, but Maya and Evie always hoped for a different answer.

"So we can have a dog once we move to another place?"

"Maybe. If we rent, it will depend on whether we're allowed to have pets. Some places allow only certain pets, and some none at all."

"We could have Vitus as our dog."

Yeah, a hundred-pound malamute was exactly the dog they'd need in the type of apartment Gen would be able to afford on a school counselor's salary. "Vitus belongs to Uncle Dane and Aunt Brooke." Dane was Gen's first cousin but almost as close as a brother. "We only took care of Vitus while Uncle Dane was traveling."

"Maybe we could get a cat."

"Maybe. We'll have to see."

Maya exchanged the cow for a mountain lion and walked it and the tiger along the edge of the tub. "If we get a cat, I'll name it Tiger." She thought for a moment. "Or maybe Cookie. Because I like cookies."

"Both solid names." Gen squirted body wash on a washcloth and handed it to Maya. "Now, don't forget to wash behind your ears."

An hour and a half later both girls, smelling sweetly of strawberries, were tucked into their beds. Despite it being a school night, they'd ended up reading all three of the new books together. Gen glanced longingly at the bathroom, the lure of a long, hot soak almost too much to resist. But that self-evaluation was due by noon tomorrow. What a great feeling it would be to turn in her last assignment.

She'd barely typed the first sentence of a new paragraph when her cell phone rang. Since it was obviously someone who knew when she put the girls to bed, it was most likely family. Sure enough, when she picked up the phone, the picture that popped up was of her brother.

"Hi, Tanner."

"Hi. Kids asleep?"

"Yes, all tucked in." She could explain she was in the middle of an assignment and would call him back later, but he'd already derailed her train of thought. Besides, he was two time zones ahead, and at the rate she was going she might not finish this evaluation before midnight. "Tell Natalie they loved the books."

"She'll be glad to hear that. I'm sure you're busy so I won't keep you, but I wanted to give you a heads-up about Saturday."

"You mean about meeting Mom at the airport? Did the flight change?"

"No, same flight, but Natalie and I will be on it as well. She's finished for the semester, and we've decided to spend the whole summer in Alaska."

"Oh, that's great!" Gen answered. And it would be. She loved her brother and his wife. But that meant before Saturday she would need to change the sheets in the master bedroom, get extra groceries, give the kitchen a deep clean...

"We're looking forward to spending lots of time with the girls." He was sincere, and Gen knew it, but she also knew her daughters.

"About that." Tanner and Natalie had been married for less than two years and, judging by all the kissing, were still in their honeymoon phase. Not that Gen had much experience in that area. In her own marriage, the honeymoon phase ended literally the day they'd returned from their honeymoon, when Larry had announced he would be spending the next weekend at a golf resort with the guys. And yet, Gen had hung on to that marriage for eight more years, until she was forced to acknowledge that many of those weekends and evenings with "the guys" had in fact been spent with other women. "I've been offered a summer job in Willow."

"Willow? I thought you were working downtown."

"I was, but that fell through. This job is for

the Susitna Peony Co-op to handle their sales and marketing while their regular manager is off. It comes with a place to stay, so we'd spend the summer there and let you and Natalie enjoy your house in peace."

"Hey, you know I've always liked having you and the girls around."

"I know, but that was when you were single. This will be better. Besides, this job sounds interesting, and it would be a good experience for the girls, to live on a farm."

"What farm?"

"It's called Jade Farm. They grow peonies. Caleb DeBoer, the farmer, says he has an extra cabin where the girls and I can live for the summer."

"I don't know, Gen. What do you know about this farmer?"

"Well, I know he's the chair of the co-op board and the father of one of the students in my school, and that he's offered me the job and a place to stay."

"Have you checked his references? Gotten a background check? I want to meet him before—"

"Yeah, well, what you want isn't really relevant." She took a breath. "Maybe you could step back a little and remember I'm thirty-five and you're not responsible for me. Okay?"

"Uh—" In the background, she could hear Natalie saying something along the same lines as what she'd just said, but more forcefully. Tanner cleared his throat. "I'm sorry. You're right, of course. So you're going to take the job?"

"Yes, I am." Ironically, Tanner's knee-jerk overprotectiveness had given her the impetus she needed to make the decision. "I'll call tomorrow and accept."

"Uh-huh. But is it okay if I stalk this guy on the internet, just a little?"

"Sure. Stalk away. Like you aren't going to do it anyway."

"You know me well."

"I do." She laughed. "And I love my big brother even when he's annoying. So the girls and I will be at the airport to pick up the three of you on Saturday."

"Thanks, Gen. Can't wait to see you. Love you, too."

"Tell Natalie we can hardly wait to see all of you. Bye, Tanner." She ended the call and set the phone on the table. Well, at least that was one thing checked off her to-do list. Decision made. She and the girls were going to Willow.

CALEB SET A box of cleaning supplies on the cabin's kitchen countertop. "Here, why don't you dust all the furniture in the living room while I do the bathroom?" Caleb handed Fleur a dust cloth and a can of furniture polish.

"Are you really making me do housework instead of letting me swim in the lake on my first week of summer vacation?" Fleur gave him that sad-eyed-puppy look she was so good at, although the extreme eyeliner diminished the effect somewhat. That look had gotten Fleur out of dozens of unpleasant chores throughout her life, and it almost worked again. But Caleb really needed the help.

"The lake is awfully cold yet—I doubt you'd last ten minutes in the water. Besides, this won't take that long. They'll be here tomorrow."

"Fine." Fleur stalked around the island to the living room and sprayed a glob of polish on the coffee table before pushing the cloth across it as if it weighed fifty pounds. Caleb almost pointed out that she'd used triple the polish necessary for the job, but there was no use starting another argument.

Thor followed Fleur to the living room and stretched out on the rug, worn out after a spirited game of Frisbee with Fleur earlier. Caleb unpacked the bathroom cleaners and rubber gloves. He kept up with painting and maintenance and stopped by for quick inspections every so often, so the cabin wasn't in bad shape, just dusty from disuse.

His parents had bought the cabin and forty acres of land with a small lake to serve as their summer home after their first year of teaching in the bush. Even after Caleb was born several years later, they'd continued to spend the school years in the village and summers here, until the year Caleb turned ten. That was when they decided to move to Willow full-time and began teaching at the high school there. And that was when they'd decided the cabin wasn't big enough for year-round living and built the main house. But Caleb had wonderful memories of summers in this cabin. He hoped Gen and her daughters would enjoy it.

Fleur had seemed pleased that her school counselor would be living on the farm. That was the only thing she'd seemed pleased about since he'd picked her up two days ago. She now considered a summer on the farm a cruel and unusual punishment for the crime of being his daughter. He couldn't even get her interested in the vegetable garden, something they'd enjoyed together since she was old enough to walk. Just like Caleb had done with his parents.

If only his parents were still around. His mom, especially, had always been good at relationships with young people. She might have been able to help Fleur understand the importance of family and tradition. This was her heritage. Farming ran in the blood of both sides of his family. Some distant cousins still ran the DeBoer family farm in Connecticut, founded more than a hundred years ago. His mother's family grew wheat, soybeans and sunflowers in Nebraska.

His parents had been the first generation from both their families to move off the farm, but they'd spent their summers cultivating an enormous vegetable garden. And that was on top of his mother's ever-expanding perennial borders and his father's experiments in cross-breeding plant varieties. Caleb's earliest memories were of working side by side with his parents, harvesting vegetables. Even the family name, DeBoer, meant *the farmer* in Dutch. Farming was there, in Fleur's genes.

But Fleur was only three when her grandparents had died, and she had no memories of them. It would be up to Caleb to teach her all the things his parents had taught him. It wasn't easy, trying to influence a child when she spent most of her time with her other parent. But he had the next three months to get closer to his daughter again, to learn about this new version of Fleur and to guide her into making better decisions. Assuming she'd let him.

He sprayed the bathroom mirror with glass cleaner. The swipe of a paper towel across the surface of the mirror revealed his own scowling image in the glass. Did he really look like that? It was no wonder Fleur was reacting badly. He tried pasting on a pleasant smile, but it looked more like a grimace.

"What are you doing?" Fleur's voice made him jump.

"Nothing. Cleaning the mirror." Caleb began wiping furiously. "Why? What do you need?"

She tilted her head and narrowed her eyes. For a moment he thought he was going to have to explain himself, but she just said, "I need the glass cleaner to do the doors of the curio cabinet."

"Here." He handed over the bottle and started cleaning the vanity, trying to think of a way to begin a conversation. It was going to be a long summer if they couldn't even talk without arguing. Inspiration struck. "You remember that cat we saw around the barn in March?" he called into the living room.

"The calico one with the torn ear?" For the first time a spark of interest lit her voice.

"Yeah, it's back. I saw it a couple weeks ago

and I've spotted it out of the corner of my eye a time or two since. It was eating with the others this morning."

"You still can't catch it?" After reading an article about pet overpopulation, Fleur had insisted they get all the feral barn cats spayed or neutered, and Caleb had agreed. It had been easy enough for her to catch the big black cat she'd christened Foodmeister. A few handouts and he was her forever friend. The other three cats were wilder, but he and Fleur had been able to catch them in a humane trap. They'd attempted to trap the calico, too, but the cat was too wary.

"No luck. I put tuna in the trap, but I kept catching Foodmeister instead. Maybe you can figure out a way to keep him occupied and lure the new cat in."

"Maybe. How was the ear?"

"From what I can tell, it's healed okay. Coat looks healthy."

"Good. I'll go check out the barn later, see if the cat is there."

"Great."

Fleur returned with the glass cleaner and set it on the counter, but she didn't leave immediately. "Those towels are kinda ratty."

Caleb followed her gaze to the stack of towels in the rack beside the tub, once forest green but now faded closer to the color of moss. Since no one used the cabin anymore, except occasionally as a place to change clothes after a swim in the lake, he'd never bothered to replace them. "Yeah, they are."

"We should get new ones before they come." Fleur ran a critical eye around the room and wrinkled her nose. "And a new shower curtain. That one is so last millennium."

He examined the shower curtain with its dizzying print of tropical foliage and parrots. A short curtain in a matching print hung over the window blinds. His mother had chosen the accessories for this bathroom—yes—in the last millennium. "You're right." It was time for an update. "Why don't you make a list, and we'll go into Wasilla this afternoon?"

"Okay." For the first time since she'd arrived, she gave one of those mischievous smiles he knew so well. "On the way home, we could get ice cream."

Caleb laughed. He didn't like to waste time and gas running back and forth, so his shopping trips often included stops for bags of fertilizer, mechanical parts and other items that his daughter didn't find particularly fascinating. An ice-cream cone from The Frosty Moose was always Fleur's treat for good behavior. Or sometimes it was Caleb's treat for putting up with her not-so-good behavior, like when she would try to slip contraband junk food into his shopping cart. Or that time she'd turned a quick stop at the hardware store into a game of hide-and-seek. He'd been this close to calling the police when someone discovered her crouching behind the nail bins. Regardless, they'd always stopped for ice cream on the way home. "I suppose we can do that. If you behave."

Fleur stuck out her tongue at him before walking away. Caleb laughed again. The old Fleur was still there, underneath all the eyeliner and attitude. He just had to coax her out.

They continued to clean. Caleb swept the floors and made up the beds while Fleur wiped down the kitchen. When he returned to sweep the living room, she asked, "Should we get some milk and stuff and put it in the refrigerator?"

"I didn't think of that, but it would be a nice gesture. Put it on the list."

She picked up her pen. "What kind should we get? Whole, nonfat, almond?"

"I don't know."

"Why don't you call her and ask?"

Caleb hesitated. Calling with a grocery question seemed like such a...domestic thing to do. Well, buying groceries at all sort of blurred the lines of professional behavior, but Fleur had suggested it and he didn't want to squelch any generous impulses on her part. "Okay, I will."

He found the number from when Gen had called to accept the job, but his call went to voice mail. He left a message and pocketed his phone. "So what else do we need to do?" He noticed a thick layer of dust still covering the fireplace mantel. "I thought you dusted in here."

"I did."

"I don't think so." He used his finger to write *Clean me, Fleur* in the dust.

"You said to dust the furniture. That's not furniture."

Caleb sighed. Fleur excelled at the loophole game. "Fleur, would you please dust the mantel and all the surfaces that need dusting in this room?"

"I guess so, once I'm done in here."

"Thank you. I'll get the vacuum with the extension wand to get those cobwebs out of the corners and then we can do the rugs." He went to the master bedroom closet, where the vacuum cleaner was stored. Two cardboard boxes sat among the extra pillows and blankets stacked on the shelf above the closet rod. Maybe he'd better have a look inside before he turned over the house to someone else. The first one almost felt empty, but the bottom bulged on the second one as he lifted it down. He had to slide a hand underneath to keep it from breaking apart.

He set both boxes on the dresser and opened the lid on the lighter one first. Inside was a piece of lace, carefully wrapped in tissue paper, and a brown folder. He opened the folder to find a wedding portrait of his parents, looking impossibly young and eager. He could see so much of his mother's face in Fleur's, not so much in the features, but in the inquisitive spark in her eyes. He uncovered the top layer of tissue paper and realized the lace pattern matched the lace brushing against Mom's cheek in the picture. His mother had mentioned once that she'd given her wedding dress away, but she must have saved the veil. Another tie to the past.

"Hey, Fleur. Look at this," he called.

"In a minute. I'm dusting the mantel like you said."

"Okay." Caleb opened the other box. Piles of loose snapshots. Mom always planned to organize them all into albums when she retired. But she'd never gotten the chance. His parents had been on a rare holiday out of state, driving a rental car in Montana, when a blown-out tire had sent a van careening across the yellow line, striking them head-on. And that quickly, they were gone, leaving the Willow property to Caleb, along with a million memories.

He smiled at the picture on top of the pile, one of his mom holding newborn Fleur. He pawed through the box. Lots of pictures of the garden. There was an old snapshot, colors fading, of Caleb as a toddler beside one of his mother's antique peonies, one he'd used in his crossbreeding experiments. The fully double pink blossoms were higher than his head, and bigger, too.

He set that one aside to show Fleur and dug deeper into the box. At the bottom, a heavy envelope was tucked among the photos. He opened the flap and pulled out a folded document. His name jumped out at him. Then he looked at the top line. *Adoption certificate.*

Adoption? He wasn't adopted. This must be some sort of mistake.

"What did you want to show me?" Fleur came in, still carrying the dust cloth.

"I   Uh   Oh, this." He set the document aside and handed Fleur the wedding photo. "Your grandparents. And your grandmother's wedding veil."

"Cool." She glanced at the photo and smiled, but her attention went to the veil. Gingerly, she pulled the rest of the tissue paper away to reveal more of the lace. "So pretty. Can I try it on?"

"As long as you're careful. Wash your hands first."

While Fleur was in the bathroom, Caleb returned the certificate to the envelope and tucked it inside his shirt. This couldn't be right. He was a DeBoer, from a long line of DeBoers, and so was Fleur. There had to be some explanation. In the meantime, there was no reason for Fleur to know. He would think about this later.

When Fleur returned, she carefully unfolded the veil and draped it over her head, securing it with a small comb attached to the underside. It wasn't one of those bunched-up net things, but a single piece of sheer netting with scallops along the edges, framing her face. Caleb gazed at his daughter, transfixed. Despite the overdone eye makeup, Fleur looked so lovely he felt a little catch in his throat. Someday, she might be wearing a veil like this, or possibly even this one, to walk down an aisle somewhere. And if he hoped to be the one walking with her, he needed to keep their relationship strong.

He'd lost his parents, he'd lost his wife, but he wasn't going to lose his daughter. Ever. He would make sure of that.

CHAPTER FOUR

A FEW HOURS LATER they'd finished with the cabin and Caleb had let Fleur loose in a big-box store in Wasilla, watching with alarm as the cart filled with piles of towels and sheets, a shower curtain printed with a copy of a famous postimpressionist painting, oven mitts with cartoon dogs and, for some reason, salt and pepper shakers shaped like rabbits that he suspected had been left over from Easter, two months ago. Now she was deliberating throw pillows.

He should rein her in, but he couldn't keep his mind on shopping, not with that adoption certificate sitting there under the socks in his dresser drawer. He hadn't had a chance to examine it closely, but it certainly looked like an official government document. But it couldn't be real.

Still, what if it was? Was it possible his parents had lied to him his whole life? One of his mother's hobbies was genealogy. She'd loved discovering snippets of history from long-dead ancestors on both sides of the family and sharing them with Caleb and his dad. Was it possible that all those stories were about someone else's family, that Caleb had no blood ties to any of them?

Did it matter? They'd raised Caleb and loved him, passed on their skills and values. It shouldn't make any difference whether they were related genetically or not. And if they'd told Caleb he was adopted, it might not have. But the possibility that they kept his adoption a secret made him wonder what other secrets might be out there.

"Caleb!" He looked up to see Vickie pushing a cart toward him. "I wouldn't expect to see you in housewares." At her voice, Fleur wheeled around and Vickie's smile grew broader. "Fleur! You're here! Come give me a hug."

Fleur's smile was almost as broad as she went willingly into Vickie's arms. "Yeah, school's out so I'm here for the whole summer." The words didn't sound nearly as resentful when she said them to Vickie.

Living on the next farm over, Vickie had been a good friend to Caleb's parents. After their deaths, when Caleb had moved his family to the house there, Vickie had stepped in and taken them under her wing. She'd been almost as brokenhearted as Caleb over the divorce, but still made a point of staying connected with Fleur. Once she'd released Fleur, she looked at the two pillows Fleur had pulled out from the shelves, one with a picture of a bluebird, and the other with shiny blue beads all over it. "Redecorating your room?"

"Nah," Fleur answered. "These are for the cabin. I told Dad we had to fix it up some, because Ms. Rockford, my school counselor, is going to live there this summer."

"I know. I'll be training her for the co-op job."

"She's bringing her daughters. They're little kids."

"In that case, you might want to rethink that pillow." Vickie pointed to the one with the baubles. "I love the color, but I suspect that if you put it in a house with children, you'd be finding beads all over the house for a month."

"Oh, yeah. I forgot you used to be a decorator. That would be such an awesome job. How come you quit and started farming instead?" Fleur asked, returning the pillow to the shelf.

"Oh, many reasons. My husband had passed, and my business wasn't as satisfying as it had once been. I had to find a way to start over. Let's see, if I remember right the couch in the cabin is navy. That bird pillow would look good with it, but if you add this solid turquoise, too, they really pop against the dark blue. See?" She crossed the aisle to hold the two pillows against a blue bedspread for Fleur's approval.

Caleb couldn't help but notice how she'd skimmed over her answer to Fleur's question. Come to think of it, it was odd that Vickie would have given up a career to move to Willow, Alaska, of all places and take up peony farming. But then, lots of Alaskans had stories like that, of packing up and leaving an old life behind. He, himself, had been a welder, working two and two on the North Slope, until he'd inherited the Willow property and decided to try farming. He still did a little freelance welding in the winter, but he considered himself a farmer now. So maybe it wasn't so odd.

Would Vickie have any information about the adoption certificate? She'd been a close friend to his mom. But she hadn't arrived in Alaska until three or four years before his parents died, so probably not, and he wasn't sure he wanted anyone else involved anyway. He watched as she and Fleur laughed at a pillow with a silly moose drawing and stacked it in the cart.

His phone rang. "Hello."

"Hi, this is Gen, returning your call."

"Oh, thanks, Gen. We were just doing some shopping and wondered if you needed us to stock the refrigerator with milk or anything?"

"Oh, that would be fabulous! I was about to run out and pick up a few things, but if you could put milk and eggs in the fridge, it would save me a trip. That's so nice!"

"It was Fleur's idea. What kind of milk and eggs do you want?"

"Two percent milk, please. Any eggs—we're not fussy. Tell Fleur that I really appreciate her thoughtfulness. I also wanted to ask about bedding. What size sheets will I need?"

He glanced at the full cart. "There's one queen and two twins, but we've got plenty of sheets and towels already."

"Oh, that's great! One thing to cross off the list, then. The girls are looking forward to staying on a real farm." In the background, a child's voice urgently asked if there were cows.

"Tell her no cows, just a dog and a few barn cats."

Gen laughed. "I'll pass that along. See you tomorrow."

"I'll look forward to it. Goodbye." He pocketed his phone and turned to see Fleur and Vickie watching him with almost identical amused expressions. "What?"

Vickie grinned. "Updating the cabin, buying groceries. I think you like this woman."

Caleb shook his head. "I was just being polite. My only interest in her is whether she'll be able to handle the job."

"Uh-huh." Vickie nodded, still with a knowing smile on her face.

Caleb ignored her and turned to Fleur. "Ms. Rockford said to tell you thanks for thinking of milk and eggs. She wants two percent."

"Okay," Fleur acknowledged.

"Well, I'll let you get back to your shopping." Vickie tucked one of the pillows more securely into his cart. "I'll plan a 'welcome to the co-op' family barbecue so everyone can meet our new employee. See you 'round."

"Bye, Vickie." Fleur pushed their cart toward the grocery section.

Caleb felt like he needed to be clear. "Look, I don't know where you and Vickie got this idea that I'm interested in Gen—"

Fleur laughed. "She was teasing, Dad. Everybody knows you're too antisocial to date."

Wait a minute. Just because he wasn't dating anyone didn't make him antisocial. But at least that was better than everyone assuming he had some sort of crush on Gen Rockford. Because if marriage had taught him anything, it was that he wasn't cut out for romance.

"Wow. This wasn't what I expected." Following Caleb's emailed directions, Gen had taken the exit in Willow, where she'd hit a major pothole, and after a few turns found herself following the gravel drive past the main farmhouse to a cedar-sided cabin accented in forest green. He'd talked about two bedrooms and a dishwasher, but he'd failed to mention the abundance of flowers surrounding the cabin. Perennials filled the area inside the split-rail fence out front and spilled out to line a trail heading downhill, toward the lake. Gen recognized some of them, the bluish-purple wild geraniums swaying on long, airy stems and white Canadian violets in bloom above mounds of heart-shaped leaves. Masses of white daisies were beginning to open, and dainty Johnny-jump-ups edged the flagstone path leading to the front door.

"Pretty," Maya commented, once Gen had released the girls from their booster seats and let them out of the car.

"Yes. But they're not our flowers, so no picking them." Evie and Maya had once taken it upon themselves to reach through the gaps in their grandmother's backyard fence to gather a bouquet of wildflowers for her. Except that they weren't wildflowers at all but the neighbor's freshly planted bedding flowers, which had resulted in a rather expensive trip to the nursery for replacements.

Evie was staring down at the lake. From their vantage point, Gen could see a floating dock on the water's edge. Nearby were a shed and a covered stand sheltering a pair of canoes, a collection of brightly colored life preservers and other assorted items. "Can we swim in the lake?" Evie asked. She and Maya had taken swimming lessons last summer and loved a chance to get wet.

"I'll have to check. I'm not sure if this lake is warm enough for swimming."

"It's warm today," Evie pointed out. She was right. They'd been lucky enough to get a particularly sunny day for the move, but that didn't mean the lake wasn't all but freezing.

"It takes more than one warm day to heat a lake," Gen told Evie. "We'll have to wait and see."

The front door opened. Fleur bounded down the steps and along the path to the front gate. "Hey, Ms. Rockford."

"Hi, Fleur. Say, at school, I'm Ms. Rockford, but here you can call me Gen."

"Really? Cool."

"This is Evie and this is Maya. Girls, say hello to Fleur."

"Hello." Evie stepped forward immediately,

always ready to make a new friend. Maya was shyer, hanging out a little behind Gen, where she could watch first.

"Hi, Evie. Hi, Maya. You want to come inside? I'll show you your room." She opened the gate, invitingly.

"Yeah!" Evie skipped up to her.

After a quick look at Gen, who nodded encouragement, Maya followed her sister, and Fleur led them inside. Gen opened the back of the minivan and leaned in to heave out the first suitcase, which seemed to weigh approximately the same as a bull moose. She thought she was being clever, packing all the books in a rolling suitcase instead of in boxes, but she'd forgotten she had to get it out of the car first. Her brother had loaded all the luggage.

Tanner had offered to come along and unload, as well, but Gen nixed that, mostly because she suspected he really wanted an excuse to check out the farm and Caleb. Just like he always used to check out potential boyfriends, to her enduring embarrassment. Although, if Tanner had been around when she started dating Larry her senior year of college, maybe he could have seen through the facade and warned her before she wasted eight years of marriage on a cheater. But that was in the past. Caleb wasn't a boyfriend, she'd already accepted the job and the cabin and she didn't need Tanner's approval for either.

Something wet brushed against the back of her leg. She let out a shriek and spun around. The enormous poodle who had licked her leg eyed her curiously. Brown curls were clipped short, except for the dog's long ears and tail. She chuckled. If anyone had asked Gen to guess what breed of dog she might find on Caleb DeBoer's farm, poodle wouldn't even have made the list.

"Thor, sit." The dog immediately plunked his back end down and Caleb stepped out the gate on the other side of the gravel pad. He leaned a hoe against the fence and closed the gate behind him before crossing to her. "Sorry about that. I was in the vegetable garden."

Gen stifled a laugh. "Did you just call him Thor?"

"Yeah." He looked sheepish. "Don't blame me. He already had that name when he moved in. Here, let me help you with that." He reached past her to grab the suitcase and effortlessly swung it out and onto the ground.

Gen rubbed her hands over the dog's curly head. He wagged his pouf of a tail. She turned to Caleb. "You must really like gardens. This—" she swept her hand to encompass the whole area "—is incredible."

"My mom planted all these. I just maintain them."

"Well, she's an amazing gardener. I guess it must run in the family, huh?"

An odd expression flitted across his face, but before she could identify it, it was gone. He picked up the suitcase, grabbed a second one from the trunk and started for the door. "Come on in, and I'll show you how to work everything."

"Okay." She grabbed a box filled with pantry items and followed. Maybe he was estranged from his mother. Although he'd sounded fond of her when giving her credit for the flowers. "Does your mother still live in Alaska, or has she moved south?"

"She died in an accident," he said shortly as he nudged the door open with his foot. "Both of my parents."

"Oh, I'm so sorry." No wonder his feelings were tender. She shouldn't have pressed.

"It was eleven years ago. But thank you." He set the suitcase down and Gen stepped inside to get her first glimpse of the interior of their temporary home, taking in the cozy couch, river-rock fireplace, built-in bookcases and an adjoining kitchen island. Thor followed them and sat on the rug in front of the door.

Before Gen could find a place to set her box,

Evie came galloping from the back room, with Maya right behind her. "Mommy! We have moose pillows on our beds and a chair in the window. Ooh, a dog!"

"Doggie!" Maya added, joyfully.

"Caleb, these are my daughters, Evie and Maya. Girls, this is Mr. DeBoer, and his dog is Thor."

"Hi. It's okay to call me Caleb." He smiled at the girls, and Maya smiled back, so intent on the dog she forgot to be shy.

"Can we pet your dog?" Evie asked, edging closer to Thor in anticipation. The dog looked eager, but he remained sitting.

"Sure. Thor, free." The dog hopped to his feet, but he approached Evie and Maya at a measured pace rather than bowling them over. Thor was not a small dog—his head was easily at Evie's chest height—but the girls, accustomed to playing with Gen's cousin's malamute, Vitus, weren't the least bit intimidated.

Maya ran her hands over the dog's coat. "Look, Mommy, she has fluffy ears."

"Thor is a he," Gen corrected.

"I thought curly dogs were girls," Maya said.

"All kinds of dogs can be boys or girls. Everybody knows that," Evie lectured.

Maya's bottom lip started to curl, but a

nudge from the dog distracted her. "He likes me!" She snuggled closer.

"He's nice." Evie was petting his head. "There's a poodle who lives on our street, but she's itty-bitty."

The dog wagged his tail, politely, but when Fleur came from the back of the house to join them, he wagged harder and pushed a step past the little girls to welcome her.

"Hey, Thoro," Fleur crooned, rubbing his ears. "You like all this attention, huh?" Soon the dog was sitting perfectly still with his eyes closed while all three girls stroked him at the same time.

Gen was easing past them toward the kitchen when Caleb lifted the box from her arms. "I'll take that. Come with me and I'll show you the appliances. The stove's a little tricky." He set the box on the island and demonstrated how to ignite the propane burners.

This was Gen's kind of kitchen, functional but pretty, with a butcher-block island, shaker cabinets and abundant sunlight spilling in from the tall living room windows. A greenhouse window over the sink looked out on the fenced backyard with a large lawn and, to Gen's relief, sturdy shrubs rather than delicate flower gardens.

They walked through the rest of the house.

The "chair in the window" Evie had mentioned turned out to be a lovely bay window with a built-in bench. Gen was thrilled to find a twin to it in the other bedroom overlooking a shady portion of the flower garden, with clusters of ferns, bleeding hearts and a plant with deep burgundy leaves. The whole house had a comfortable, lived-in feel to it, although she noticed a few blank spots on the walls. In the bath between the two bedrooms, Gen spotted a price tag still attached to one of the thick gray towels that hung beside the double sinks on the outer area. She flipped the light on the inner compartment and stopped in surprise at the shower curtain. "Oh, wow, it's Monet's *Water Lilies*."

"Do you like it?" Fleur had slipped in behind her and was holding her breath like Gen's answer really mattered.

"It's one of my favorite paintings! How did you know?"

"I saw it on your screen saver once, at school."

"Oh, Fleur, that's so sweet. Thank you!"

"No problem. I picked out the moose pillows for the beds, and the ones on the couch, too." She looked at her father and then back at Gen. "Dad let me choose them."

"Well, you made wonderful choices. Everything looks great, and the girls love the moose pillows. It's so kind of you and your father to make us welcome. You didn't have to do all that, but we appreciate it."

Caleb didn't say much, but he looked pleased. They returned to the living room, where Thor had rolled onto his back on the rug in front of the fireplace to give Maya and Evie a chance to rub his belly. "We'll leave you to get settled in," Caleb said. "I'll be by tomorrow with the laptop and all the passwords for the job. Vickie Faramund, another co-op farmer, will be calling to schedule some training for you."

"Great. I can't wait to get started."

"Good. Your house keys are on a wall hook in the laundry room. Oh, that reminds me. I need to turn on the valves for the washing machine."

Gen followed him through the kitchen to the adjacent laundry room. A small built-in desk beside the dryer had a corkboard hanging on the wall behind it, with a few curling snapshots pinned on. She removed one of a toddler, all chubby knees and giggles. An attractive older couple beamed proudly in the background. On the back was written *Fleur, Bram and Jade DeBoer* and a date thirteen years ago. "Aw, Fleur is adorable."

"What?" Caleb turned from where he'd been

adjusting something behind the washer. "Oh, yeah. Those are my parents with her."

"Bram and Jade. The farm is named for your mother?"

"Yes, because she loved peonies." He took the photo from her hand and then briskly removed the other pictures from the bulletin board. "Sorry, I thought I'd taken all the family pictures out of here, but I forgot these." His face grew serious. "By the way, if you should happen to come across any documents hidden away somewhere, please let me know."

"Why? What sort of documents should I be looking for?"

"Nothing in particular. I just—I came across something when I was cleaning yesterday and it's possible… Well, if you find anything personal, or any other photographs, please call me."

"Of course."

"Thank you. And thanks for taking this temporary job. It really helps us out."

"It helps me out, too. And seriously, thank you for making me and the girls so welcome. I love this cabin."

"Good. Until tomorrow, then."

"Until tomorrow."

Gen spent the next few hours settling in. An alert on her phone reminded her that the girls hadn't talked with their father in two weeks. She was tempted to leave it until later, but Florida was four time zones ahead. She texted, Up for a chat with the girls?

The answer came quickly. Watching the game. Call in an hour?

Of course it was too much to ask that he might pause a sports event for five minutes to speak with his daughters. *Fine.* Gen set another reminder so that she wouldn't get busy and forget to call. Sometimes she wondered why she bothered, but it was important that the girls maintain some relationship to their father. And she would do most anything for her girls.

CHAPTER FIVE

NOT A CLOUD in the sky the next morning when Caleb stepped outside. A robin perched in the tallest birch in Caleb's front yard, singing his heart out. Caleb sincerely hoped the bird found a mate and settled down soon, because as cheerful as the birdsong sounded, Caleb hadn't particularly appreciated hearing it through his bedroom window at four thirty in the morning. It was going to be a warm day, at least on Alaska standards, with a high in the midseventies. The sun wouldn't be setting until well after eleven. On days like this, Caleb could almost watch his peonies grow.

Strolling along the pathway between his fields, he kept an eye out for any sign of botrytis fungus, but it had been a cool, dry spring and the leaves looked healthy. He reached the farthest field, the reds, which would be the first to harvest. Earliest were the Mary Lou peonies, with their spectacular burgundy double flowers that reliably reached seven inches in diameter. After that would come the Kathryn's

Hearts, a beautifully formed crimson bloom, beloved by florists. Caleb opened the valves to start the drip irrigation on the first six rows. He was lucky enough to have a reliable well that supplied his irrigation and drinking water, but his pump could only produce so much at a time. He set a reminder on his phone to come back in two hours and change over to the next six rows. This process could be automated, but he'd never set aside the time or money. Besides, he liked an excuse to spend more time in the fields.

As he turned to leave, Thor suddenly raised his head and stared toward the cabin. Caleb followed his gaze to see Gen, wearing plaid pajamas and carrying an oversize mug, step out onto the cabin's back porch. She sat down on the top step and gazed out at the yard. Probably enjoying the still of the morning before her daughters woke up. She looked happy there, peaceful. For a moment he felt the urge to join her, to sit quietly in her company for a little while, but she might not appreciate anyone intruding on her few moments of solitude. Besides, he had plenty to do today, including getting her set up in the job.

He chose to walk through the rows rather than on the main driveway on the way back, partly to inspect the plants and partly because he didn't want Gen to see him and feel like her privacy had been compromised.

His next stop was the experimental gardens, near the main house. This was his own outdoor laboratory, which predated his career in peony farming by a good fifteen years. It was his dad, the science teacher with a special fascination of botany, who had taught him about developing new varieties of plants. By crossing some lesser-known heirloom seeds with the earliest-producing modern varieties, Dad had created a cool weather-tolerant bush bean that began production a full two weeks earlier than average in their area. He'd never bothered to patent it, but most every vegetable gardener around would grow a row of Bram's early beans.

Following in his father's footsteps, Caleb experimented with crossing some of the antique varieties of peonies his mother had collected, many grown from seed she'd exchanged with other gardening enthusiasts from around the world. When Caleb was a teenager, he and his dad had set up this special garden. Even after he left home, Caleb would come out on his days off to work it with his dad, trying to improve disease resistance, hardiness and vase life and to develop new forms and colors.

Most of Caleb's experimental crosses were

no better than the favorite varieties already on the market, but there were a few that showed promise and one possible star. Its official patent listed the name as JF-143C. For the past few years, clones of this variety had been growing in test gardens all over the United States and Canada to see if the characteristics that made it so special here would translate to other climates. If the major seed company that Caleb had partnered with liked the trial results, the royalties from the patent could make a world of difference for Caleb.

Those royalties could finance breaking out another ten acres for production and hiring help. It could mean Caleb would no longer need to work welding jobs in the winter to supplement his income from the farm. If he was right and florists loved the flowers as much as he thought they would, the royalties could pay Fleur's way through college, and even graduate school if she so desired. Assuming she got her act together and passed her classes.

"Dad!" The shout came from the direction of the house. Caleb looked up to see Fleur leaning out of the upstairs bathroom window. "Dad, there's no water pressure." Judging by the panic in her voice, this was an emergency on par with a fire or earthquake.

"Oh, sorry." He'd forgotten that Fleur hadn't showered yet. "I have the irrigation running."

"Well, can you turn it off? I need to wash my hair."

"All right." According to the timer on his phone, the two hours were almost up anyway. He went into the well house to shut off the main valve to the irrigation system. He would just need to remember to turn it on before he walked back out to the fields to set up the next six rows. The door was slightly ajar. He made a mental note to fix the latch before winter. When he opened the door, the calico cat darted out. So this is where she'd been hiding. Thor crowded behind Caleb until the cat was gone. Having once chased Foodmeister and gotten a swat across his nose, Thor lived in terror of cats.

Caleb closed the valve and went to leave, but a mewling sound stopped him. A pair of yellow eyes looked up at him from behind the tank. When he leaned closer to check on the black kitten, another one appeared from under the tank, this one white with blue eyes. So much for spaying the calico. He checked carefully but could only find two kittens.

When he reached out, the black kitten rubbed its head against his hand. Surprising, since their mother was so wild. Caleb would guess them to be two or three months old. A mouse their mother must have just delivered confirmed she was feeding them solid food. He would get Fleur to bring cat food to the well house. Later, they could take the kittens to the vet for vaccinations and find them homes.

When he went inside to tell Fleur that she could shower and about the kittens, he found her standing in front of an open refrigerator with her phone pressed to her ear. "Where? But—" She paused, slammed the refrigerator door and wheeled around to pace across the kitchen. "But what if—" Another long pause. "Yeah, he's right here." She moved the phone away from her head and looked at Caleb. He wasn't sure if the irritation on her face was directed at him or whoever was on the phone. "Can I shower now or is that too much to ask?"

"You can shower." He would mention the kittens later when she was in a better mood.

She thrust the phone at him. "Mom wants to talk to you." She turned and stomped up the stairs. "Plug in my phone when you're done."

"I will, since you asked so politely." The sarcasm appeared to roll right off her back as she didn't even slow her ascent of the stairs. He pressed the phone to his ear. "Mallory?"

"Caleb. Good. I just told Fleur. Charles has just gotten a major promotion, so we'll all be moving to Atlanta in August, right after our honeymoon." She made it sound like good news.

"Wait. What?" Caleb shook his head. "You can't move my daughter across the country." At the time of their divorce, Mallory had been working for—and involved with—an insurance agent in Anchorage, and so Caleb hadn't paid much attention to the out-of-state rules in the custody agreement, but he remembered there were restrictions.

"Calm down, Caleb. You'll still get her summers and every other Christmas just like you do now. And you can talk with her on the phone every day if you want."

That wasn't enough. Even with all the phone calls and a visit every other weekend, he hadn't known about Fleur's grades slipping. "No, Mallory. That's not going to work. Don't you have to go to court before you can take a child out of state?"

"Not if the parents agree. Don't make this difficult, Caleb. The move will be good for her. She'll love Atlanta."

"She didn't sound too happy about it a few minutes ago."

"She hasn't had a chance to get used to the idea yet, but once I tell her about the new school, with horseback riding, and send her pictures of the house we're looking at buying there—"

A private school with horses? When Fleur was five, she'd begged for a horse, but it wasn't in the budget. Did she still want one? And how had Mallory already picked out a house? "How long have you known about this move?"

"Just since last week. But Charles knew he was on the short list for this promotion since late February, so we've done some research."

More secrets. How he hated secrets. "You've known for more than three months you might be relocating, but you didn't see fit to mention it to me or Fleur?"

"There was no use bringing it up until we were sure."

There was every reason as far as he was concerned. "The answer is no. I'm not going to agree."

"If you don't, we'll have to take it to court. If we can show them why it would be in Fleur's best interest—and a private school with an excellent reputation should tip the scales—the court will agree. Besides, Fleur is old enough to weigh in on the decision. If she wants to go, the court won't stop her." She sounded confident, as though she'd already gotten legal advice on this.

"What if she wants to stay here?"

"With you? In Willow?" Mallory scoffed.

Caleb didn't find it so ludicrous. "Fleur was born here. She's grown up in Alaska. What makes you think she would want to leave?"

"You're projecting your feelings onto Fleur. You're the one who loves the farm so much."

"Fleur loves it, too." Or at least she used to.

"Seriously, Caleb. Would you go to court to make Fleur stay if she wants to go?"

Caleb stopped to consider. His goal was to get closer to his daughter, but forcing her to stay with him against her will would only drive a wedge between them. "I guess not. No, if she really wants to go, I'll agree to it. But if she wants to stay, you'll do the same?"

"Sure." Mallory didn't even hesitate. "But she won't."

"We'll give her the summer to think it over. She can give us her decision in August."

"Why not let her choose now so that we can make plans?"

"No, it's a big decision. She'll need time." And Caleb would need time to show her the reasons to stay.

"Fine. We'll get her answer when Charles and I get back from our honeymoon. If Fleur says she wants to stay in Alaska, we can flip the custody agreement so that she's with you during the school year and I get her summers. If she wants to go to Atlanta, you won't fight it."

"Agreed."

Caleb ended the call and headed upstairs to plug Fleur's phone into the charger as she had so charmingly requested. Judging by the recent state of their relationship, if Fleur moved across the country, he might lose touch with her completely. As she got older, there might be summer jobs and friends and boyfriends keeping her there. Her visits would dwindle from the whole summer to half the summer to a couple weeks, and instead of a constant presence in her life, he would be practically a stranger. He couldn't let that happen. He had a little over two months to convince his daughter to stay.

It might take every minute.

"Mommy, have you seen my other sock?" The familiar call came from across the hall.

"I put it on your bed with the rest of your clothes," Gen called. She had showered, done her hair and makeup and was digging through a suitcase she hadn't yet found time to unpack, trying to decide between black pants with a black-and-white-striped shirt or linen pants and a short-sleeved sweater. She supposed it really didn't matter, but Caleb had said he would be dropping by with the stuff she needed for her new job, and she wanted to look nice. Professional, that is, not nice as in dressing up for a good-looking man. Even if Caleb was interested in her, which he clearly wasn't, romance was far down her list of priorities right now. Ahead of skydiving maybe, but well below learning to scrapbook, which was something she'd probably get around to sometime after the girls left for college.

"I can't find it!" Maya called.

"It could be under the bed." Gen pulled the two outfits from her suitcase and held them up. The linen pants needed ironing, so that left the black pants. But did the striped shirt say *competent professional* or *Mommy's lunch out*? "Evie, do you see the sock?"

"No," Evie answered immediately.

Gen laid the clothes on her bed and crossed the hall, where she found Evie still in her pajamas sitting cross-legged on the floor with a book in her lap. Meanwhile, only Maya's legs were visible, sticking out from under a half-made bed, one foot bare, the other in a red sock. When Gen moved to straighten the sheets and pull up the comforter, the missing sock appeared under the corner of the pillow. "Here it is."

"Oh." Maya, in her hurry to scramble out from under the bed, bumped her head. "Ouch!"

"Did that hurt? Let me see." Gen hugged her daughter with one arm while parting her hair to make sure she hadn't broken the skin on her scalp. "No blood, but you might get a bump." She dropped a gentle kiss on the spot.

Maya sniffed but didn't cry. With a tendency to rush in before she thought, Maya collected bumps and bruises like punches on a frequent customer card, but she usually just shrugged them off. Evie, on the other hand, seldom got hurt, but when she did, there was big drama. "Can I have a Band-Aid?" Maya was a big believer in the magical healing power of plastic strips.

"I think a Band-Aid would get stuck in your hair, but I'll get a bag of ice. Put on your sock while I get it. Evie, put down the book and get dressed." Gen went to the kitchen for the ice. When she returned, Maya had forgotten all about her accident and was trying to look at the book over Evie's shoulder, but Evie was deliberately blocking her view. Gen took the book from her hands and set it on the dresser. "Get dressed first. Then you may read. Here, Maya. Hold this against the bump."

Evie groaned, but she got to her feet and reached for the clothes Gen had laid out for her. Maya pressed the towel-wrapped ice bag against her head.

"Caleb is coming over in a little while to bring me the things I need to start my new job, so I'll need you girls to read or play quietly while he's here. Okay?"

Maya nodded, as she picked up her pajamas and stuffed them under the pillow. Evie had pulled on a T-shirt.

"Evie, did you hear me?"

"Yes. I just want to read my book."

"As soon as you're dressed." Once she was confident that the girls were making progress, Gen returned to her bedroom. Yes, stripes were too…something. She pulled out a knee-length, forest green sleeveless dress. Perhaps with a light jacket? Why was she obsessing like this? She'd been working for an entire semester without second-guessing her fashion choices. Working from home should be easier.

Someone knocked at the front door. Well, so much for making a professional impression. Gen shucked her bathrobe, pulled on the dress since it was fastest, shoved her feet into a pair of leather flip-flops and hurried through the living room. "Coming!"

When she opened the door, Caleb stood waiting, carrying a nylon computer bag. His eyes swept over her dress to her feet before returning to her face to give her a smile. "Hi." He didn't seem perturbed by her lack of professional attire. Of course, he wasn't particularly dressed up himself, in faded jeans and a gray T-shirt.

"Hello." She smiled back. Before she could say anything else, Thor shoved past Caleb through the door, wagging his tail, and trotted straight back toward the girls' room. Gen laughed. "I guess we don't stand on ceremony. Come on in."

"Thanks." He stepped inside. "Where do you want everything?"

"Let's use the kitchen table. Would you like coffee?" She was already moving toward the coffeemaker on the kitchen counter.

"Sure."

She reached into the cabinet, chose a mug and filled it. She looked at him. "Let me guess. Light milk, no sugar?"

He stared at her. "How could you possibly know that?"

"I don't know." She chuckled as she reached into the refrigerator for the milk he and Fleur had left there. "It was a game we used to play when I worked as a barista in college. We'd try to guess what people would order before they reached the front of the line. I got to be pretty good at it." She added the milk, stirred and set the mug in front of him.

He took a sip of the coffee. "It's perfect."

"Good." She poured a cup for herself and set it in front of the chair beside him, but before she could sit, a crashing noise and a bark came from the back of the house. "Excuse me." She hurried down the hallway.

The bedroom looked like a tsunami had passed through. All the blankets were dragged off Evie's bed and draped over the top of a pole lamp, which was now leaning against Maya's bed. It looked like the girls had used books, shoes and toys to anchor the edges of their "tent" to the tops of their beds. Only someone—Gen's guess would be Thor—had gotten tangled in the blanket and pulled the whole thing down on top of them.

Low laughter came from over her shoulder. Caleb had followed her, probably to make sure his dog was still alive. Thor crawled out from under the edge of the blanket, pulling a couple more books down as he did. Two little faces appeared from under the blanket, eyes wide in innocence. "You said to read, so we were making a reading fort."

"I see that." Gen pulled back the blanket and turned off the pole lamp. "But this fort has a problem. Don't ever drape clothes or blankets over lamps because they could catch on fire."

"But what can we use to make our tent?" Evie asked.

"Well…" Before Gen could either come up with suggestions or divert their attention onto some other project, Caleb snapped his fingers.

"I've got an idea. Be right back."

Gen had no clue what he was thinking, but she righted the lamp, glad to see the shade hadn't been crushed in the collapse. A minute later Caleb returned, carrying a metal pole with a tripod stand in one hand and a lantern in the other.

"Is that a music stand?" Gen asked.

"Yes." Caleb positioned the stand in between the girls' beds, raised the telescoping pole to its highest setting of around five feet and tightened a nut to hold it in place. With Gen's help, he draped the blanket over the stand, creating a center pole for the tent. Then he clicked on the battery-powered lantern and set it inside to light up their new reading space. "How's that?"

"Yay, our reading fort is ready!" Maya clapped her hands.

"Thank you," Evie told him, and Maya sang out her thanks as well. Thor wagged his tail.

"You're welcome." Caleb's smile seemed

genuine. There was something so attractive about a man who was comfortable around kids.

Mentally, Gen shook off the thought. She had no business noticing anything attractive about Caleb. He was her employer and landlord for the summer. That alone was enough to disqualify him for any sort of romantic relationship even if she was open to one, which she wasn't. "Do you play an instrument?" she asked Caleb as they watched the girls lug pillows and books inside. Thor crawled in to snuggle up between them.

Caleb shook his head. "I remembered seeing that old stand in the furnace closet the other day. My mother must have left it. She played the cello and gave private lessons. She tried to teach me, but I never could seem to get the hang of it."

"I feel that way when my brother tries to teach me to tie flies. Do you still have your mother's cello?"

"No. When she died, I gave it to one of her students. He's with the Anchorage Symphony Orchestra now."

"That's wonderful. I'm sure your mom would be proud."

"Yes." He was silent for a moment and then seemed to shake off whatever he'd been thinking of. "Are you ready to take a look at the computer?"

"Yes, please." She bent down so that she could catch both girls' gazes. "We're going to be working now, so I need you to read or play quietly. Understood?" Gen asked.

"Yes, Mommy." They spoke in unison. Looking at their sweet faces, you'd think the little angels had never given anyone a moment's trouble in their lives. Gen knew the cooperative spirit would be short-lived, but hopefully it would at least last long enough for Caleb to show her what she needed to know, so she could make this new job a success.

"So you're Gen. I'm Vickie. So nice to finally meet you!" The woman at the door was a surprise. After reading Vickie's profile on the co-op's website, mentioning a long career in interior design before becoming a peony farmer thirteen years ago, Gen had expected someone in her sixties. But at first glance this woman looked to be ten or fifteen years younger. With her colorful tunic, white capri pants and cute flats, she wasn't dressed like Gen's idea of a farmer, either. Before Gen could register more than that, she was engulfed in a hug.

Surprise rendered Gen motionless for a second before she reciprocated. Vickie stepped back and grinned. "I know. I'm a hugger. Caleb says I should be required to have a warning signal like big trucks use for Reverse."

Gen laughed. "Well, consider me warned. Come in. And thanks so much for coming over to train me. I have a lot of questions."

"I'll bet." Vickie moved two tote bags she'd set on the porch inside and casually kicked off her shoes as though she was a frequent guest. "But first, who are those two pixies peeking at me?"

Gen turned to see Maya and Evie at the end of the hall, leaning out to see who was at the door. She had bribed them with the promise of a trip to town for ice cream if they stayed in their room, but it didn't seem to be working. Although, technically, with their feet inside the door, they hadn't yet broken the pact.

"These are my daughters, Evie and Maya."

"Well, hello, Maya and Evie. Come meet me," Vickie called.

Maya started to step forward, but Evie put out an arm to hold her back. "We can't," she called. "Or Mommy won't let us have ice cream."

Gen could feel the warm flush rising up her neck toward her face, but Vickie just laughed.

"You don't need to hide them away on my account. The more, the merrier."

"Okay. Girls, come meet Ms. Faramund."

"Vickie," she insisted as she knelt and opened her arms. "Who's up for a hug?"

Evie bolted up the hall and right into Vickie's arms. Maya hung back, but after examining Vickie's face while she hugged Evie, Maya must have decided she looked trustworthy because she stepped up for her turn. Now that Gen had a chance to look more closely, she noticed smile lines around the corners of Vickie's mouth and eyes, like Caleb's but deeper. Must be a side effect of working outside during the long days of Alaskan summer. Strands of silver, which Gen had originally taken to be highlights, ran through Vickie's chin-length bob. Vickie probably was sixty or so. It was her slim figure and the energy she radiated that gave the impression of youth.

"Okay, better scoot back to your room so Vickie and I can work."

"They can stay in here as far as I'm concerned," Vickie told her. "I love kids."

"Can we, Mommy?" Maya begged.

"We'll be quiet," Evie promised.

Vickie looked just as hopeful as the girls. "All right. Here." Gen pulled new hundred-piece jigsaw puzzles she'd set aside for such an occasion from the bookshelf near the fireplace. Two puzzles, to discourage fighting. She pulled a quarter from the bowl near the door where she dumped her keys and change. "Evie, heads or tails?"

"Heads."

Gen flipped. "It's tails. Maya, you get first choice."

From the excruciating thoroughness of her thought process, one would think Maya was making a life-or-death decision but eventually she picked the bird puzzle and Evie got the rabbits. Gen set them up at opposite ends of the coffee table in the living room and then ushered Vickie to the kitchen table.

"Sorry about the delay," Gen told her as she opened and signed in to the laptop Caleb had delivered yesterday.

"Don't be. I love spending time with little ones."

"Do you have children?" Gen asked, thinking Vickie would be a wonderful grandmother.

"I—no." The look of pain that flashed momentarily across her face made Gen suspect there was more to that story. But Vickie had reached across her to bring up the co-op sales reports, and obviously didn't want to talk about it. "Did Caleb show you how this works?"

"No. He just gave me the computer and sign-in codes and showed me how to forward the phone number to my cell phone. He said you were the computer genius who would teach me everything I needed to know."

Vickie laughed. "There's a little Tom Sawyer in Caleb. Let's start with the basics. Early in the spring, the sales manager surveys all the farmers in the co-op about how many stems of each variety they expect to produce this season and creates a sales inventory. From there..." Vickie went on to explain exactly how the co-op took the orders and collected payment and then distributed the orders to the various farms for direct shipment. "We usually have at least half and often more of the crop sold a month before harvest. Peonies will only last six weeks in storage after cutting, and that's why Alaskan peonies are special. By ordering from us, late summer brides are able to have the sorts of bouquets that only spring brides could get before."

"Six weeks? That seems like a long time."

"The cold rooms are held at exactly thirty-four degrees and high humidity."

"Wow. Like a big refrigerator?"

"Most are small rooms with big air conditioners and special thermostatic equipment. At least mine is. Caleb has three times the number of peony crowns I do, so his cold room is a lot bigger. You'll have to get him to show you sometime."

"I will. This sounds like the sort of thing that would be interesting to post on the website and social media."

It took a long time to go through all Gen's duties and responsibilities for the sales manager part of her job. They were going over the social media when the girls, who had been working quietly, suddenly erupted into a squabble over a puzzle piece that had somehow wandered into neutral territory.

Gen sighed. "Excuse me."

Vickie chuckled. "Of course."

Gen confiscated the disputed puzzle piece. "Once you've used up all the other pieces, we'll know where this one goes. In the meantime, I'll hang on to it."

"But—" Both girls started to protest, but a stern look reminded them they could be banished to their room at any time. Maya went back to her puzzle, but Evie announced, "I'm hungry!"

Before Gen could answer, Vickie said, "Me, too. I brought a picnic lunch for all of us. It's a beautiful day, and I thought we could have lunch by the lake."

Puzzles forgotten, both girls jumped up and

ran over. Maya tugged on Vickie's hand. "I want to go on a picnic with you!"

Gen was touched. "Thank you, Vickie. That's so thoughtful of you."

"I like an excuse to feed people." She gestured toward one of the totes she'd left by the door, which Gen now realized was an insulated shopping bag. "I brought plenty of food, but you might want to gather some drinks."

A few minutes later they all headed down the hill toward the lake. Gen had been meaning to check it out since they arrived two days ago, but with unpacking, trying to get a handle on the new job and refereeing the girls, she hadn't had a chance. Flowers lined the pathway all the way down to the shoreline, with sun lovers like daisies and shrub roses transitioning into a woodland garden of ferns, forget-me-nots and bleeding hearts as they passed under a canopy of tall birches. Vickie stopped at a shed, almost hidden behind a huge lilac, and manipulated the lock on the door. "The combination is nine-oh-seven, same as the Alaska area code."

"Is this your shed?" Gen knew Vickie's farm was next door but wasn't sure exactly where Caleb's ended and hers began.

"Oh no. But when Caleb's parents were alive, we all used to spend a lot of time here."

She handed out two lawn chairs. "Let's take these down to the dock."

Gen handed the bag of water bottles and juice boxes she'd been carrying to Maya and the jug of iced tea to Evie so that she could take the chairs. "Caleb won't mind if we use these?"

"He never minds. You can use the boats, too, if you want." Vickie gestured toward the two orange canoes.

It was tempting. When Gen was in high school, she'd done a bit of canoeing with her friends. Were the girls old enough to take out on the lake? Or was that just asking for trouble? Speaking of trouble, she set the chair on the dock and went to collect two child-size life preservers from the collection hanging near the canoes. "Girls, come here and put these on. Whenever you're near the lake, you have to wear a life jacket."

"Even when we swim?" After a few weeks of lessons and a blue ribbon for swimming the length of the pool, Evie was convinced she could swim the English Channel given the opportunity. But there was a big difference between swimming in a pool under the watch of a lifeguard and swimming in a lake.

"Especially when you swim," Gen confirmed. "And any other time you're near the water. Otherwise, we won't be coming to the lake. Got it?"

"Okay." Evie sighed and pulled on the life jacket.

Gen helped Maya get hers buckled. Meanwhile, Vickie had carried down a folding table and laid out a feast of sandwiches cut into perfect triangles, a tray piled with fruit kabobs and a plastic bowl shaped like a starfish with carrot sticks and other veggies arranged around a cup of yogurt dressing. "Lunch is ready."

"Everything looks wonderful," Gen said as the girls swarmed the table.

"Don't fill up. I made brownies for dessert."

Gen helped the girls get settled sitting on the edge of the dock and set plates down beside them. Then she took a plate for herself and sat in one of the lawn chairs. She bit into the sandwich, a delicious chicken salad made with pecans and apples. Occupied with eating, the girls were quiet. Gen leaned back and enjoyed the feel of the sunshine on her face and the soft birdsong in the background. Suddenly, the birds stopped, startled by the sound of something thundering down the hill toward them.

"Thor!" Fleur called from the top of the hill, but the dog either didn't hear or pretended not to, because he continued down the pathway at a full gallop, leaped onto the dock, landing between Maya and Evie, and then launched himself into the lake with a splash that showered Evie and Maya with lake water.

The girls squealed. Fleur came running up, looking mortified. "I'm so sorry! If I'd known you were on the dock, I wouldn't have let Thor—"

But she was interrupted by Vickie's guffaw. Gen couldn't help but laugh, as well, shaking her head. Thor, who had paddled himself quite a way into the lake, grabbed a stick that happened to be floating by and turned to paddle back in their direction, a doggy grin surrounding the stick. Maya and Evie looked at each other as though trying to decide what their reaction should be, but taking their cue from Vickie, they giggled.

"It's okay, Fleur. It's not your fault." Gen stood up and shook the water droplets off her arm. "I never realized poodles love water so much."

"Oh, yes," Vickie said, still chuckling. "They were originally water retrievers. In fact, Francine, Thor's dog mom, told me the name *poodle* comes from a German word that means *splash in water*."

Gen was confused. "Thor's mom? Doesn't Thor belong to Caleb?"

"Francine and her husband ran the farm store in Wasilla for years," Vickie explained. "When he died winter before last, Francine moved to a senior apartment building in Palmer. Thor needed more exercise than she could give him living in an apartment, so she passed him on to her son, who took over the farm store and also runs an animal rescue. But he'd already adopted a possessive potbellied pig who didn't care for Thor, so Caleb volunteered to take the dog. Technically, Francine still owns him. She comes out every week and takes Thor to visit at nursing homes and hospitals. He's a certified therapy dog."

"Really?" It was hard to imagine the dog paddling across the water as a therapy dog, but then Gen had discovered in the teachers' lounge that some of the calmest, most unflappable teachers would tell hilarious stories of their misadventures outside school. Everyone needed off-duty time, even dogs. Thor reached the edge of the dock, climbed out of the water and shook, spraying water everywhere. Not that it mattered—the girls were good and wet already.

Evie pulled her T-shirt away from her body and squeezed some of the water out of it. It was a warm day, but with the breeze coming off the lake, she and Maya would be getting chilly before long. "Come on, girls. We'd better get you into dry clothes."

"I'll take them, if you want," Fleur volunteered, to Gen's surprise. Maya and Evie looked delighted. They'd already decided Fleur was the coolest.

"Thank you," Gen answered. "I'd appreciate that."

"You and Vickie can stay here. Don't worry. Thor only does one cannonball when he first gets to the water. After that, he calms down." She grinned at the girls, who had come to stand beside her. "Race you!" She turned and dashed up the hill. Thor bounded over Vickie's legs and galloped after her. Laughing so hard they could hardly run, the girls followed.

Gen collected the plates the girls had dropped when Thor splashed them. Vickie held the tote bag open. "Put them in here."

"Thanks. This was lovely, but I guess we should get back to work. I'm sure you have things to do besides tutoring me."

"Nothing urgent. Besides, we haven't eaten the brownies yet. Fleur loves my brownies. When she was about Maya's age, she used to come over and bake with me all the time."

"She doesn't anymore?"

"Not as often." A wistful smile crossed Vickie's face. "Of course, since Caleb only sees her every other weekend during the school year, he wants to spend that time with her, so he isn't particularly eager to drop her off with me."

"I can understand that." In fact, she could understand Caleb's reaction much more easily than her own ex-husband's. Almost three years ago, Larry had suddenly announced he was quitting his job to become a professional comedian. Oh, and incidentally, he would be moving out to live with a woman with whom he'd been having an affair. At first, Gen had planned to remain in their home in Florida so that they could co-parent the girls, but it soon became clear that parenting was one of the main things Larry was trying to escape. And since he had no income, he paid no child support so she couldn't make the mortgage payments anyway. That was when she had accepted Tanner's invitation to come home to Anchorage and live with him.

She'd been concerned that Larry might protest, but if anything, he'd seemed relieved that he wouldn't be expected to spend regular time with his daughters. He'd since given up comedy and gotten another job, so he now sent regular child support payments, but he still showed little more than polite interest in the girls.

Vickie pulled out a plastic tray and opened the cover. "Here. Enjoy your brownie and a little peace and quiet before we go back to work. You'll need to meet everyone in the co-op to get ideas for the blog, that sort of thing. I'll see if we can't get everyone together next week at my house for a family barbecue. That way you can meet them all at once and we can brainstorm."

"That would be great. Thank you." Gen poured more iced tea into their glasses and they both sat back and looked across the lake. She had just finished the last crumb of fudgy brownie when she heard the slap of the screen door shutting. Maya and Evie appeared on the trail, now dressed in mismatched but dry clothes.

Evie came skipping up to the dock. "Fleur says Ms. Vickie makes the best brownies in the whole world."

"I want one!" Maya pushed up beside Evie.

Fleur was right behind them, carrying a wad of paper towels. "I thought you might need these."

"Thanks." Gen took the towels and passed them to Vickie. "Girls, how do you ask?"

"May I have a brownie, please?" Maya recited.

"May I please have one, too?" Evie asked.

"Of course." Vickie passed brownies to the girls and to Fleur.

"Thank you," Fleur said and looked expectantly at Evie and Maya.

"Thank you, Vickie," they chimed.

Fleur got the girls settled on the edge of the dock and gave them juice boxes to go with their brownies. Too bad she hadn't been there all morning to keep them entertained while Gen and Vickie worked. And then it dawned on Gen. Why hadn't she thought of this earlier? "Fleur, how would you like a job?"

CHAPTER SIX

CALEB PINCHED OFF the last secondary bud on the sixth row of Barbara's Beauties. They were a mainstay peony, the delicate appearance of the fluffy pink flowers belying their iron constitution. Cold, insects, disease: nothing fazed them. Florists loved them, too, because with proper care the eight-inch blossoms would last more than a week in a vase. The crop looked healthy, with plenty of good-size buds. A rumble in his stomach reminded Caleb it was lunchtime. Fleur had been watching a movie when he went to bed last night and was sound asleep when he peeked into her room this morning. Presumably, she'd dragged herself out of bed by now.

He whistled, but Thor didn't come running. Caleb tried to remember when he'd last seen the dog. Probably about two hours ago, when he'd been sniffing around the barn. Perhaps he'd gone looking for Fleur. Caleb whistled again and started for the house. Just as he reached the door, Thor came galloping down the drive that led to the lake and the cabin. Caleb shouldn't have been surprised that Thor had been visiting. The dog loved kids. Hopefully, he hadn't been making a pest of himself.

Caleb let himself and Thor inside, washed up in the mudroom and then went into the kitchen. "Fleur? Want some lunch?" He pulled out the makings for turkey sandwiches. "You want tomato on your sandwich? Fleur?" Surely, she wasn't still asleep. He checked her bedroom, but it was empty. The door to the bathroom stood open. She couldn't drive, but she could have taken a walk. He pulled out his phone and texted. Lunch?

Can't. Babysitting.

Babysitting? She must mean she was watching Gen's two girls, but she should have talked to him first. If she wanted a job, there was plenty on the farm she could be doing. But maybe it was just a one-time thing.

After returning the turkey to the refrigerator, he headed for the cabin. Thor, once he sensed the direction, galloped ahead. As Caleb drew closer, shrieks and giggles floated in the air. There, in the backyard behind the cabin, was his daughter, a bandanna tied over her eyes, calling "Marco." Meanwhile, the two little girls fluttered around her like birds, with their answering calls of "Polo." He smiled, remembering how much Fleur had loved this game when she was that age.

He came to lean on the fence, waving at the two little girls. Thor effortlessly bounded over the four-foot fence, stirring a fresh gale of laughter. Fleur pulled the blindfold from her face. He nodded. "Hey, Fleur."

She grinned and rubbed Thor's head. "Hi, Dad."

"What's going on?"

"Oh, Gen hired me to watch the girls every day. Isn't that cool?"

"Huh." Caleb didn't think it was cool at all, but he didn't want to get into an argument in front of the little girls. "Where is Gen?"

"Inside, working."

"Okay. I need to talk with her." Gen had overstepped. He needed to make it clear that Fleur was his daughter, and he should be consulted on decisions like this. He stalked around the cabin to the front door, which was standing open, with just the screen door closed to keep out the bugs. Gen sat at the kitchen island, her laptop in front of her. She spotted him, pointed to the headset on her ear to indicate she was on the phone and motioned him inside.

"Yes, I got your email about changing from

pink peonies to blue," Gen said. "Unfortunately, peonies don't come in blue, and we don't dye our flowers. But one of our growers does have some incredible delphiniums in several shades of blue. Perhaps we could change the peony order from pink to white and add the delphiniums. They would be lovely together in a bouquet. I'm emailing you some photos of her delphiniums and a picture of a white peony and delphinium bouquet, just to give you an idea."

She listened for a moment. "I agree. Or blush peonies would be stunning against the cobalt blue of the dress in the link you sent." A pause. "Yes, the slightest hint of pink. We also have a variety called Dawn Dreams. It's more of a salmon pink semidouble with a yellow center. I'll send pictures of bouquets using both of those for reference."

Wow, she was good at this. He would have just told the bride there was no such thing as a blue peony and that canceling the order would mean losing the deposit.

Gen tapped on her computer for a moment while she listened. "Of course. But I just checked inventory, and we're almost sold out on the Dawn Dreams, so if you decide to go that route, sooner is better. Good. I'll look forward to talking with you tomorrow, then." She laughed. "Of course. Happy to help. Thank you for ordering Alaska peonies."

She ended the call, removed the headset and smiled at Caleb. "Hi."

He paused, realizing if he flew off the handle with her, she just might quit. And if she did, he would be the one dealing with calls like that. "I, uh, that was impressive."

She chuckled. "What? Talking to a bride?"

"Yeah. Giving her options instead of canceling the order. Who is selling delphiniums, by the way?"

"Jolene Svoboda. Not commercially—she just has a row of them all along her back fence—but she said she'd be willing to fill a small order to keep the bride happy. And they really would look amazing with the Dawn Dreams Jolenc grows."

"Yeah, they would."

"So did you need something?"

"Yes. I came to talk about Fleur. She says you hired her."

"Yes," she said slowly, "but I can see you're not happy with the idea."

"No."

"I'm sorry. It was kind of a spur-of-the-moment thing. The girls kept interrupting my work, and then Fleur stopped by and occupied them, and it seemed like the perfect solution, but I should have talked with you before I said anything to Fleur."

Okay, it was hard to stay mad at someone who admitted she was in the wrong. "Yes, you should have."

"You're right. If you want, I'll tell her I've changed my mind and find childcare somewhere else. But she is really great with the girls, and it's only from ten to two, Monday through Friday. It gives her a chance to earn a little extra money, and studies have shown part-time jobs can be good for teens. Of course, I know that getting those school assignments done is her highest priority, so if you feel like she can't handle both—"

A twinge of guilt poked Caleb. "Actually, she hasn't been working on school assignments."

"Oh?" Gen's expression was neutral, but he felt the need to defend himself anyway.

"I thought I would give her a few days' break first."

Gen nodded. "That's reasonable. You might not want to wait too long, though. It doesn't take long to form a habit, which can either work for or against us. If she can get into the routine of starting her lessons at a certain time of day—"

"Yes, I understand." He'd come in here to

blast Gen for hiring his daughter without consulting him first. How come he was the one feeling defensive?

She grinned. "Sorry. I guess all those classes I've been taking are spilling over. I didn't mean to lecture you."

"It's all right. I needed the reminder."

"So do you want me to talk to Fleur?"

"Talk to Fleur about what?" Fleur stepped in from the laundry room door, carrying a tray of empty picnic plates.

"I'll take that." Gen whisked the tray from her hands and carried it to the sink. "I was just apologizing to your dad because I should have consulted with him before I offered you the job watching Maya and Evie."

"Why?" Fleur demanded. "It doesn't have anything to do with him."

"Of course it does. He's your father."

Fleur wheeled to face Caleb. "You're not going to make me quit, are you? I really want to do this. I like Evie and Maya, and I can earn money for—" She hesitated.

"For what?" Caleb demanded. "What do you need extra money for?"

"For boots, okay?"

"Boots?" She had at least three pairs of snow boots and some nice leather ones he'd bought her for Christmas last year. And then he remembered another conversation. "Oh, you mean those overpriced knee-high rubber boots with the fancy patterns on the lining?"

She raised her chin. "They've got awesome designs."

"I love the new sockeye in waves pattern," Gen commented.

Fleur flashed Gen a smile. "I know, right? I'm trying to decide between it and the octopus."

Caleb shook his head. "I don't get it. They're rubber boots and they cost two hundred dollars. And the pretty pictures are on the inside, where nobody can see them."

"No, Dad, you turn down the cuff to show the design. You wear them over skinny jeans. They look amazing."

It sounded like a ridiculous waste of money to him, but he could remember some skater clothes he'd coveted when he was Fleur's age that were a lot less practical than rubber boots. And working to save toward a goal would be a good lesson for her. But there was still the matter of the schoolwork.

"What about all those assignments you have to make up?"

Fleur didn't hesitate. "I can do both."

"Can you? Because you didn't have a job when you fell behind—"

"That was different," Fleur insisted. "I can do this."

"If your dad is agreeable, we could have a probation period," Gen suggested. "We could try it for a week, and then evaluate how much progress you've made in turning in your school assignments. If you find the job is getting in the way—"

"It won't. I promise."

"Well, then," Caleb told her, "today is Wednesday. Next Wednesday I'll expect to see progress on your schoolwork."

"You will."

"In that case, I guess you'd better get back to your job."

Fleur flashed him a grin. "Thanks, Dad." She hurried out before he could change his mind.

"Thanks from me as well." Gen smiled at him. "And I am sorry. I won't make the mistake of bypassing you again."

"Apology accepted."

Her phone rang and she looked at the screen. "Oh, it's the bride again. She must have made a decision about the delphiniums already."

"I'll leave you to it, then."

She waggled her fingers in goodbye as she answered the phone. "This is Gen."

As he let himself out the door, the last sound

he heard was her cheerful laughter as she spoke with the bride. In the past fifteen minutes, she'd figured out a way to get the bride what she wanted and a way to motivate Fleur to do her homework. Maybe that unexpected meeting at the counselor's office was Caleb's lucky day, after all.

VICKIE'S HOUSE LOOKED exactly the way Gen would have expected. It was a simple white two-story, which had most likely started with a small porch tacked on to the front, like a hundred other homes built in Anchorage and the Mat-Su Valley in the seventies. But now a deep covered porch ran the entire length of the house, with white-painted posts topped with corbels. A lantern hung from each post, smaller versions of the two flanking the deep red double doors. Crisp black shutters lined each window. A porch swing, several rockers and a few wicker chairs were already occupied by clusters of people. Four long tables spread with red-checked cloths had been set up on the grass out front.

A group of men gathered around two smoking grills in a paved area on one end of the yard. At the other end, a few children played together. Gen held on to her girls' hands, Maya's for support because she tended to be shy, and Evie's so she wouldn't go dashing in before Gen had a chance to greet the hostess. The front door opened and Vickie came outside, carrying a tray. When she spotted Gen, she handed the tray off to someone on the porch and came forward, a welcoming smile on her face.

"You're here! Come meet everyone. Let's start with the most important people." She led them to the yard, where a boy about ten or so was throwing rings toward a spindle. He missed the first two, but when the third landed on the pole, he whooped.

"Good job, Peter." Vickie offered a high five. "Meet Evie and Maya. Peter raises rabbits. His Dutch Lop won a blue ribbon at the 4-H show this spring." Quickly, she introduced the other children in the group, which included Peter's two sisters and two preschool-age children from another farm family, reciting some special detail about each of them. Five minutes later Maya and Evie had been absorbed into the group and Gen was on her way across the lawn to meet the members of the co-op.

"Here, I brought potato salad." Gen reached into the tote she had draped over her shoulder and pulled out the covered bowl.

"Wonderful!" Vickie accepted the offering and set it on a table near the grill that looked as though it already contained at least three kinds of potato salad. Darn, Gen should have made coleslaw.

When they reached the porch, all conversation stopped, and everyone turned to look as if a performance was about to begin. The names and pictures of the families were all on the website, so Gen had a head start, but it was still overwhelming to meet this many people at the same time. The co-op members ranged in age from the Svobodas, a couple in their early seventies, to the Garcias, parents of the two preschoolers. They all offered a friendly welcome, until one of the men working the grill, who looked to be about Gen's age or perhaps a few years younger, strode over to the porch. "You the new saleslady?"

Vickie gave a little eye roll before turning toward him. "Gen Rockford, this is Clancy Latham."

Gen smiled. "Hello, Clancy. Yes, I am the sales manager for the summer." From the corner of her eye, she saw Fleur setting yet another container of potato salad on the table. Someone from the grill area called Vickie and with a nod of apology to Gen, she drifted that direction.

"If you're here," Clancy demanded, "who's answering the phones?"

"I would imagine any calls are going to voice mail," a familiar deep voice said from behind Gen's shoulder. "Just like they always do after office hours. Clancy, don't chase away our employees with unreasonable demands. People have lives, you know."

Gen looked back. One of Caleb's eyes flicked a tiny wink, and she held back a laugh.

"I just don't want to miss any sales," Clancy explained.

"That's why we set up the online ordering system," Caleb replied. "So that people can place orders anytime."

"Have you checked your email today?" Gen asked Clancy.

"No. Why?"

"I think you'll be pleased. We got a big order in from Denver for single reds." Clancy was the only grower who had listed any in inventory. "She wants all you have."

"No way. Are you sure she said singles?"

"Yes. She's got a big event in August using red and gold as the colors and was asking about gold. I told her we didn't have any gold peonies, but the single reds have golden-yellow centers." Gen had been going over all the materials and memorizing all the different varieties they had to offer. "I sent her a picture, and she loves the look and is using them for all the tabletop arrangements."

"All right, then." Clancy didn't quite smile but he managed to look smug as he turned away muttering, "Guess I better check on those hot dogs."

Gen watched him go, resisting the urge to shake her head. No thank-you, she noticed, even though he was obviously pleased. He must be a curmudgeon prodigy.

"Don't mind Clancy." Jolene Svoboda stepped forward, holding a pitcher and an empty glass. "Would you like some iced tea?"

"Yes, thank you." Gen took the glass and held it while Jolene poured the tea.

"Clancy is still sore about the singles," Jolene explained. "He thought he got a good deal on Mary Lou crowns, but two years later when they bloomed, half of them were single reds instead of what he'd ordered. Personally, I like singles. I have several in my perennial flower garden. They're beautiful and they don't need staking. But brides tend to prefer the doubles—the bigger and fluffier, the better. So Clancy hasn't always had an easy time selling his singles."

"I see." Behind Jolene, Caleb went to the table and poured a glass of tea.

Jolene glanced out to where the children

were playing. "I see you have daughters. Could your husband not make it this evening?"

"I'm divorced," Gen told her, getting that out of the way.

"Oh, I'm sorry." But Jolene's expression looked closer to delighted than sorry. "I have a nephew, Orson. He's thirty-eight and has a good job with the road maintenance department—" behind Jolene, Caleb, obviously eavesdropping, pressed his lips together in a forbidding line "—in Wasilla. I was wondering if you'd like to meet him?"

"That's so sweet of you," Gen said, while wondering what Jolene's nephew had done to inspire such disapproval from Caleb, "but I'm not dating right now. I'm so busy trying to learn this job and take care of my girls, and at the end of this summer when your regular sales manager returns, I'll be moving back to Anchorage."

"Anchorage isn't that far away. If you change your mind—"

"I know where to find you. Thank you, Jolene. Now, tell me more about your flowers. If I were to start a perennial garden, what plants would you recommend?"

"Oh, well, it all depends on your garden site. Whether it gets full sun or shade, and the soil…" Jolene happily launched into the possibilities. It would be years before Gen saved up enough for a place with a yard, so she didn't really listen too closely, but she was happy to have diverted Jolene away from matchmaking mode. If she'd really wanted gardening advice, Caleb was obviously the person to ask. The gardens surrounding the cabin were spectacular. In fact, Gen half expected him to join the conversation with Jolene, but instead he took his tea and went to sit in one of the rockers a little distance from the others.

Fleur came bounding up, though. "Hi, Jolene. Hey, Gen, I want to take the kids down to the bog to see the frogs. Is it okay if Evie and Maya come?"

"Wait. What?" Had she known the barbecue included frog wrangling, Gen would have brought the girls' rubber boots instead of dressing them in cute outfits and clean shoes.

"Nobody's going to the bog." Vickie had returned and she answered before Gen could. "Dinner's almost ready, and I don't want mud monsters at the table."

"Oh. Whatever." Fleur quickly shifted into her nonchalant, bored-teen attitude.

Vickie patted Fleur's arm. "Sorry you're the only teenager here today. The Sullivans had some family event and couldn't make it." As

Gen recalled, the Sullivans had a large farm near Wasilla.

Fleur just shrugged. Her overly casual response made Gen wonder if one of the Sullivan boys might just be a teenager.

"How is the babysitting going?" Vickie asked.

"Great," Gen replied. "Except for that little incident with the sandwiches."

Fleur grinned and looked down. Vickie raised her eyebrows. "What about sandwiches?"

"Oh, I ran into town to pick up the new brochures and cards from the printers, and Fleur was supposed to feed the girls sandwiches for lunch."

"Sandwich. Two slices of bread with a filling in between," Fleur quoted. "You didn't say what kind."

"Graham crackers do not qualify as bread," Gen insisted. "And s'mores are not sandwiches."

Vickie chuckled. "Well, technically..."

"Don't you start," Gen said, but she smiled as she said it.

Vickie caught the eye of someone near the grill, who gave her a nod. She clapped her hands. "Okay, everyone. Dinner is ready. Hope you all like potato salad."

Laughter spread through the ranks as the

co-op members and families made their way toward the serving table. Gen stood back and waited for Caleb to bring up the rear, stopping him before he went down the porch steps. She spoke in a low voice. "Thanks for defending me with Clancy, but it wasn't really necessary."

"I didn't want him discouraging you before you've even had a chance to settle into the job."

"I wasn't discouraged. Every group has that person who can find a dark cloud in any silver lining."

"That's Clancy. Good job on that sale, by the way. It's great that you've familiarized yourself with the inventory enough to make recommendations."

"Thanks." All the kids had run forward to take their places in line. "Guess I'd better help Evie and Maya fill their plates."

"Sure." Caleb touched her back. She was sure it was just a gesture to indicate that she should go first down the stairs, but his hand felt warm through the fabric of her shirt, creating a little zing of attraction. What was that all about? All the reasons she'd given Jolene for not dating were valid, not to mention that Caleb was her boss.

She glanced back at his face once and then turned resolutely away and marched down the stairs. Okay, he was attractive. She could acknowledge that. But an instinctive tug of attraction was just that—instinct. She didn't base her decisions on instinct. She couldn't. Not with two girls to support and a new career to build. Nope, no romantic complications for her. Not now anyway. Maybe not ever.

CHAPTER SEVEN

COFFEE: LIQUID MOTIVATION. Gen smiled as she folded the embroidered kitchen towel. She was finally getting around to unpacking the last couple of boxes she'd brought with her. Even though the kitchen at the cabin was fully equipped, Gen liked to have a few of her own favorite things: the collection of aprons and humorous tea towels her mother had embroidered for her over the years, the ice-cream spade that worked so much better than a scoop, and the set of coffee mugs with curved handles that felt just right in her hand.

Gen had allowed Fleur to take the girls for a walk along the trail that paralleled the lakeshore, with strict instructions to stay away from the water unless she was there to supervise. Since Gen had put in a couple of hours of work on Saturday, helping a do-it-herself bride with all her floral decisions, she didn't feel bad about taking a little time to unpack while Fleur kept the girls occupied. She opened the drawer to put away the tea towels, but something caught, keeping it from opening all the way. When she reached back to readjust, an oven mitt fell over the back of the drawer and into the cabinet.

Gen pulled the drawer all the way out, tilting it to unhook it from the drawer stops, and set it on the counter. When she reached back to retrieve the oven mitt, her fingers brushed against something that crinkled. A crumpled envelope was wedged there, partly behind the drawer underneath. She found a corner and fished it out.

The envelope was addressed to Mr. and Mrs. Bram DeBoer, with a return address of Vital Records in Connecticut. The top had been slit open, but she didn't check inside. This might be the mysterious document Caleb had mentioned. She called his cell phone. "Hi. It's Gen. I found an envelope addressed to your parents stuck behind the kitchen drawers. You said to call—"

"Yes, thanks. What's in it?"

"I didn't look. Do you want me to send it home with Fleur when she's done here?"

"No. Did Fleur see it?"

"No, she's at the lake with the girls."

"Good. I'll be there in ten minutes."

It was closer to five when Gen heard steps on the porch, barely giving her time to put the drawer back in place. "Come in," she called before he could knock.

He stepped inside. From his furrowed brow, Gen got the idea whatever he was looking for wasn't good news. "Hi. Thanks for calling."

"No problem." Gen handed over the envelope.

Caleb immediately unfolded the paper inside. The lines on his forehead smoothed. "It's just my parents' marriage license. I have another copy in my firesafe at home. They must have misplaced this one and ordered a duplicate."

"So this wasn't the document you were concerned about before?"

"No. And I don't really know that there is another document, but—" He looked down at the certificate for a moment and then looked up at her. "You're a counselor. You deal with kids every day. Maybe you can give me some advice."

"About what?"

"I've recently come across some information and I'm not sure how to tell Fleur. Or even if I should."

"Okay." Gen checked the clock. "Fleur and my girls aren't due back for another half hour. How about you tell me the whole story over a cup of coffee?"

"Coffee sounds good. Thanks."

Gen motioned for him to sit at the kitchen table while she started the pot, mostly to give him a moment to collect his thoughts. Once she'd measured the coffee and started the machine, she came to sit across from him at the table. "So tell me about this information."

He explained how he'd stumbled across the box of photos when cleaning the cabin and happened to find the adoption certificate at the bottom of the box. "I was shocked, to say the least."

"You didn't know you were adopted?"

"Not a clue. At first, I thought it was some sort of mistake, or a forgery. That's why I asked you to contact me, in case you found something else that might either confirm or deny its validity, but it certainly looks genuine. The dates are right. And I can't figure out any reason anyone would want to forge an adoption certificate with my name on it. So I've come to accept that it's most likely genuine."

"Hmm." The machine beeped and she went to pour coffee, added milk to his and set their cups on the table before sitting down again. "Do you have any idea why your parents would keep that information a secret?"

"I don't. It seems completely out of character for them. They valued honesty. When I was growing up, they stressed time and time again that I should never be afraid to tell them the truth. That if I found myself in a situation I couldn't handle, I could call them and they would be there for me." He picked up his mug and set it down, without drinking. "My mother liked to research genealogy, and she would mention things like, 'Your great-great-grandfather's uncle was wounded at Gettysburg.' How could they have lied to me all my life?"

"Maybe they didn't consider it a lie. If you were adopted, then legally, he was your great-great-grandfather's uncle. They may have felt you were better off not knowing about the adoption for some reason. People don't share everything with their children." She gave a wry smile. "I know as a teenager, I had a few lapses in judgment that I hope my daughters never find out about."

"Okay, point taken, but this is different. One is personal privacy, the other is keeping secrets that affect the other person."

She nodded. "I see what you mean, but would your life have been different if you'd known?"

"Not really, but all the more reason they should have told me." He took a sip of coffee. "I hate secrets."

"Why?"

"They always come out, and usually in the most painful way." A moment or two later he set down his mug. "I don't know why I'm telling you all of this. You're a professional counselor. You don't need to listen to my problems for free."

"How about if you just talk to me as a friend?"

He met her eyes. "Are we friends?"

"I'd like to be, if you're okay with that."

After a short pause he answered, "I think I'd like that."

"Good." She smiled. "So do you want to tell me about this painful secret? It's okay if you don't."

He blew out a long breath. "My ex-wife, Mallory—well, you've met her. Our marriage ran into problems fairly early on. I worked a two weeks on/two weeks off schedule as a welding supervisor on the North Slope, which was fine at first but after Fleur was born Mallory resented me leaving them alone for such long periods. When my parents died and I inherited this place, she was the one who suggested I turn it into a peony farm. Vickie had already established her farm, so we knew it was feasible, and I've always been a farmer at heart.

"But Mallory wasn't prepared for all that was involved in the transition. I did all the soil preparation and planting during my two weeks off between hitches, so in effect I was working two full-time jobs and had even less time to contribute to the family. It took three years before the peonies were producing enough that I could quit my slope job, but by that time she'd had enough."

"How does that relate to secrets?"

"She never told me she wanted to leave. She was office manager for an insurance agent in Wasilla. He was opening a new branch and asked her to temporarily move to Anchorage to help him get it running. It was only supposed to be for a year, and then she would return to run the Wasilla branch. Fleur had started kindergarten here, and Mallory said it was my turn to take care of Fleur while she pursued her career, which was fair. But what I didn't know was that Mallory and her boss were having an affair. I discovered that when I had to run into Anchorage for a tractor part. I brought Fleur and we dropped in on Mallory at her apartment without calling."

"And he was there." Gen was thankful she hadn't had to experience that particular humiliation.

"Yes. Exactly. Fortunately, we didn't literally catch them in the act, but it was clear enough. I think Mallory was relieved to get it out in the open and start divorce proceedings. But what I don't get is how she had been coming home every weekend for months and acting as though everything was fine. She let Fleur and me believe she would be moving back at the end of the year, even though she admitted later she never had any intention of doing so." He let out a long breath. "I suppose I should have seen the signs, but I trusted her."

"I understand. I was the same way, except my husband had multiple affairs during our marriage and I never suspected—or at least I never acknowledged my suspicions—until he announced he was moving out to live with a girlfriend."

He gave a smile of sympathy. "How long ago?"

"Almost three years now."

"I'm sorry. Not an experience I'd wish on anyone."

"No. But I'm happier now. I don't have this constant sense that there's something wrong and I don't know how to fix it. You know?"

"I do. But it hit me hard, knowing she lied to me. And now I find out my parents lied as well."

"Omitted."

"Same thing."

"Okay. So you're deciding whether to tell Fleur about it?"

He gave a wry laugh. "It would be pretty hypocritical not to, wouldn't it, after all I've said about honesty and secrets?"

"Unless you have some overriding reason she shouldn't know, yes, I'd agree."

"So any suggestions on how I tell her?"

"I think you just need to be straightforward with her, like you were with me today." She smiled. "Maybe not the part about your wife cheating with her boss, but about finding the adoption certificate and how you feel about it. How do you feel, by the way? Not about the adoption but about your parents?"

He raised an eyebrow. "Is this a counselor question or a friend question?"

"Whichever you want it to be."

"Truthfully, I don't know. I'm upset with them, obviously, but they're gone. It's not like I'm going to get an apology. And I couldn't have asked for better parents. I miss them."

"So you forgive them?"

"I mean, yeah. Of course. But I still want to know why."

"Naturally. But you may have to live with the fact that you'll never know." She sipped her coffee. "Have you considered looking for your birth parents?"

"I'd never do that." He spoke without hesitation.

"Why not?"

"I know who my parents were. That's all I need to know."

"I understand. But be prepared. Fleur might ask about them."

"That hadn't occurred to me. I'll think it over and make sure I have my answers before I talk with her." He stood and tucked the envelope into his shirt pocket. "Thanks for the coffee, and for listening. It helped."

"Anytime." Gen came to stand beside the door. "And needless to say, I won't be talking with anyone about this."

He nodded and reached for the knob. Before he opened the door Gen remembered. "Speaking of Fleur, she's great with my girls. I hope she's been doing her homework as promised."

Caleb sighed. "She's turned in a history worksheet and is halfway through a math assignment."

Gen frowned. "That's—"

"Not good enough. I know. But she and I have been getting along fairly well since I agreed to let her work for you, and I hate to do anything to mess that up."

"I understand, but you and I both know parents can't always be the nice guy."

"Well, if I'm not, I might not have the chance to be in her life at all. My ex-wife is getting married and moving across the country, and we've agreed to let Fleur decide whether to live here or there. And Mallory has some attractive bribes in place to make sure she chooses there."

"Oh. I can see why you're worried." Especially since the counseling session had exposed that Fleur's mother wasn't particularly inclined to keep Caleb involved in his daughter's life. "But wouldn't she still be with you summers?"

"In theory, but I hear teenagers aren't always willing to leave their friends and activities for three months."

When Gen was that age, she would spend much of the summer at her grandparents' remote cabin. But she'd had her brother and cousin, and friends in the area. Fleur's situation was different. She might very well decide to skip summers on the farm. "I understand. Do you want me to bring up the subject of her assignments and nudge her in the right direction? I am a professional nudger."

He chuckled. "Couldn't hurt."

"Consider it done."

"Thanks. For…" He waved his hand, taking

in the room and the coffee and her. "Thanks," he repeated.

"You're welcome. See you around." She shut the door behind him. Gen had to admire Caleb for caring so much. While she would hate to get into a tug-of-war with her ex-husband over the girls, it would be nice if he showed some interest in their lives.

Fleur might not realize it, but she was lucky to have Caleb as her father.

THE NEXT AFTERNOON Caleb made a point of debudding in the field closest to the driveway around two o'clock. If he didn't remove the smaller buds, the Kathryn's Heart peonies would produce boatloads of medium-size blooms instead of the larger blossoms that their customers paid a premium for. That made it a wonderful landscape flower but a high-maintenance commercial grower. Still, he'd included several rows of the anemone-shaped flowers in his field because Kathryn's Heart was one of his mother's favorites. In another month the cardinal-red blossoms would burst into bloom all along the fence at the cabin and beside the porch at the main house, perfuming the whole yard.

It was two thirty before he saw Fleur and Thor making their way up the drive toward their house. Fleur had her head down, reading something on her phone, but Thor saw him and wagged his tail. Caleb jumped across the ditch onto the driveway. "Hi."

"Oh, hi, Dad." Fleur put the phone in her pocket. "I was just on my way to work on my math assignment."

He suspected that was a story she'd invented on the spot, but it didn't matter. "That's good, but I wondered if you'd like to go to the Frosty Moose first."

She frowned. "Why? What's wrong?"

"Does something have to be wrong for us to get ice cream?"

"No, but you usually don't leave the farm in the middle of the day unless you need to go to town for some other reason."

"Okay, yes. I'd like to talk with you about something. Two things, actually. You're not in trouble or anything. It's just about your grandparents and—"

She held up her hand. "Whatever it is, it will be better over a raspberry-mocha-swirl cone. Let's go."

Fifteen minutes later they were sitting at a café table on the covered patio outside the Frosty Moose. None of the other tables were currently occupied. Fleur rotated her cone to lick evenly around the circumference. As

Caleb worked on his own caramel-pecan cone, he decided ice cream wasn't conducive to conversation after all. It took too much attention to keep it from dripping onto your hands to focus on words. Fleur seemed to agree, because she waited until she'd finished the last bite of cone before sitting back in her chair. "Okay, what's this all about? Are you going to tell me that the DeBoers are actually aliens from another planet and I'll soon begin experiencing the first hints of my burgeoning superpowers?"

Caleb laughed. "As far as I know, the DeBoers have no superpowers. But you're not completely off the mark. Remember when we found the veil and photos at the cabin the other day?"

"Yeah, of course."

"Well, at the bottom of the photo box I found a certificate. Of adoption." When she looked blank, he added. "My adoption."

"You're adopted?"

"Apparently."

"Wow. And you didn't know?"

"No, I didn't."

"Huh. So we might not be Dutch at all. We could be, like, German or Spanish or, ooh, Czech. That would be fun, because nobody knows how to spell Czech. We should get one of those DNA test things."

She seemed more excited than upset. Which was good, he guessed, but it made him wonder if she really understood. "That's not the point."

"What is the point?"

"The point is that my parents… That is, our heritage… Okay, I don't know what the point is." Just because this information had felt like a blow to him didn't mean Fleur had to react in the same way.

She drew her eyebrows together. "You're really upset about this, aren't you?"

"I guess I am."

"Why?"

"I don't know, exactly. I guess because I feel like my parents lied about who I really am."

"I've known some kids who are adopted. It's no big deal. Their parents are still their parents."

"That's true." Maybe Fleur was better at seeing the big picture than he was.

"Are you going to look for your birth parents?"

Why did everyone ask that? "Definitely not."

She shot him a sidelong glance but didn't question his decision. "Okay. So I'm not adopted, am I?"

"No." He chuckled. "You've seen the pictures." They had a whole album of pregnancy and baby photos.

"Just checking. Pictures can be Photoshopped, you know."

"They weren't."

"Then I don't see that this changes a whole lot."

He thought about it. He still had his farm. His memories. His daughter. "I guess you're right."

"So what's the other thing you wanted to talk about?"

Caleb blinked and shifted gears. "About you. I know your mom told you she's moving to Atlanta after the wedding."

This earned a full eye roll. "She sent me a bunch of stuff about some school there. They have horses and they go on field trips to, like, NASA and the Smithsonian, like I'm going to be all fangirl or something."

"It does sound pretty amazing," he had to admit. Equestrian lessons weren't in the cards for her at the farm, although if she decided to take up dog mushing, he had plenty of neighbors who could teach her those skills.

"Would have been nice if somebody asked me first."

"That's what I wanted to talk with you

about. If you don't want to go to Atlanta, you can stay here, with me."

She frowned as if the possibility had never occurred to her. "And go to school here?"

"Yes."

She tilted her head. "Does Mom know about this?"

"Yes. We agreed that it's your choice. If you choose to stay here, you can spend your summers with her."

"Really? You're letting me decide? What about—" she dropped her voice an octave "—*because I'm your father and I said so*?"

He laughed. "Well, in this case, your mother and I are at a stalemate, and you have the tie-breaking vote."

She thought for a moment. "So either way, I have to start a new school."

"I'm afraid so. I know it will be hard to leave your friends—"

She scoffed. "Like I have friends."

He frowned. "What about Emily?" Emily and Fleur had been best friends since kindergarten.

"Emily lives in Eagle River now. She's got lots of new friends." The implication being she didn't have time for old ones, like Fleur.

"Well, what about…" He tried to remember the name of the girl whose slumber party had preempted one of their usual weekends a couple months ago. "Brooklyn?"

Fleur grimaced. "Brooklyn's not my friend anymore."

"Oh." He felt stupid for bringing her up. "I'm sorry." For Emily moving, for this Brooklyn person and whatever had happened there, and for not knowing about any of it. He had to find a way to keep closer tabs on Fleur's life.

"Whatever." Fleur threw their napkins in the can. The sun came out from behind a cloud and brightened the planter filled with orange and yellow nasturtiums at the edge of the patio. "It's nice today."

"It is."

She gave a wry laugh. "Spending winters in Alaska and summers in Georgia doesn't seem like great planning."

"Valid point." He decided his best course was to be frank. "Honestly, I hate that your mother is moving and that one or the other of us isn't going to see you for months at a time, but I don't have any say in that. I would love to have you here full time, because I'm afraid if you move across the country, we'll lose touch." Even more than they already had. "But I'm sure your mother feels the same way. Take the summer, think it over and make the best choice for you."

"So I don't have to decide right now?"

"No. Your mom says you can tell us when she gets back from her honeymoon in August."

"Okay." She adjusted her chair. "And, Dad, I'm sorry your parents didn't tell you you were adopted."

"Thanks." He smiled at her. "But you were right. It doesn't really change anything. Family is still family."

GEN GATHERED UP the LEGOs scattered across the coffee table. Fleur had taken the girls to see swallows' nests at the barn, and Tanner had called to say he and Natalie were at some event at Big Lake and wanted to drop by the cabin on the way home, so Gen was doing some quick housekeeping before they arrived.

The front door flew open. "Mommy! Look!" Evie and Maya came inside, each cradling something against their chests. Fleur and Thor followed, Fleur with a guilty smile on her face, like the one she'd worn when the girls told Gen about the s'mores for lunch. What now?

"Come see, Mommy. There's one for each of us," Maya said. "Mine is white."

Uh-oh. Whatever Maya was holding looked furry.

"Mine is black. See?" Evie held up a black kitten with a spot of white on its chest, who regarded Gen with thoughtful yellow eyes. The kitten's oversize ears gave him, or maybe her, a comical look. And, as if he wasn't already adorable enough, he tilted his head to one side. "Isn't he cute?"

"Very cute," Gen said. "Who do these kittens belong to?"

"To us!" Maya shouted.

"Fleur says the kittens are big enough to leave their mother now," Evie explained. "So they can live here!"

Gen turned to Fleur. "I thought you were showing them a bird's nest."

"I did. But then we heard the kittens. Their mom is a barn cat. Dad's been trying to trap her to take her for shots and spaying for a long time. She finally went into the trap this morning and Dad took her to the vet. The kittens were crying, so we went inside to cuddle them. Evie said you promised they could have a cat when you moved to a place that allowed it. And Dad allows pets, so—"

"Please, Mommy?" Both girls chimed in. "They need us." Thor gazed at Gen with imploring eyes, as though he was just as concerned about the fate of these two tiny creatures.

Gen hesitated. Since she didn't know what school, if any, would hire her this fall, Gen hadn't made any moves toward finding an apartment in Anchorage. Pets would limit their choices. Plus, there was the extra work involved.

As if she could read Gen's mind, Evie claimed, "We'll take good care of them."

"We will." Maya's eyes were wide and solemn as she gently stroked the white kitten. "We'll feed them and cuddle them and everything."

Gen didn't doubt that her girls were sincere but caring for a pet on a daily basis was more responsibility than first and second graders could be expected to take on, and she doubted they would be as enthusiastic about cleaning the litter box.

"Here, Mommy. You can hold her." Maya set the white kitten on Gen's lap. Gen ran an exploratory finger over the soft fur.

The kitten closed its eyes, rubbed its head against Gen's arm and made little rumbling sounds that, as Gen continued to stroke its fur, grew into a full purr. Gen was a goner. "Are you sure they're ready to leave their mother?" she asked Fleur in a last-ditch effort.

Fleur grinned. "Yeah. Dad and I took them to the vet two days ago for their first shots and he said they're old enough to be adopted now."

The kitten turned wide blue eyes toward

Gen. Cats would be more practical in an apartment than a dog. Two of them could keep each other company during the day when they were all in school.

"Knock, knock." Natalie and Tanner stood at the still-open front door.

In all the excitement, Gen hadn't noticed the sound of their car. "Come in!"

Natalie looked around the room. "Nice place! And I love the gardens."

"Uncle Tanner, Aunt Natalie, we've got new kittens!" Evie thrust her kitten into Natalie's willing hands.

"Adorable." Natalie cuddled the black ball of fur. "What's his name?"

"I haven't named him yet. Maybe Ferdinand?" Evie had recently fallen in love with a character named Ferdinand from an old book Gen's mom had saved.

"You might want to rethink that." Tanner had turned the kitten over and checked underneath. "I believe this is a her."

"What's mine?" Maya asked, taking the white kitten from Gen and handing it to Tanner.

"Yours is a girl, too, I think," he told her and returned the kitten.

"Now, wait just a minute. I haven't said you could keep them," Gen reminded them.

"Please, Mommy?" Evie begged.

"Please?" Maya echoed. All eight pairs of eyes—yes, including the dog's and the kittens'—gazed at Gen with such longing she couldn't hold out any longer.

"Okay, we can adopt them, *if*—" Gen held up a finger to make sure they paid attention "—Caleb agrees that they're ready to leave their mother and doesn't have other plans for them."

"Yay!" The girls paid absolutely no attention to the qualifiers at the end of the sentence.

"I'm going to name mine Snowflake," Maya declared. "Or Tiger."

"Tigers aren't white," Evie argued.

"Some are," Maya retorted.

"You could call them Salt and Pepper," Tanner suggested.

Both girls scoffed at such prosaic names. Gen had a feeling this naming process would go on for some time. She went to give her brother and sister-in-law hugs. "Hi. Have a seat. This is Fleur. Fleur, my brother, Tanner, and his wife, Natalie."

"Hi, Fleur." Natalie readjusted the kitten she was carrying to offer a wave. "Gen told us what a great job you've been doing watching the girls."

"Thanks." Fleur smiled proudly.

If Gen had known Fleur would be handing out kittens, she might have been stingier with her praise. "Anybody need something to drink?"

"I'm good," Tanner told her. "Actually, we stopped by to bring something for the girls, but we didn't realize we'd have to compete with kittens."

Evie lifted her head like a pointer that had just picked up a scent. "What did you bring us, Uncle Tanner?"

"Come outside and see."

"Here, Mommy, will you hold my kitten for a minute?" Maya handed the white kitten to Gen and all three girls raced outside with Tanner close behind, as eager as any of the children. Natalie and Gen looked at each other and laughed. By the time they made it to the porch, still carrying kittens, Evie and Maya were already straddling a pair of brand-new bicycles, complete with training wheels and baskets on the front.

Tanner pulled two helmets from the bed of his truck and handed one to Fleur. She adjusted the straps and helped Evie put hers on while Tanner helped Maya.

"Since you mentioned the long driveway to the cabin with no traffic, we figured this would be the perfect place for them to learn to ride," Natalie explained to Gen.

It was a great idea. Gen just wished she'd thought of it first. She would have picked up a couple of secondhand bikes, knowing the girls would soon grow out of them and need bigger frames. Tanner, as usual, had spent far more than he should have, but it was hard to stay mad at someone who got such a kick out of making her girls happy.

"Mommy, Uncle Tanner is going to show us how to ride. Can you watch the kittens for us?" Evie asked.

"Sure. Let's go in and get comfortable, Natalie. I'm sure they'll be a while, and I want to hear all the latest news." They'd had a few days together in Tanner's house between the time she'd picked them up at the airport and when she and the girls had moved to the farm, but Gen had been so busy packing and organizing they hadn't had much time for conversation. It was nice to play with the kittens and talk while someone else took charge of Maya and Evie.

The black kitten in Natalie's lap mewed and was looking around nervously. "Where's the litter box?" Natalie asked.

"I need to get one. The kittens arrived literally minutes before you did." They took the kittens out and found an area with bare soil, which both kittens took advantage of. "The local grocery should have food and kitty litter, but I don't know if they'll have litter boxes and collars."

"The hardware store might. And didn't I see a pet store of some sort on the north edge of Willow?"

"Not a pet store. That one's for sled dog supplies. There are lots of mushers in the area. In fact, Caleb told me that the people he hires to help harvest the peonies run a small kennel not far from here."

"Caleb, the man who owns the farm? You like him?"

"Yes. He's a good boss, and it's very generous of him to let us use this cabin."

"But do you like him? As a person?"

Gen laughed. "As opposed to as a plant? Or mineral?"

"You know what I mean."

Gen knew, but she wasn't going there. "Sure, he's a nice man and a good father. Oh, look, here they come. Wow, Evie's really getting the hang of this."

Maya still looked wobbly, with Tanner running along beside her, but Evie peddled on ahead in a straight line. "Remember how to stop, Evie?" Tanner called.

When Evie got to the cabin, she reversed her

peddling, brought the bike to a stop and put her foot on the ground, all in one smooth series. "Wow, you're doing great," Natalie told her.

"You really are." Gen scooped up both kittens. "I'm so impressed."

"Uncle Tanner says I'm ready for my training wheels to come off. Maya isn't, though."

"Well, Maya is younger than you, so that makes sense." Gen was glad it hadn't worked out the other way around, because Evie would have been embarrassed if Maya had graduated from training wheels before she did. "Where's Fleur?"

"Her dad said she had to go home and do her homework. When she's done, she's going to get her bike out and ride with us."

Maya arrived and, with a reminder from Tanner, braked to a stop. "Good job, Maya." Tanner grinned at Gen. "They're naturals."

"I can see that."

"I'm going to take Evie's training wheels off. Maya may need a couple weeks, but she'll be ready soon."

Maya's bottom lip rolled out. "I want to practice some more."

"Okay. You ride up and down while I work on this bike." Tanner pulled out his tool kit and knelt beside the bike to work on the training wheels.

Evie reached for the black kitten. "You can ride in my basket."

"I don't think so," Gen told her. "The kitten might jump out and get hurt."

"Oh, okay." Evie snuggled the kitten. "Fleur says I should name her Midnight."

"That's a good name for a black cat."

Evie stroked the kitten's glossy fur. "She looks like your dress. The pretty one you wore to the party at Christmas."

"The black velvet?"

"Yes! Her name is Velvet."

"That's a great name," Natalie said, dangling a piece of grass for the kitten to bat with her paw.

Maya pedaled up more smoothly than before, but when she braked, the bike wobbled, and it was only the training wheels that kept her from falling over before she could get her foot on the ground.

"I'm naming my kitten Velvet, like Mommy's dress," Evie told her.

"Then I want to name mine after Aunt Natalie's dress." She turned to Natalie. "The white one. When you and Uncle Tanner got married."

"My lace wedding dress?"

"Yes. Lacey."

"Velvet and Lacey." Natalie stroked the white kitten. "Perfect."

"Okay, Evie. I've got the training wheels off." Tanner rolled the bike away from his truck. "Give it a try."

Evie handed the kitten to Natalie and then mounted the bike and rode off down the driveway as though she'd been doing it for years. Maya followed, pedaling furiously.

Gen smiled as she watched them go. She turned to Tanner, shaking her head. "You spoil them."

Natalie wrapped an arm around his waist. "I have to take the blame for this one. I saw the bikes at the store and mentioned it to Tanner. And since we were coming out here to Big Lake anyway, it seemed like a good time."

"Well, thank you. They love the bikes."

"Bikes and kittens." Natalie nuzzled Velvet. "It's been a big day for them."

Tanner packed his toolbox in the back of his truck. "We should head out. Give me a call if you need me to take the training wheels off Maya's bike once she gets the hang of it."

"I can manage, but thanks. It was so sweet of you both to do this for the girls. Here, let me hold the kittens while you say goodbye." Gen watched while Evie and Maya came to give hugs and profound thanks for the new bicycles without her even having to remind them.

Once they'd gone, the girls retreated into the house to play with the kittens. A little while later a knock sounded and Fleur walked in, carrying a small pail and a plastic tray filled with sand. "I brought you some cat food from the bin in the barn and rigged up a litter box until you can get some kitty litter."

"Fleur! We named the kittens. Mine is Velvet and Maya's is Lacey."

"Cute names!" Fleur handed the items to Gen.

"Thanks." Gen set the pail in the kitchen and the tray in the laundry room. "Just out of curiosity, how long have you been planning this?"

"Planning what?" Fleur's eyes widened in mock innocence.

"This." Gen's hand swept over the scene of the two girls dangling bits of string for the kittens to chase. "Kitten matchmaking."

"Oh, well, I've been feeding and petting the kittens for a couple weeks, taming them."

"You didn't consider keeping them yourself?"

"We can't have them in the house because of Thor."

"He would hurt them?"

"No, he's scared of them. One time he chased Foodmeister, one of the big barn cats, and the cat turned around and clawed him on the nose. Since then, he's been terrified."

"He was with you when you brought the kittens."

"Yeah, but you notice he didn't get too close."

"So you decided the kittens should move in here."

"Dad mentioned taking them over to Palmer, where the vet runs a cat adoption, but you know, two kittens, two girls..."

Gen tried to look stern. "And it never occurred to you to talk to me first, before you let Maya and Evie bring them home?"

Fleur grinned. "I figure why tell you when I can show you? Kittens are pretty irresistible."

Gen shook her head and chuckled. "You're incorrigible."

"What does that mean?"

"Look it up. And speaking of looking things up, how are the assignments progressing?"

"Okay, I guess. Oh, look. Velvet is hugging Lacey!" Fleur hurried over to join the girls.

Gen let her go, but she planned to follow up about the assignments later. Fleur's success was becoming important to her, and besides, she'd promised Caleb. And Gen believed in keeping her promises.

CHAPTER EIGHT

Two days later Gen bumped her way down a gravel road leading to the large Sullivan farm, north of Wasilla. From what Janet Sullivan had told her on the phone, their main crops were seed potatoes and carrots, but they'd planted a field in peonies three years ago and were expecting their first full harvest this year. Gen parked in front of the house, but before she got out, she checked her phone. It was her first time to leave the girls alone with Fleur for more than a half hour, and she wanted to make sure there were no SOS messages she might have missed. But her phone showed three bars and no alerts, so she grabbed her camera and got out of the car.

In the meantime, a welcoming committee of four dogs and a goat had assembled. A scruffy terrier, a black-and-white border collie, a husky mix and an enormous St. Bernard crowded in. So did the fawn-colored goat, bleating, as though complaining that she wasn't getting her fair share of attention. Gen took a step back and found herself pinned against her minivan, hemmed in by overaffectionate animals.

Four kids, ranging in age from midteens down to about twelve, spilled out the front door. The youngest, a girl, waved and dashed off toward a nearby orchard, calling, "Mama, the lady's here."

The three dark-haired boys, all with brilliant blue eyes, dispersed the pack of animals. "I'm Matthew," the oldest said. "This is Mark and Luke and she—" he waved toward his sister "—is Joan."

"Hi. I'm Gen Rockford. From the co-op."

"We know," Mark, the middle one about Fleur's age, answered. "Mama said you were coming to take pictures."

"Hello, there." A fresh-faced woman had emerged from the orchard gate and was walking toward them. "I'm Janet. And you must be Gen. I'm so glad you came. Brian's on the tractor this morning. Did the kids introduce themselves?"

"Yes, they did. I'm so glad to meet all of you."

"You, too. Sorry we couldn't make it to the thing at Vickie's. Matthew and Mark had a soccer game." She set the plant trimmer she'd been holding on one of the big rocks that someone had positioned around the perimeter of their front yard to discourage parking on the lawn. "You said something about pictures for the website?"

"Yes. I'd love to get some shots of you and your family out in the peony field."

"Hmm. I'm not sure I want the kids' pictures out there on the internet." The kids groaned, but Janet ignored them.

"I understand and that's fine," Gen told her. "I could just post farm scenes. Or, if you wanted, I could take photos of the kids but from angles that don't show faces, so they wouldn't be recognizable. I'll show you the photos in advance and won't post anything without your permission."

Joan's eyes grew wide and eager. "Let's do that!"

Janet laughed. "You're just trying to get out of your reading assignment. But we can try it and see how the pictures come out. The peony field is this way." She gestured toward a path that ran past the house.

The kids and dogs ran on ahead, leaving Janet, Gen and the goat to follow. The goat bumped Gen's hand and she reached over to scratch her neck, earning an approving glance from Janet. "You homeschool year-round?" Gen asked Janet.

"Yes. We slack off a little in the summer,

but we've found that the kids retain knowledge better if we don't let too much time go by. Especially this year, because Matthew and Mark have decided they want to try public school this fall, and we want to make sure there are no gaps in their curriculum."

"That must be a big job. I was trying to help a middle schooler with an algebra problem recently and discovered I'm hopelessly rusty at math."

"Oh, me, too. But my brother is a math whiz. He comes over every Thursday evening and tutors all the kids. Is this Caleb's daughter, Fleur, you were helping?"

"I, uh—" Gen should have realized Janet would guess. She hadn't meant to share Fleur's academic situation.

"Never mind." Janet smiled. "But if Fleur, or whoever you were helping, would like to join my brood for Thursday Math Night anytime, she's welcome."

"Thanks. I'll pass that on."

"You do that. Now, where do you want us for the pictures?"

Two hours later Gen had dozens of pictures and a growing admiration for Janet's organization skills. She somehow homeschooled four children, cultivated an apple orchard and an enormous vegetable garden, canned or froze the produce from the garden, raised chickens, made incredible quilts and was now in the peony business as well. Her husband, Brian, who had returned from the field in time to meet Gen over cookies and milk, had his hands full with the root crops.

But the family passion was giant vegetables. They'd let Gen see their special patches and greenhouse devoted to growing record-setting pumpkins, cabbages and zucchini. The kids had shown Gen the collection of photos and state-fair ribbons. Gen would have loved to post pictures of the vegetables in progress, but apparently, giant vegetable growing was top secret and highly competitive.

Gen left the Sullivans with a cardboard box overflowing with salad greens, green onions and dill. Such a great family. She couldn't wait to tell her girls about the giant vegetables. But when she turned in to the driveway at Jade Farm, her heart stopped. Evie's bike lay sprawled on one side of the drive, tire still spinning. Fleur, Caleb and Maya crowded next to it, at the edge of the ditch. Evie?

Gen jumped from the car and ran to see them all bent over her daughter, who was sitting in the mud of the ditch, holding her knee. A quick visual inventory showed no damage to her helmet, no blood on Evie's face and all four limbs intact. Most likely just a scraped knee. You'd never know it, though, from Evie's heartrending sobs.

"Let me see, sweetheart," Caleb was saying. "Is your knee the only place you're hurt?"

Evie nodded. "I'm b-b-bleeding."

"That's good," Caleb told her in a calm voice as he examined the scrape. "That means you didn't hurt your heart."

"W-what?"

"If you're bleeding, your heart must be pumping, right? Can you wiggle your feet?"

"Yes." Evie was so caught up in the concept of her heart pumping and feet wiggling, she forgot to cry.

"Can you wiggle your hands?"

Evie made jazz hands and wiggled her fingers.

"Good. Can you wiggle your ears?"

Evie giggled. "No."

"No?" Caleb looked surprised. "You can't wiggle your ears?"

"Nobody can wiggle their ears," she insisted.

"Are you sure? Let me try." Caleb closed his eyes tight and wrinkled his nose for a moment. "Hey, you're right. I can't wiggle my ears, either."

Evie and Maya were both laughing now, and

so was Fleur. Caleb smiled. "Let's go inside and get you cleaned up. I'm going to carry you, okay?"

"Okay."

Caleb scooped her up, ignoring the mud that was smearing all over his T-shirt. Evie leaned against his chest, her face entirely trusting. Caleb turned to see Gen. "Oh, hi. Evie had a fall, but I'm pretty sure she'll live."

"That's good news." Gen stepped up to pat Evie's arm. "Maybe Uncle Tanner got a little ahead of himself. I can put the training wheels back on if you want."

"I don't need them," Evie protested.

Maya ran to Gen. "It wasn't Evie's fault she fell. Something ran right in front of her."

"Thor flushed a rabbit," Fleur clarified. "Evie swerved to miss it. I'm really sorry." Fleur looked like she might cry herself. "I didn't mean for Evie to get hurt."

"It happens," Gen told her. "I gave you permission to ride bikes with the girls while I was gone. It's not your fault."

Fleur let out a breath. "I was afraid you were going to say I couldn't babysit anymore."

"No, you handled this very well, calling your dad to help."

"I didn't call him," Fleur confessed. "He

was working and must have heard Evie scream because he came running over."

"Let's all go inside." Caleb, still carrying Evie, led the way across the front lawn to the farmhouse. The gardens here weren't as extensive as those at the cottage, but there were still abundant flowers. Thor met them on the porch. Fleur opened the front door and held it while everyone else filed through and followed Caleb through a living room furnished with leather chairs and sofa, craftsman-style bookcases and thick rugs over hardwood floors. At the end of the room, a wide pass-through opened into the kitchen. Caleb went through the arch next to the pass-through and set Evie on the countertop, beside the porcelain farmhouse sink.

He pulled a washcloth from a drawer and handed it to Gen. "If you want to clean her knee, I'll get the first aid kit."

"Thanks." Gen took the cloth, wet it with soap and water and managed to clean the dirt and gravel from Evie's knee. Most of the bleeding had stopped. Usually at this point, Evie would be sobbing and trying to escape, but today she endured the process bravely, with only a few hisses when Gen had to clean a tender spot.

Once she'd finished, Caleb smoothed on a

layer of petroleum jelly and covered it all with a big Band-Aid. "There you go. You'll be good as new before you know it."

From a hallway behind the kitchen that Gen assumed led to a mudroom came the sound of a door opening. "Hello!" Vickie's voice called. "Caleb? Fleur?"

"We're in the kitchen."

She came in with a tote bag over her arm and carrying a glass platter covered with a floral-painted metal dome. "I saw the bikes and the minivan on the driveway. Is everything okay?"

"It's fine now," Caleb told her. "Evie had a spill and scraped her knee."

"I'm sorry. I'm blocking the drive," Gen said. "I'll go move my car."

"It's fine. I parked behind you. Evie, I've got just the thing to make you feel better." Vickie set the platter on the counter beside Evie and lifted the lid to reveal a tall cake covered with swirls of chocolate frosting. "It's Caleb's birthday cake!"

"Today is your birthday?" Evie asked.

"Are you going to blow out candles?" Maya wanted to know.

"He is," Vickie answered before Caleb could. "I have the candles right here." She set her bag on the counter and pulled out a package of candles and a small box wrapped in brown paper and fastened with jute twine. Two sprigs of rosemary had been tied into the bow.

"If we're doing your birthday stuff now, I've got your present, too." Fleur ran off and returned with a blue gift bag stuffed with tissue paper.

Although he looked embarrassed at all the attention, Caleb was smiling. Evie slid off the counter. Maya crowded close to watch Vickie. "That's a lot of candles. How old is Caleb anyway?"

"He's thirty-nine," Vickie told her without hesitation. "Practically still a kid."

Fleur, who had been gathering plates from one of the cabinets, snorted. Vickie carried the cake to the round oak table at one end of the kitchen, set it in the center and then pulled a box of matches from her pocket to light the candles. By the time she had the last one lit, the first ones were dripping wax. "We need to sing fast."

Caleb's cheeks reddened as they all sang "Happy Birthday" to him, the girls a little off-key but making up for it with enthusiasm. As soon as they'd finished, he took a deep breath and managed to blow out all thirty-nine candles.

"Happy birthday," Gen told him. "I wish

I'd known. We would have gotten you a present, too."

"You three can help me by eating some of this cake," Caleb declared. "Save me from myself. Once I taste one of Vickie's cakes, I can't stop until it's gone."

Vickie removed the candles and began cutting slices. Fleur opened the freezer and pulled out an ice cream container with the Frosty Moose logo on the side. Caleb raised his eyebrows. "How did that get there?"

Fleur smirked. "Francine picked it up last week when she brought Thor home. It's caramel pecan."

"Well, in that case—" Caleb held out the plate with a slice of cake Vickie had passed him "—put a big scoop right there."

They all enjoyed the cake and ice cream and watched Caleb open his gifts. Fleur's was a shirt in a deep forest green. When he held it up against his chest, Gen realized Caleb's eyes, which she'd thought were brown, had splashes of green circling the darker center. The green also brought out coppery highlights in his hair, which he'd passed on to Fleur. "Thank you. I love it."

Then he unwrapped Vickie's gift. Gen didn't recognize the label, but Caleb must have because he eagerly opened the box and pulled out a pair of pruning shears. "Wow, where did you find these?"

"It wasn't easy," Vickie told him. "But I found a private seller." At Gen's questioning look, she explained, "A company in the UK made the best-quality secateurs I've ever used, but last year the company folded. As soon as I heard, I placed an order for a dozen, but every gardener in Britain must have had the same idea. Anyway, I found this pair."

While Vickie spoke, Caleb had been trying them out. "They fit my hand perfectly. Thanks, Vickie."

"You're welcome." She beamed, clearly thrilled that Caleb found pleasure in her gift. It was interesting that they were so close. From what Gen understood, Vickie had moved to Alaska fifteen years ago, so it wasn't as though Caleb had known her from childhood. But they were neighbors and good friends.

The girls, not terribly impressed with garden tools, finished their ice cream. Thor had been sitting politely to one side of the table, but when Maya leaned over to look at him, he took the opportunity to clean a smear off her chin with a swipe of his tongue. Gen decided it was time to round up the girls before they got restless and decided to get into something they shouldn't.

"We'd better go. I have a basket of vegetables in the van I should put away. Thank you, Vickie and Caleb, for sharing birthday cake and ice cream with us."

Evie, without prompting, thanked Caleb for taking care of her knee. They all wished Caleb a happy birthday and said their goodbyes, but before they slipped out the door, Gen leaned closer to Caleb and spoke quietly. "Call or stop by when you get the chance. It's about Fleur. Just an idea."

"Okay. I'll call later." He raised his eyebrows, clearly curious, but he didn't ask more. "Bye, girls. Thanks for helping me eat this cake."

"Bye, everybody," Maya sang out. "See you tomorrow, Fleur."

Gen herded the girls out the door and then looked back once more before following, only to see Caleb watching her. He smiled. "Later," he mouthed.

She nodded. "Later." Why did it feel like a promise?

CALEB HELPED HIMSELF to one more sliver of chocolate cake. Fleur was in the living room, watching some superhero movie. This morning they'd struggled together over one of her math assignments, which had almost resulted in a mutiny, but in honor of his birthday Fleur had declared a truce. Tomorrow, though, Caleb was going to have to get a handle on the math concept. He had been a decent student, but it had been a while since quadratic equations had played any role in his life. He scraped a stray bit of candle wax from the top of his cake and took the first bite.

The first aid kit still sat on the kitchen counter. It had been like old times today, watching the little girls practice riding their bikes up and down the drive. When he'd heard Evie's cry, he'd felt that same heart-pounding surge of adrenaline he used to feel whenever Fleur was in danger, along with the same sense of satisfaction when he'd managed to tease Evie out of her fear and distress. It didn't hurt, either, to see Gen looking at him like he was a hero when he carried Evie to the house.

Now, as to why he would care one way or the other what Gen thought—well, that was something he didn't really want to examine too closely. He liked her, liked her easy way with people and the patient and loving way she interacted with her daughters. He respected her, earning an advanced degree while rais-ing two daughters alone. Maybe that was rea-son enough. She'd asked him to call, but she'd implied it had something to do with Fleur, so he'd decided to wait until Fleur was busy elsewhere, and now it was too late in the evening. Or was it?

From long habit, he'd been about to head upstairs, but he wasn't tired, and most people weren't early birds like he was. The little girls should be asleep, but Gen might still be up. "Fleur, I'm going for a walk."

Thor, hearing the "w" word, got up from his spot at Fleur's feet and trotted over to join Caleb. Fleur, absorbed in the show, didn't even look up. "Okay."

Caleb decided to walk through the fields instead of along the drive. At nine thirty this close to summer solstice, the sun was still high in the sky. It would continue to shine until it set a little before midnight tonight. If he was very still, Caleb could almost hear the peonies growing under the almost midnight sun. He made his way through his whites, Snowfall, a mainstay for brides, with pure white double blooms, and Glee, almost a twin to Snowfall but with the tiniest flecks of crimson on some of the petals around its heart. Then came the pinks, the prolific Barbara's Beauty, with her huge double blooms, and the Peggy's Pink that opened a deep fuchsia and faded to raspberry. Then there was the Grace, a Japanese form beloved by floral designers, with the rounded guard petals and a fluffy white center. Elsewhere, Grace was a white flower, but something about the long days and cool nights of Alaska summers caused the blossoms grown here to open blush pink. And finally, he came to the reds, the crimson Kathryn's Hearts and burgundy Mary Lous. It was almost a shame that they would all be cut and shipped in the bud form, because a field of peonies in full bloom would be a sight to behold.

Between the reds and the vegetable garden opposite the cabin lay the corals. He'd planted a single row each of Dawn Dreams and Coral Globe, more as an experiment than an investment. The commercially available coral varieties had proven finicky for Alaskan growers. They might yield a bumper crop one year and almost no blooms the next. This year looked to be a lean one, and he'd only put a minimal bud count into inventory for sale with the co-op. The corals' tendency to underperform was why he held such high hopes for the peony he'd bred, JF-143C. Even this year, under conditions that discouraged the other corals, the ones in his experimental garden were robust and filled with buds. Once trials were complete this growing season, the company he was partnering with would decide whether to offer him a deal. Until that time, he couldn't sell or distribute any of the flowers, but he'd planted five rows of JF-143C here two years ago. Once his partner company signed the agreement, if they did, he would be free to start selling the flowers. In the meantime, he'd snipped off the buds to encourage the plants to put their energy into healthy root stocks. Building for the future.

The cabin was quiet, so perhaps they were all in bed. He was about to turn back toward his own home when he heard the familiar creak of the front screen door. Gen stepped outside, walked to the edge of the porch and looked up at the sky before sitting down on the top step. She looked tired, but happy, which as mother of two little girls, was probably her normal state at the end of a day. He almost slipped away without disturbing her, but Thor had other ideas. He galloped over to the porch.

"Oh, hi there." Gen rubbed the dog's head. "Are you here alone?"

"No, I'm here." Caleb stepped from the shadow at the edge of the vegetable garden fence. "Sorry, I didn't mean to sneak up on you."

"It's okay. I just got the girls tucked in a little while ago and thought I'd sit outside for a few minutes and enjoy the garden." Gen scooted over on the step. "Come join me."

"All right." As Caleb crossed the yard, his foot brushed against the cheddar pinks adjacent to the walkway, releasing a burst of clove scent. Behind them, blue and white columbines swayed in the slight breeze.

Gen closed her eyes and breathed in. "That smells so good. I love being out here in the evenings. Every day the perfume changes."

"Yes." Caleb sat on the step beside her. "My mom loved fragrant flowers. She planted all these perennials, but she used to pop in a few annuals like nicotiana and alyssum just for the scent."

"That would explain why there are so many different types of lilacs in the backyard."

"Yes, and later you'll have rugosa roses."

"Your mother was an amazing gardener."

"Both my parents were."

"And you're carrying on the tradition. They would be so proud."

"I think they would." He scratched that itchy spot at the base of Thor's neck. The dog closed his eyes and moaned in pleasure.

Gen laughed. "That's how I looked eating Vickie's chocolate cake today. Thanks for letting us crash your birthday party. The girls loved it."

"I'm glad. Thirty-nine is too old to be blowing out candles but try telling Vickie that."

"I disagree. There's no upper limit for birthday candles. Does Vickie always make you a cake?"

"Yes. My mom always went big on birthdays. The first year after my parents died, I didn't feel like celebrating. I even told my wife not to do anything, but then Vickie showed up with a cake and said that's what my mom would have wanted. And she's been doing it every year since. She bakes for Fleur's birthday, too."

"Nice. I know from her bio on the co-op website that Vickie moved to Alaska and started her farm about the time Fleur was born. Were she and your mom old friends?"

"No. In fact, the first time my dad mentioned they'd met the new neighbor who was moving in next door, I got the idea my mother wasn't too taken with her. We were living in Anchorage then, and I was working two and two on the slope, so I didn't get around to meeting Vickie until a few months later, when my parents had a big barbecue at the lake and invited several of the neighbors. They must have worked out whatever the problem was, because it seemed like practically every time I came to visit, Vickie would be there, or would drop by. And after I inherited the land and decided to grow peonies, she got Jade Farm into the co-op and gave me lots of great advice."

"Speaking of advice, I was at the Sullivan farm today. You know they homeschool, right?"

"Yeah. They always have." He hoped Gen wasn't going to suggest he homeschool Fleur. Just trying to assist with algebra was testing his limits.

"Well, Janet tells me every Thursday evening, her engineer brother does a math help session with all the kids, and she said Fleur would be welcome to join them if she wants." She leaned a little closer. "Just so you know, the invitation came out in conversation. I wasn't discussing Fleur's academic situation or sharing anything private."

He smiled. "I didn't think you were. Have you mentioned this to Fleur?"

"No. I wanted to run it past you first. See if you thought it would be a good idea."

He thought for a moment. "I confess, I've been dreading working with Fleur on her math assignment tomorrow. It would be great if she could get expert advice. Although I feel a little guilty, pawning off my sarcastic teenager on some poor unsuspecting soul—"

The corners of Gen's eyes crinkled up in

amusement. "I wouldn't worry. It sounds like he's used to working with teenagers, and kids are seldom as annoying with others as they are at home. I don't know how many times I've shocked parents when I mention how polite their children are to me at school."

"Well, let's give it a try. Why don't you bring it up, so Fleur doesn't think I'm trying to put something over on her?"

"Aw, reverse psychology." Gen chuckled. "Do you plan to forbid her to step foot on that farm?"

"I can be a little more subtle than that."

"Good, because she would see right through that. You didn't raise a fool, Caleb DeBoer."

"I hope not." She wasn't raising any fools, either. Today, when Evie was hurt, Gen had exhibited just the right balance of concern and calm, and the girls had picked up on it right away. And even though he'd seen a moment of panic on Gen's face, she'd been understanding and compassionate with Fleur, reassuring her that she wasn't to blame.

"Oh, look." Gen pointed. A cinnamon-colored hummingbird with a green head darted to one of the columbine flowers and hovered there, drinking the nectar, before moving to the next flower. "It's the first one I've seen."

"It's a Rufous hummingbird. They migrate

all the way down to Mexico in the winter and return to Alaska in the summer, but they're not common this far north."

"Then we're lucky to be able to see them. Oh, look, there's another one." This one had more green on the back. "His mate, I'll bet." Delight transformed her face from merely attractive to beautiful.

"I'll bet you're right." Caleb watched the hummingbirds for a moment, but he couldn't help turning to watch Gen instead. Sunlight picked up the subtle colors in her hair, making the golden strands shimmer against the cocoa undertones. That faint citrus scent he'd noticed the first time he met her mingled with the floral aromas of the garden to create a heady perfume. Her soft-looking lips parted slightly as she watched in wonder.

After a moment the tiny birds darted away. "Beautiful," Gen breathed and turned to look at him, and their eyes locked. He leaned closer, and she didn't pull away. Should he kiss her?

And then, before he could make up his mind, she leaned into him. Their lips touched, once, twice and then found the perfect connection and came together. Her hand gently touched his face and trailed down his jaw in a soft caress. He slanted his head a little and the kiss deepened. His eyes closed, and for a long moment nothing mattered except for the feel of her mouth against his.

When he drew back, her eyes met his, wide open and beautiful. Her breath came faster, and if she was experiencing anywhere near the same thing he was, her heart must be racing faster than that hummingbird's. He leaned in for one more kiss, this one shorter, because if he lingered, he might never be able to pull away. He stood up. "Early morning tomorrow. I'd better get to bed. My bed, I mean."

"Of course." Gen chuckled. "Goodnight, Caleb. And happy birthday."

"Thanks." He walked away, but he couldn't help the smile that crossed his lips, the lips that had just kissed the most amazing woman he'd ever met. Happy birthday, indeed.

CHAPTER NINE

TWENTY MINUTES BEFORE time to start work, Gen was up to her elbows in dough. She'd brought a jar of her family's heirloom sourdough starter to the cabin but hadn't taken the time and effort to make bread until this morning. But if anything called for the soothing rhythm of bread making, last night's kiss qualified.

It had started out as a friendly chat. She couldn't say exactly when that changed, when she became aware of the man beside her, close enough to feel the heat from his body. Close enough to notice little things like a tiny moon-shaped scar at the base of his thumb. Close enough to see the desire in his eyes when they met hers. When she'd sensed that he wanted to kiss her, she'd realized she wanted it, too. He'd leaned closer, but he'd hesitated, and before he could talk himself out of it, she'd leaned in and kissed him. And she couldn't say she was sorry.

Yes, he was her boss, or at least chairman

of the board who hired her. And he was her landlord as well. And the father of one of the students at the school where she had done her internship. Okay, on paper, he was off-limits. Way, way off-limits. But that hadn't been her boss, or her landlord, or a school parent she was responding to last night. It was the man. The warm, caring man who coaxed beautiful flowers from the earth and took in a homeless dog and carried a little girl with a scraped knee with such tenderness. Caleb.

She stretched and folded the dough a few more times and set it aside to rise. The breakfast dishes were still stacked beside the sink. Since they were using the plates that belonged with the cabin, Gen had temporarily suspended the girls' kitchen chores for fear of breakage. To make up for it, she'd added cleaning the bathroom counter to their chore chart, and right now she could hear them arguing because Evie had just wiped the sink and Maya wanted to wash her hands.

Velvet, fleeing the commotion, ran to Gen and rubbed against her ankle. Lacey dashed into the kitchen and pounced on her sister. The two kittens rolled across the floor in a wrestler's hold, and then broke apart and nonchalantly licked their paws. As Gen loaded the breakfast dishes, a few drops of milk from a cereal bowl landed on the dishwasher door. Both kittens immediately stretched up on two legs like prairie dogs and licked up the spill.

The front door opened and Fleur appeared, carrying a plastic zipper case on a hanger. "I forgot to charge my phone. Am I late?" Thor was right behind her.

Gen looked at the clock. "You're still five minutes early. What's that in your hand?"

"My mom took me shopping on Saturday to pick out a dress for her wedding." Fleur rolled her eyes. "You wouldn't believe the dress she had in mind for me. Even Evie would think it was too frou-frou. We finally found two we both like, but I can't make up my mind. I brought them to see what you think. She'll return the other one."

"Oh, wow." Gen was flattered that Fleur wanted her opinion. But before she could say anything, Lacey pounced on Velvet, who broke away and dashed across the floor toward Thor with her sister at her heels. Thor tucked his tail and backed up until he bumped the door.

Gen laughed. "He really is afraid of cats, isn't he?"

"Told you."

Lacey, noticing the dog, dropped low and stalked in Thor's direction, her little tail twitching back and forth. Thor looked right and left, and then, as the kitten got close, jumped over her and ran across the room to hide behind Fleur. Gen scooped up the kitten. "Be nice, Lacey." She turned to Fleur. "We have five minutes before I need to start working. Why don't you try on both dresses and show me?"

"Okay." Fleur disappeared into the bathroom.

The girls stopped fussing to greet her. When the door opened, Maya ran out first and came to grab Gen's hand. "Mommy, come see. Fleur looks like a princess."

"Come out here where we can all see," Gen called.

Fleur tramped out from the bathroom, the dazzling blue satin of her dress in contrast to the army-green hiking sandals on her feet. After taking in the strapless bodice, beaded sash and box-pleated skirt of the dress, Gen was hard-pressed to imagine the dress that Fleur had rejected as being too frou-frou. But despite the mismatched footwear and Fleur's awkward modeling job, she looked amazing. Gen could see why her mother had approved it. "Great color on you, and the fit is perfect." She smiled. "You do look like a princess."

Fleur's nose wrinkled. "At least it doesn't look like it's made out of a lace tablecloth like the one Mom picked out."

"When is the wedding anyway?"

"August fifth. And then they're going on their honeymoon and after that, I have to decide if I'm going with them or staying with Dad."

"That's a tough choice. Are you leaning one direction or the other?"

Fleur shrugged. "Either way, I have to go to a new school."

"That's true. If you want to talk about it sometime—"

"Whatever. Let me show you the other dress." Fleur was in and out of the bathroom in two minutes flat. This dress was a long chiffon in a Grecian style gathered onto a beaded band that encircled Fleur's throat. The shade of blue was similar to the satin, but it looked softer, nipping into a fitted waist and then flowing to the floor. In it, Fleur appeared about four years older than she really was.

Gen felt a little catch in her throat. "Oh, that's lovely."

"Twirl around," Evie ordered.

Fleur obliged, sending the chiffon tiers swirling around her. Maya clapped her hands. "You're so pretty."

"Maya's right," Gen agreed. "You look wonderful in both of them. Which one do you like best?"

Fleur frowned. "I don't know. Mom likes the other one, but she says I can choose. I kind of like this one because it isn't strapless."

Gen smiled. "I know what you mean. I wore a strapless dress with a meringue skirt to my senior prom. My mom offered to add spaghetti straps, but I said no. I spent the whole evening tugging at the top and living in fear I'd step on my hem and flash everybody."

Fleur's eyes widened. "You didn't, did you?"

"No, although I almost knocked over a table with my skirt. It's hard to navigate in giant petticoats."

Fleur laughed. "Yeah, I'll bet." She smoothed her hands over the soft chiffon. "I think this one's the best."

"I agree. You look amazing." Gen glanced at the clock. "Okay, I need to get to work. It's supposed to rain this afternoon, so if you want to take the girls out on their bikes, you might want to do it this morning, once you've changed."

Fleur stepped closer. "Are you sure you still trust me to take them on bikes?"

"I'm sure. Like I told you yesterday, falls happen, and it's good for Evie to get back on her bike so she won't build this up in her mind as bigger than it really is. Oh, and if you don't mind, could you help the girls make invitations to our Fourth of July cookout?"

"Invitations?"

"That's right. I'll send out an email invitation to everyone, but it's fun if they can do homemade invitations, too, for a few special people. I thought black construction paper with glitter fireworks on the front, and the invitation I printed out glued inside." She nodded toward the supplies she'd set aside. "Let's see, there's my brother and his wife, my mother, my uncle, Vickie and you and your dad. So we'll need five invitations to mail."

"You're inviting me and Dad to your party?" Fleur looked surprised and pleased.

"Sure, I thought it would be fun. Do you have other plans?"

"I don't think so. We usually go to the parade in Wasilla in the morning."

"We're doing that, too. The cookout isn't until afternoon." She crossed the room to hand the kitten to Maya. "You girls mind Fleur."

With a general murmur of agreement, Maya and Evie trailed Fleur back into the bathroom.

Gen poured a cup of coffee and settled at the table with the co-op laptop. Several new orders had come in overnight, and she got busy sending them out to the members of the co-op. Sorting through and cropping the photos she'd taken at the Sullivan farm took the rest of the morning, and she spent the afternoon scheduling social media posts and answering questions from the manager of a wedding venue in Arizona. By now, after studying all the pictures, talking to the farmers and absorbing all the written information on peony culture, Gen felt confident in her answers. She could hardly wait for the upcoming harvest when she would get to see the peonies in person.

But despite her busy workday, her mind kept returning to that kiss. To that man. Was this the start of something, or was it a one-time thing? She wasn't in the right place for a relationship right now. She had just spent the past two years earning her master's degree so that she could support herself and her daughters. She'd been financially dependent on her husband, and then on her brother, but now it was time to stand on her own. Any sort of romantic relationship might get in the way of her main goal. Still, that kiss was… She smiled to herself.

At two, she closed the laptop. She found Fleur and the girls on the back porch, blowing bubbles for Velvet and Lacey to chase. The kittens were having a grand time scampering after the floating bubbles and watching them burst. Thor appeared to be napping in the corner, but Gen noticed he kept one eye open. Soft rain pattered on the roof overhead and dripped from the edge.

"Bubbles. What a great idea." Gen sat down in an empty rocking chair.

"I found them at the back of the pantry," Fleur explained. "Winter before last when it got really cold, my friend Emily and I made a video with them."

"I'd love to see it."

"It's on the internet. Just search for 'Two Alaskan Girls at Twenty-three Below Zero.'"

"I want to see!" Maya set down her bubble jar and hurried toward the door. "I'll get your computer."

"Maya, put the lid on the bubbles if you're done with them," Gen told her. "I'll get the computer." Maya sometimes got ahead of her feet when she was excited, and Gen wasn't going to risk the laptop. "I'll be right back."

The video was quite well-done, with Fleur and a girl Gen didn't recognize taking turns throwing water into the air, where it would instantly freeze and form a cloud of white powder over their heads. Then they'd filmed close-ups of bubbles, which would go from clear to frosted in intricate crystal patterns and then burst in a matter of seconds. "This is really good," Gen told her. "Emily doesn't go to Goldenview, does she?"

"No, she was in my elementary school, but her family moved to Eagle River the summer after sixth grade." Fleur tried to imply that it didn't matter to her, but Gen could tell it did. That must have been how Fleur had ended up with Brooklyn and her crowd when she moved to middle school.

As a school counselor, Gen tried to meet each student where they were and understand the forces that had led them to make good or bad decisions, but she found it hard to empathize with people like Brooklyn. Gen hadn't counseled the girl, but she had worked with one of Brooklyn's former friends, who'd finally grown tired of the way Brooklyn's little comments always made her feel small. She'd found other friends and was much happier. The kids who still hung out with Brooklyn seemed decent enough, but sometimes they let her lead them in the wrong direction. It might be good that Fleur would be changing schools next year. "Oh, I almost forgot. I was at the Sullivan farm yesterday. You know the Sullivan kids."

Fleur raised her head in interest before she remembered to act cool. "Kinda."

"Well, they homeschool, and it turns out that

every Thursday evening, their uncle comes to tutor them all in math. And they've invited you to join them if you want."

"You told them I'm doing summer school!" Fleur looked horrified.

"No, I didn't tell them anything. And technically, you're not in summer school. You're just finishing your regular semester assignments. But I wouldn't worry about it. The Sullivan kids do school all year. They won't think it's odd if you had questions about certain concepts you might have had trouble with during the school year."

"Would Mark be there?" Fleur's question was so deliberately casual, it was almost painful.

"As far as I know, they'll all be there."

"Does Dad know about this?"

"I mentioned it to him. I don't know that he's wild about the idea, but he said if you wanted to go, he'd take you." More or less.

Fleur ran a hand over Velvet's back. "I'll think about it."

"Okay, but think fast. Today is Thursday."

"Oh my gosh, it is." Fleur jumped to her feet. "When is the thing?"

"Janet said after dinner, about seven to nine."

Fleur glanced at her phone and then remembered it wasn't charged. "What time is it now?"

"About two thirty," Gen told her.

"Okay. I gotta go. See you tomorrow." Fleur gave Evie and Maya pats on their heads, called Thor and took off, muttering something about washing her hair.

Gen gave a little chuckle. Maybe Caleb was onto something with this reverse psychology. Or maybe Mark Sullivan was the draw. All the Sullivan boys were good-looking, with those amazing blue eyes, but Mark also had a killer grin and an adorable cleft in his chin. Definitely a boy Gen would have looked at twice when she was Fleur's age. Whatever the reason, Gen was glad Fleur would be getting the help she needed in math.

SATURDAY TURNED OUT to be one of those perfect summer days that Alaskans remember fondly in the middle of January. For once, Fleur was up early and had even volunteered to help Caleb with weeding and harvest in the vegetable garden. "Look at the size of this one!" The zucchini Fleur held up was nearly as big as a loaf of French bread.

"Oops." Caleb had been so busy with the rest of the farm he hadn't been here to harvest vegetables in over a week, and sometimes they grew that fast. "Throw it on the compost pile."

"How about if I take it to the Sullivans' house next week?" Fleur suggested. "They can feed it to their goat."

"Good idea!" Come to think of it, he could trace Fleur's good mood to Thursday afternoon, when she'd suddenly announced he would be taking her to the Sullivans' house that evening. When Gen had mentioned the Sullivans' math night, Caleb had figured the chances that Fleur would agree to go were slim, and that she would get anything out of it were slimmer. But he'd been wrong on both counts. When they'd arrived Thursday evening, Fleur had settled right in at the long dining table with the four Sullivan kids, their uncle and a big bowl of popcorn. Meanwhile, Caleb had walked the peony fields with Janet and Brian, helping them debud some of their whites while they chatted about crops, weather and all the things farmers talked about when they got together. On the drive home, Fleur had explained all about her new understanding of quadratic equations and on Friday afternoon had finished off and submitted two math assignments after returning from her babysitting job. She was now more than halfway through her list of assignments. Gen just might be a genius.

Gen. Caleb had never known a woman like her. Smart and pretty. Compassionate and yet practical. Strong. Funny. Adaptable. He could go on all day listing her positive qualities. Not to mention, she was an incredible kisser.

"What?" Fleur's voice broke into his thoughts.

"What, what?"

"What are you smiling about? Did I do something funny?"

"No. I, uh, was just thinking about the Sullivans' goat that thinks he's a dog." Caleb bent down to pick some of the tender spinach leaves. Shoot. Now he was lying to his daughter, after he'd condemned his parents for doing the same thing. Of course, there was a big difference between not sharing every private thought and not telling your child he's adopted.

Fleur laughed. "Mark raised the goat for a 4-H project but when the time came to sell, he couldn't. His brothers were razzing him about it, but I wouldn't be able to let somebody eat an animal I'd raised, either."

"Then it's good we raise peonies instead of cattle."

Fleur moved on to the yellow squash, and Caleb picked a selection of salad greens and added them to the basket. Later, he would wash and dry them, pack them in plastic bags and take them to the local food bank, along with much of the squash. There were quite a few people in the Willow area who depended on that bit of extra help, and they were always delighted to get fresh produce. Next, he went to work thinning the carrots, onions and a second planting of lettuce. The food bank wouldn't want these tiny vegetables, but there were more than he and Fleur could eat. Maybe Gen would like some.

He gathered up a handful, along with some mixed greens and one of the yellow squash Fleur had picked. "I'm going to run these over to the cabin."

"I'll do it." Fleur stood up from where she'd been crouching beside a squash vine.

"It's okay. I'll be right back."

"But I want to tell Gen about the math assignments." She retrieved the squash from his hands.

"Fine, we'll both go." He'd been hoping for a moment alone with Gen, but that was wishful thinking. Besides, even if he did catch her alone, what was he going to do, kiss her again? With the little girls right there in the house, ready to burst in at any second?

He probably shouldn't be kissing her at

all. Well, no *probably* about it; he absolutely shouldn't. One, she worked for the co-op and he was part of the board that employed her. Two, they both had their hands full with their respective daughters and jobs, and any sort of kissing-type relationship would only complicate that. And three, she would be going back to work in Anchorage in the fall and he might well never see her again after that. And yet, he couldn't help but wonder if she made a habit of sitting on the front porch in nice weather after she put the girls to bed. Last evening had been rainy, but today would be sunny and clear. If he happened to walk by…

With Thor tagging along, he and Fleur made their way up the curving path through the garden to the porch. Before he climbed the stairs, Caleb noticed a purple object almost hidden under the leaves of a bleeding heart. He reached in and recovered a small shoe. The front door stood open behind the screen door, and Caleb could see Maya sitting on the rug in front of the fireplace, wiggling a feather duster for the two kittens. They'd obviously settled into their new lives as house pets without much difficulty.

Gen's voice carried from the back bedroom. "I don't see it under here. Did you look in the hamper?"

"Are you looking for a purple shoe, by chance?" Caleb called through the screen.

Gen stepped into the hallway, dressed in denim shorts and a T-shirt the exact shade of coral as Caleb's new peony variety. He held up the shoe and she smiled. "There it is! Come on in."

Caleb stepped inside and handed the shoe to Evie, who was already wearing its mate on her right foot. "Thank you." She slipped on the second shoe and went to join her sister and the kittens. After greeting Gen, Fleur set the squash on the island and followed Evie. Thor watched from a safe distance.

Caleb handed Gen the rest of the vegetables he'd brought. "Fleur and I were working in the garden this morning and thought you might like these."

Maybe he was imagining it, but her smile seemed somehow more personal. Intimate. "Thank you. A salad would be perfect on a warm day like today." Then she noticed the thinnings. "Aw. Evie, Maya, look at these tiny carrots."

"Just thinning the rows so the rest have room to develop," Caleb explained. "They're good in salads or stir-fried."

"I'll bet."

The girls came to look, carrying their kittens. Evie got there first. "They're like doll-house vegetables."

"Can I eat one?" Maya asked.

"Sure. Let me wash off the dirt." Gen carried the bunch to the sink.

"What else do you grow in your garden?" Evie asked.

"All kinds of things. Spinach, chard, cabbage, lettuce, peas, beans, onions, squash—"

"Do you grow oranges?" Maya asked. "We had an orange tree at our old house."

That was right. Gen had said they'd lived in Florida before her divorce. "No, oranges don't grow up here. We have a few apple trees at the house, but the garden is just for vegetables."

"Can we see the garden?" Evie asked.

"Sure. Fleur and I have some weeding to do."

"I can pick weeds." Maya seemed full of confidence. "At Grandma's house, we pick candy lions out of her grass."

"Dandelions," Evie corrected.

Maya shook her head. "They're candy lions, because they're the same color as lemon drops but they have a mane like a lion. Right, Caleb?" Maya gazed up at him in perfect confidence.

"Um, they are dandelions, but I think candy lions is an even better name." Judging by the frowns both girls shot his direction, his attempt at neutrality was unsuccessful. "Would you like to help us with the weeding? If your mom doesn't already have plans."

"I don't." Gen handed each of the girls, including Fleur, a few of the tiny carrots. "Other than to spend as much time as possible outside today, so yes, now that Evie has her shoe, let's all go work in the garden for a while." She bit into one of the carrots. "Oh, these are so good. They're not going to make it into the salad." She offered some to Caleb.

He took two and ate them as he started for the door. "Okay, then. Let's go."

Two hours later the garden was weed-free. Fleur had discovered a few early snap peas and decided to wash them with a hose so she and the little girls could taste them there in the garden. Of course, that led to a mud puddle, which in turn meant both little girls, Thor and, to a lesser extent, Fleur, were covered with streaks of mud.

Caleb put away the hoes in the toolshed and returned to see Gen grinning as she watched the three girls detour to splash through the puddle on the way to the gate. "They look like swamp creatures."

"Nothing a little water won't cure." He checked the time on his phone. "Want to go for a swim before lunch? The lake should be warm enough."

"I'd love that. We'll get changed, then, and after we swim I can make a salad and sandwiches, and we can have a picnic."

"Great. I'll be down at the dock."

"Don't you need to go home to get your swimsuit?"

"No." He lifted his T-shirt to show the black waistband above the level of his jeans. "I came prepared."

"All right, then. See you in a few minutes. Hey, girls! Want to swim in the lake?"

Evie gasped. "Really?"

Maya squealed. "Yes!"

"Come on, then," Fleur told them. "I'll help you get your swimsuits on."

Fifteen minutes later Fleur, Maya and Evie came barreling down the hill, giggling all the way. Spotting them, Thor climbed onto the dock, shook and galloped up the hill to meet them. Fleur wore a bikini Caleb had never seen before. He supposed it covered more of her than some swimsuits, but it made him nostalgic for days when she used to wear suits like Maya's one-piece printed with mermaid scales and a ruffle across the body. Or Evie, whose suit consisted of yellow shorts and matching sunflowers on a top that covered her middle.

But Fleur was a teenager now, and he'd better get used to it.

Gen came down the hill at a slower pace, carrying a huge pile of towels. She stopped at the canoe rack. "I did a little canoeing when I was a teenager. Would it be all right if the girls and I tried out one of these sometime?"

"Sure. Anytime, if the weather's good and you all wear life jackets. It's a little breezy today. You'd spend most of your time fighting the wind." Caleb looked through the row of life preservers and chose two smaller ones.

"We should take them to the waterfall sometime," Fleur suggested.

"What waterfall?" Evie wanted to know.

"There's a place on the other side of this lake," Fleur told them. "The only way to get there is by boat. There's, like, a beach, and then you follow the creek a little while and you come to this waterfall. It's really pretty."

"I want to see that," Maya said. "Mommy, can we go see the waterfall?"

"I don't know. I'm not sure where it is or how far."

"Caleb, will you take us?" Evie asked. "Please?"

"Please?" Maya added her plea.

"Not today." He slipped one of the life preservers over Maya's head. "Like I said, it's too windy to take the canoes out today. But maybe next weekend if it's nice, and if the peonies aren't ready to harvest before then."

"Yay. We get to see the waterfalls." Evie did a little happy dance while Caleb buckled Maya's life preserver. It took a few minutes to get Maya's straps adjusted and then to repeat the process with Evie. By then, Gen had made it to the dock. When he turned around, Gen was kicking off her slides and pulling the loose T-shirt she'd worn over her head. Her legs looked a mile long under the diagonal-striped suit that, while modest, hugged the curves of her body.

He must have stopped and stared a little too long because Gen grinned at him and looked pointedly at the jeans he still wore. "This isn't all a trick to entice me into a freezing cold lake while you stand on the shore and laugh, is it?"

"No tricks." He toed off his sneakers, slid out of his jeans and pulled his T-shirt over his head. At the last minute he remembered his farmer's tan. He looked over to see if Gen would tease, but her attention had shifted to Evie, who was now backing away from the edge of the water, eyes wide.

"What's wrong?" Gen asked her daughter.

"I forgot about the alligators."

"Alligators?" Gen looked as confused as Caleb did.

"You said," Evie insisted. "You told us we always had to swim in the pool and never go too close to lakes, because of alligators."

Gen's lips twitched. "Oh, Evie, that was in Florida. There are no alligators in Alaska."

Evie still looked doubtful. "Are you sure?"

"I'm absolutely sure."

"But somebody could have brought one from Florida."

"It's too cold for alligators in Alaska. They're cold-blooded. They'd freeze in the winter."

"But what if somebody brought an alligator from Florida in the summertime and let it go in the lake? It wouldn't freeze until winter."

Caleb had to give Evie points for logic, even if her grasp of probability was a little faulty. "I'll go into the water first and make sure there are no alligators. Okay?"

Gen shot him a grateful smile. Evie considered. "I guess so."

"All right, then." Caleb stepped to the edge of the dock. "Cannonball!" As always, the cool water was a shock, but by the time he'd surfaced, it felt good. All four of the ladies on the dock looked a bit wetter, thanks to his splash, and Evie didn't seem nearly as worried. Thor had jumped in after him, and barked now at the girls, urging them in. Caleb made a show of swimming to the far side of the dock. "Any alligators here? No?" He swam back to the other side. "How about over here? Alligators? Nope?" The temptation was strong to pretend something had him by the leg, but if he did, Evie might never get into the lake. Instead, he swam back and stopped in front of Evie, treading water. "Inspection complete, ma'am. This lake is certified alligator-free."

Evie giggled, and Caleb winked. "Ready to come in?"

She screwed up her face. "I don't know. Is it cold?"

"It's nice."

"I'll jump in," Maya volunteered, and before anyone could say anything, she'd held her nose and jumped into the water, her life jacket bobbing her to the top almost immediately. She gasped. "It's fun. Come on, Evie!"

"I'm coming, too." Fleur jumped in after Maya.

But Evie still looked doubtful. Caleb held out his arms. "Want me to catch you?"

Evie nodded.

"Okay. One. Two. Three." On three, Evie left the dock and leaped forward. Caleb caught her in the air and eased her into the water so that she didn't bob under at all. "Good job. Gen, you coming?"

She grinned. "Wild horses couldn't keep me away."

CHAPTER TEN

LATER THAT DAY Gen waved at Maya as she pedaled after Evie. Maya was really starting to get the hang of bike riding. Soon, Gen would be taking off her training wheels, too. A sudden gust had Gen clutching at her straw sun hat as she walked along the driveway, watching until the girls disappeared around a curve ahead of her. In a minute or two they would reach the end of the driveway and ride back.

Gen was thoroughly enjoying this lazy summer Saturday with her girls. Once Evie was convinced she wasn't going to be eaten, they'd all had a great time splashing around in the lake and picnicking afterward. It was so sweet the way Caleb had teased Evie's fears away by going into the water first and pretending to hunt for alligators. After lunch Caleb and Fleur had gone, Caleb to work in the fields and Fleur on her lessons. Gen and her girls had stayed at the lake for a little while, but it wasn't as fun without the others there and soon the girls decided they'd rather ride bikes.

The girls came riding back, and this time Fleur was with them on her own bicycle. She rode up to Gen and stopped. "Hi."

"Hi. I thought you were working on your history paper."

"All done, but would you mind looking it over for me before I send it in?" Fleur asked.

"Sure. Just email it to me."

Fleur grinned. "I already did. Thanks." She pushed her bike forward and took off. "Hey, Evie, Maya, let's ride this way." A minute later they'd all three vanished in a puff of dust.

Gen continued along the drive toward the road, knowing they'd be back along soon. As she drew nearer the farmhouse, she saw Caleb walking between peonies, which were chest-high now with round buds forming on the long stems. Caleb looked up and waved. She waved back and made her way to him. "Hi. What are you working on?"

"Debudding. I've already gone over this patch once and nipped off all the smaller buds, but now I'm doing it again, so that all the energy goes into the bigger ones."

Gen looked at the round buds, already the size of a small Brussels sprout. "How big will they get?"

"They're already double A, but in about

three weeks when they're ready to harvest, most will be triple A."

She looked more closely at the buds to see if she could determine the color of the bloom, but they were still in the green stage. "What variety is this?"

"Glee. They're white, but—"

"With a few drops of crimson. I've seen pictures. Just beautiful. I can't decide between them and the Coral Globes as my favorite. I love the shape of Glee, but that coral color is amazing."

Caleb seemed extraordinarily pleased at her comment. He reached for her hand. "Come with me."

"Where are we going?" She allowed him to lead her across the field since the girls were with Fleur.

"Over there." He waved toward what looked like a temporary greenhouse formed from metal hoops and heavy plastic film. Through the film, she could see splashes of an orangey color. He pulled back an overlapping sheet of plastic to allow Gen in. The fragrance hit her immediately, a light but enticing scent. Inside were the most amazing flowers. Each bloom was almost the size of a dinner plate, consisting of an outer edging of rounded guard petals, with rows and rows of fluffy inner petals. The color was deeper than it had looked through the plastic, a rich rosy coral with a few darker maroon flecks in the center petals.

Gen cradled one of the blossoms between her hands and bent closer to inhale the fragrance. "These are incredible! Why haven't I seen any of these on our website?"

"They're not for sale yet. They're still in development."

"Why the greenhouse? Are they not as hardy as the other varieties?"

"No, they're quite hardy. I grew these inside so that I could use early supplemental heat to simulate how they might grow in gardens in the lower forty-eight, for research purposes."

"Is that why they're already blooming?"

"Yes. In fact, this same peony outside in my experimental beds is the last to bloom. Once we go commercial, they'll be available to ship well into September."

"These would be absolutely beautiful in a September wedding. What's this variety called?"

"Its patent name is JF-143C."

She laughed. "Not a very inspiring name."

"Well, like I said, it's in development. It will get a new name at some point."

She straightened so that she could look at his face. "What does that mean, *in develop-*

ment? Did you buy a few to try before you plant more?"

"No, I didn't buy these. I bred them from crosses of several varieties from my mom's garden."

"Wow! You bred these?" Gen looked at the peonies again. They were arguably the most beautiful of any she'd seen. "That's impressive. I didn't know you did that."

He shrugged. "Not many people do. I've been tinkering since I was a teenager, but this is the first one I've developed that might have commercial potential."

"You mean to sell to other peony farmers?"

"Yes, and to landscapers and home gardeners as well. It's in trials right now, which means it's growing in several places throughout the United States and Canada to see how it does in different climates and soil conditions. So far, my partner has been pleased with the results."

"Your partner?"

"A big seed company who specializes in bringing new plant varieties to market. I've been working with them for four years now. This is my make-or-break season. At the end of the summer, when they've collected all the data, they will be deciding if JF-143C is worth bringing to market."

"And if they do, what does that mean for you?"

"It depends. I would get a royalty on each root sold. It could mean money to clear the rocks out of that area to the south and plant it. Eventually, it could mean the money to send Fleur to a college or training program without having to worry about cost or loans. And I feel like it would honor my parents. My mother collected all sorts of different peonies. Some she even grew from seed other gardeners had collected from their heirloom varieties. My father, a biology teacher, is the one who taught me how to make the crosses."

"JF-143C. JF is for Jade Farm?"

"Yes. One-four-three just means cross number 143, and the *C* is for coral."

"One hundred and forty-three crosses?"

"Way more than that, but most crosses I threw out immediately due to weak growth or some other problem. Only a fraction did I grow long enough to see how they would bloom, and most of those were inferior to their parents or to other blooms already on the market. So only a very few are still growing in my experimental garden. Of those, this is the best."

"It's beautiful. I know on the co-op website, coral peonies sell for a premium. Is that because they're more in demand?"

"Partly. And partly because they're harder to grow, at least up here. The corals I have now never produce as many buds per plant as the Barbaras, Glees or Peggys, even on their best years. This is a lean year for corals. I'll be lucky to get five buds per crown. But so far—" he crossed his fingers "—JF-143C seems to be a good producer. Still not like the Barbara's Beauty—I get fifteen triple A buds per crown from Barbaras—but my most mature 143s look like they're making ten or more. That's good. And the florists we've given samples to say their vase life is excellent."

"This is so exciting!" She smiled up at him. "Thank you for sharing this with me."

His face changed just a little. His eyes flickered to her mouth. And the next thing she knew, he was reaching for her, and she was putting her arms around his neck to pull him closer. Her hat fell off, but she hardly registered the loss as their lips came together. Her heart beat faster, and she tipped her face to one side so that they fit together. Perfectly.

Too soon, she heard the sounds of her two girls laughing and calling to Fleur. Reluctantly, she drew back. "I guess I'd better go see what they're up to."

"I guess so." But Caleb didn't immediately release her.

She rose on her tiptoes and planted one more quick kiss on his lips before she stepped back and picked up her hat. "I really have to go."

"One second." Caleb pulled the pruning shears Vickie had given him from his pocket and cut three long stems that were beginning to unfurl. "Here. Take these with you."

"Thank you." Gen clutched the flowers to her heart. "So..." She motioned toward the opening, which was behind Caleb.

"Right." He stepped outside and held the flap for her to follow. Together, they walked toward the driveway, where the girls were still riding up and down.

Gen lifted her head to breathe in the fresh air. "I'm so glad you offered me this job. Living on the farm has been wonderful for the girls."

"Just for the girls?"

"For me, too." She sighed. "It's going to be hard to move to a city apartment after spending the summer here."

His face, which had looked so content, clouded. Gen wished she hadn't mentioned summer's end. It was barely July. They had another month and a half before she would need to be at work, assuming she found a position at one of the Anchorage schools.

"Well, those peonies aren't going to debud

themselves." Caleb moved farther down the row, away from her. But then he called, "I checked the weather reports, and they're forecasting clear and calm next Saturday. Unless something changes, we can canoe to the waterfall. If you still want to."

"I do."

"All right, then. It's a date."

ON MONDAY THE windshield wipers on Gen's minivan caught a stray birch leaf and dragged it back and forth across the glass. She'd hoped for a bright day so that they could walk among the peonies, but it looked like Vickie's video interview would be taking place indoors. She turned in to Vickie's gravel driveway and splashed through a puddle.

"Are you sure Velvet and Lacey will be okay while we're gone?" This was the third time Evie had asked in the three-minute drive from the cabin.

"I'm sure."

"Why couldn't we bring them to show Vickie?" Maya chimed in.

"Because you don't bring pets to other people's houses without asking first."

"Why didn't you ask? She would have said yes. Vickie's nice."

Gen pulled up in front of the farmhouse.

"We're here. Get your bags of books and things. And pull up your hoods. Oh, and grab that invitation for the cookout." Gen zipped her rain jacket as she got out of the car and removed the leaf from the wiper. By the time she had both girls out and was herding them toward the porch, Vickie had stepped outside.

"Good morning!"

"Hi, Vickie. Thanks for letting me bring the girls. Fleur is spending the day with Francine and Thor, visiting a nursing home in Wasilla."

"Francine will love having her along. Come in out of the rain."

Gen and the girls toed off their rubber boots and left them on the porch before following Vickie inside. "This is for you." Evie handed Vickie the homemade invitation to their Fourth of July cookout. Some of the overabundant glitter scattered on Vickie's immaculate floor. Gen winced, but Vickie didn't seem to mind.

"How beautiful! Did you girls make this?"

"I made that one," Maya told her. "Evie did other ones."

"It's beautiful. Look at all the shiny glitter." She opened it and read the message on the inside. "Your mother already invited me via email, but I'm thrilled to have a real handmade invitation. I can hardly wait for the party."

"We're going to have Popsicles and ice-cream bars."

"Yummy. I'll bring my special Fourth of July flag cake with strawberries and blueberries." After helping the girls out of their rain jackets, Vickie gave each of them a hug. "I'm so glad you could come with your mother today. Tell me what you've been doing lately."

"We got bikes," Evie said. "Maya has training wheels, but I got mine off the first day!"

"Mommy says mine can come off, too, as soon as she finds her crescent wrench."

"That's wonderful." Vickie was leading them from the entry hall into the living room as they talked. A fire burned in the massive stone fireplace anchoring one end of the room. A wooden cart on big iron wheels served as a coffee table between twin couches. The fireplace mantel displayed a row of antique glass bottles in different shapes and sizes, several holding tiny bouquets of wildflowers. Vickie set the homemade card right in the center of the mantel.

"We got kittens, too," Maya was telling Vickie. "Fleur found them. They were living in the barn."

Vickie turned in surprise. "They didn't happen to be one black and one white, did they?"

"Yes. Mine is the black one," Evie said. "Her name is Velvet."

"Mine is Lacey," Maya added. "She's white."

Vickie put her hand to her heart. "My goodness. I'm so glad to hear that. Is the deaf one settling in okay?"

Gen blinked. "Deaf?"

"Yes, the white kitten is deaf. Blue-eyed white cats often are. They were living under my porch for a while. The mother was wild, but I fed and played with the kittens when she wasn't around, and I noticed the white one never seemed to be startled by loud noises. I'd planned to take them over to the cat adoption center in Palmer when they were old enough, but the mother cat must have taken offense, because she moved them. I'm so happy they found a home with you."

Gen nodded. "That explains why the kittens were so tame, even though their mother was feral. I hadn't even realized the kitten was deaf, so yes, I'd say she's settling in fine. Caleb managed to trap the mother cat, by the way, and got her spayed and vaccinated. He says she was not happy about it, and the minute he let her out of the crate, she was gone."

Vickie chuckled. "I'll bet. Here, girls. Come this way." She took them to another corner of her living room, where bookcases lined both walls and a round oak game table nestled into the ell. A wooden box waited on the table. "I thought you might like to play with the dominoes while your mom and I are filming."

Maya abandoned her bag full of quiet activities like coloring books, climbed onto a chair and opened the box. "Can we make towers and knock them down?"

"Absolutely." Vickie smiled and turned to Gen, gesturing toward a heavy door. "We can use my home office to do the video."

Gen made sure the girls had what they needed and were settled at the table. "We'll be inside Vickie's office there, but we'll have the door closed." She cleared her throat and waited until both girls were looking at her. "No disturbing us unless it's an emergency. I mean a real emergency, like blood or fire, not like your sister isn't sharing her crayons. Understand?"

Both girls nodded and went back to the dominoes. Gen followed Vickie into her office. Creamy yellow walls with crisp white trim made the room seem sunny, despite the rain. A whitewashed wall unit held books, pots and botanical prints above a shallow desktop that supported a computer monitor. In front of it was a matching desk with a swivel chair so that Vickie could turn back to work on the computer or swing around to use her writing desk. Two wing chairs in a subtle print flanked a low table near the triple window.

Gen took mental notes. She would love a similar setup if she ever lived in a home big enough for a dedicated office space. "What a beautiful room. I'm tempted to put you in the armchair, but I think the backlight from the window would wash you out on video. Let's film you at the desk." She set up a tripod while Vickie closed the office door.

Vickie checked her reflection in a mirror near the door and added a swipe of lipstick. "How is Fleur working out for you and the girls?"

"She's great. The girls adore her." Gen chuckled. "I have to be specific in my instructions, though. Last week, for instance, we'd just gotten home from the bookstore, and I suggested she choose one of the new books in the bag to read to the girls. When I passed by, instead of reading one of their books, she was reading them the romance novel I had picked up for myself. Thank goodness there weren't any steamy scenes."

Vickie laughed. "She's a character, all right. Has been since she was tiny. Caleb and Mallory didn't see eye to eye about a lot of things, but between them they've managed to raise a fine young woman."

"I agree. She's been a lifesaver for me this summer, keeping the girls busy and happy." Gen was pleased with the progress Fleur had made toward completing her assignments, too, but that information was confidential. "We're all supposed to try canoeing next Saturday, to some waterfall Fleur mentioned."

"Fleur's taking you? The waterfall is back in a little cove, kind of tricky to find. Is she sure she knows the way?"

"Caleb is coming, too."

"Oh, Caleb is coming." Vickie got a sudden gleam in her eye. "He'll be at the July Fourth party, too, I expect?"

"Of course. Everyone's invited. Fleur mentioned the waterfall and got the girls all excited. They begged Caleb to take them, and he agreed. I think he's just being a good sport."

"Hmm." Vickie gave a knowing smile. "The waterfall is a particularly romantic spot."

It was easy to see where Vickie's mind was going. And while it was flattering that Vickie wanted to set Gen up with one of her favorite people, they didn't need that kind of pressure. Gen laughed. "Despite the book, I don't think my girls are particularly interested in romance quite yet. Okay, I've got this tripod set up. Sit there behind the desk, and we can start the interview."

When Gen looked at the screen on her phone, she noticed that Vickie's blouse coordinated perfectly with the pinks and greens of the botanical prints behind her. She adjusted the phone and pressed the start button. "We're here today with Vickie Faramund, one of the founding members of the Susitna Peony Cooperative and something of a peony pioneer here in Alaska. Vickie, can you tell us a little bit about what got you started in peony farming? Why peonies?"

"I lived in Colorado for many years, working as an interior designer, but I always had a passion for flower gardening, especially perennials, and peonies have always been a favorite of mine. Is there anything sweeter and more feminine than the ruffled pink Barbara's Beauties, or more voluptuous than deep red Mary Lous?"

Gen made a note to add in clips of close-ups of those two varieties when she edited the video. Vickie continued. "After my husband died, I carried on for several years, but I needed a change. I decided to visit Alaska. On my flight up I happened to sit next to an extension agent connected to the university, and he told me about a farmer at North Pole, Alaska, who was growing peonies commercially. And the idea took root, so to speak."

Gen chuckled. "Was that your first time in Alaska?"

"Oh my, no. I'd been to Alaska many times before. I even worked here for several months when I was twenty." An odd expression flitted over Vickie's face, but her warm smile returned quickly.

Gen tried to draw her out a little more. "So many people here planned to spend one summer, and then either never left or found a way to come back."

"Yes. For a certain subset of us, Alaska feels like home."

Gen continued the interview. Vickie would have been right at home on a late-night talk show, telling funny and interesting stories, but always working back to the peonies. She was in the middle of a story about matching peonies from an old wedding photo for a fiftieth wedding anniversary celebration when a knock sounded at the door.

"Oops." Gen turned off the video. "Sorry about that." She opened the door to find Maya standing there shifting from foot to foot.

Evie had her arm, trying to drag her away from the door. "Mommy said not to—"

Maya looked panicked. "I have to go to the bathroom, and I don't know where it is!"

"Right past this room at the end of the hall," Vickie called out.

Gen pointed and Maya turned and ran that direction.

"Sorry, Mommy," Evie said, stepping in and wandering over to the window. "I told Maya it wasn't fire or blood."

"That's okay. That really was an emergency." Gen put her hands on Evie's shoulders and guided her toward the door. "But Vickie and I really do need to finish this video. We won't be too much longer."

"Once we're done here, we can have lunch," Vickie told her. "Do you like quesadillas?"

"With lots of cheese?"

"Of course. And we have homemade cookies for dessert."

"What kind of cookies?"

Gen chuckled as she nudged Evie out of the room. "The sooner you leave us to finish up, the sooner you'll find out." She shut the door behind her eldest daughter. "Sorry about that."

"Don't be sorry. Your daughters are treasures, both of them." Vickie blinked rapidly. "Hold them tight and never take them for granted."

"You're right. They can try my patience, but

the joy they bring into my life is immeasurable."

Vickie nodded, but she sniffed again and wiped at her cheeks with her fingertips. "Are you okay?" Gen noticed a box of tissues on the table by the window. She brought it to the desk.

"Thank you." Vickie blotted her cheeks. "I don't know what's gotten into me. I just…"

"It's fine." Gen handed her a tissue and gently rested a hand on her shoulder. "Vickie, is it something to do with a child? That is, if you want to talk about it. If you don't, that's okay, too."

Vickie drew in a shuddering breath. "I lost a child." She reached for another tissue. "But not in the way that sounds."

Gen didn't answer, just rubbed Vickie's shoulder and waited to see if she wanted to say more. After a moment Vickie reached up to rest her hand on top of Gen's. "I gave up my baby for adoption."

"Oh. That must have been so difficult."

"Hardest thing I've ever done. But there were reasons." Vickie let out a breath. "The man I'd been seeing—he'd become abusive, toward me and then after I broke it off with him, toward my roommates. We had to get a restraining order. So when I discovered I was pregnant…" She shuddered.

"I'm so sorry, Vickie."

Vickie nodded. "One of my roommates had an aunt in Wasilla who was willing to let me stay, so I took off a semester and lived with her until the baby was born and then for the rest of the summer." Vickie smiled. "He was a beautiful baby. It was so hard, letting him go, but I knew if the man I'd dated found out, he would never give up. And I couldn't let that man anywhere near an innocent child. So I lied. Told them I didn't know who the father was. And I gave the baby up."

"Oh, Vickie." Gen wrapped her arms around Vickie's shoulders and gave her a long hug. "Have you ever tried to find your child? Signed up with a registry to see if he was looking, too?"

"Years ago. He wasn't on the registry." She blew her nose. "That's the main reason I moved to Alaska after my husband died. To find my son."

"And did y—" Gen started to ask when something in Vickie's face made the connection for her. "It's Caleb, isn't it?"

Vickie looked up, startled. "You can't tell him. Ever."

"Why not?" Not that it was her place to tell,

but why was Vickie keeping it a secret? "Are you still afraid of your old boyfriend?"

"No, no. He's gone. Killed trying to hold up a liquor store a few years after Caleb was born. But it would devastate Caleb to find out he was adopted. His parents never told him."

"But—" Gen almost told her he had found out, but she'd promised Caleb to keep that private. Before she could say anything else, Vickie continued.

"Caleb was so close to his parents. When they died in that accident, he was overwhelmed with grief. It took him a long time to get over that. I'm not sure he ever really has. Finding out they'd been keeping this secret all his life would be..." She shook her head.

Now what? Gen had promised Caleb she wouldn't talk about his adoption, and now Vickie was asking for her promise that she wouldn't tell Caleb. It would be better for everyone if the whole story was out in the open, but was that Gen's decision to make? "I think you're underestimating Caleb. You're already as close as family. Sure, he'd be upset at first, but once he has a chance to process, he'll be thrilled to have his mother close by."

"I'm not his mother. I'm just the woman who gave birth to him. Jade and Bram raised him. They loved him so much, and they never wanted him to feel different or rejected."

"You love him, too."

"Yes. And I've tried to fill a little bit of that void after his parents died. But Caleb hates secrets. If he ever finds out I've been keeping this from him, he'll cut me out of his life."

"Surely not. Caleb loves you."

"It's the people we love who can hurt us the most. I promised his mother. After Jade and Bram died, I considered breaking my promise, but I couldn't compound Caleb's grief by throwing this bombshell on top of everything else. And the longer I waited, the more difficult it became to tell him. Now it's impossible."

A timid knock sounded at the door. "Uh, Mommy? We're hungry."

Vickie smiled, wiped the last few tears from her eyes and got briskly out of her chair. "I think we've got enough video, don't you? Let's feed those precious girls of yours."

"Vickie—"

Vickie patted Gen's arm. "It will be okay. This way I can be in Caleb's life, and he need never know I kept this from him. Come on. Your girls are waiting."

CHAPTER ELEVEN

CALEB REACHED INTO the back of his truck for the folding camp chairs he'd packed, passed one each to Gen and Fleur and hoisted the other three to his shoulder. "Let's go find a good spot." Some years he spent the Fourth of July cutting peonies, but a cool spring had put all the peonies a little behind, so he was taking Fleur to the Fourth of July parade in Wasilla. And since they were going, too, it only made sense to invite Gen and her family along, which should be fun. Fleur was way too cool now to get excited about people throwing candy from homemade floats, but he'd bet Evie and Maya weren't.

Gen walked ahead, all decked out in a sundress with red-and-white stripes on the top and a dark blue skirt that made her look even more attractive than usual, he couldn't help but notice. When he'd arrived at the cabin early to carry folding tables from the shed by the lake to the cabin for her party, he found she'd already dragged one up the hill by herself, covered it with a red-and-blue-striped tablecloth and anchored the cloth with colorful rocks he suspected had been painted by Evie and Maya, obviously with a little help from Fleur since the ladybug rock had Fleur's unique style all over it.

The backyard had been transformed into an Independence Day extravaganza, reminding him of the summer parties his parents used to throw, although Dad would never have allowed the red, white and blue stars Gen had spray-painted on the freshly mown lawn. Personally, Caleb liked them.

"Vickie!" Gen waved.

Vickie crossed the street to see them. "You made it!" She hugged the girls while flashing an uncertain look at Gen, who gave her a smile of reassurance. What was that about?

"Yes. I didn't know you were coming, though. You should have driven in with us."

"I needed to get here early. My book club is riding in an antique car in the parade."

"How fun!"

Vickie smiled at the girls before she left. "I'll try to throw a little extra candy your way."

They were early enough to find a good vantage point to set up their chairs, with the two smaller chairs at the curb so that Maya and Evie would have an easy view, while the three of them grouped behind the girls. Caleb set his chair on one end. When Gen chose the other end, leaving the middle for Fleur, Caleb felt a little stab of disappointment.

While they waited for the parade, Fleur entertained the little girls with a game of I Spy. Caleb wasn't sure how Fleur had developed all these babysitting skills, but she was good. She'd been making steady progress on her lessons, too, especially after her second math night at the Sullivans'. And speaking of the Sullivans, there they were, the whole family making their way up the sidewalk across the street. He waved, and Janet waved back.

Their second son—Mark, if he remembered correctly—looked over, said something to his mom and jogged across the street. Fleur jumped up and went to meet him, far enough away that Caleb couldn't overhear. After a few moments Mark rejoined his family. When Fleur turned, she had a big smile on her face. Uh-oh. Wasn't it too soon for Fleur to be thinking about boyfriends? It seemed like five minutes ago she'd been riding a tricycle. She almost skipped back to her chair. "Mark's family is helping one of their cousins with a float in the parade. They're all meeting for pizza after, and he asked if I can come. Okay?"

"Um, what about the Fourth of July cook-out at the cabin?" Caleb nodded toward Gen and the girls. "Didn't you promise you'd help set up?"

"I won't be that late. Mark said they would give me a ride home."

"The party doesn't even start until four," Gen volunteered. "There's plenty of time."

Darn, he'd been hoping Gen would give him an excuse to say no. "Well, then, I guess you can go."

"Thanks!" The delight on Fleur's face made him glad he'd agreed, but he made a mental note to learn more about Mark Sullivan.

Maya jumped up from her chair. "Look! That lady has a wiener dog dressed up in a costume! Can we go see?" The woman she'd pointed out was indeed holding a small dachshund wearing a star-spangled coat and, somehow, a striped top hat.

"What's the rule about dogs you don't know?" Gen prompted.

"Ask before we get close enough to pet them," both girls chanted in unison.

"Okay, then." Gen stood up, but Fleur was faster. "I'll take them over." Holding both their hands, Fleur took them across the street.

Gen slid over to the chair Fleur had vacated next to Caleb and winked. "What's wrong, papa bear?"

He raised an eyebrow. "Papa bear?"

Gen laughed. "Judging from the expression on your face, I suspect you're considering hiring a bodyguard to accompany Fleur everywhere she goes for the rest of her life."

"Not a bad idea." He grinned. "But FYI, male bears aren't protective of cubs. In fact, they're often what the mama bear is protecting them from."

"You're right. Bad analogy. Hmm. Ganders can be quite protective, but papa goose just doesn't resonate. Let's go with papa wolf. I can see some alpha wolf in your expression." Gen chuckled. "Fleur is fourteen, you know. That's old enough for group dates."

He groaned. "Please don't use the d-word and Fleur in the same sentence. What do you know about Mark Sullivan?"

"I haven't been around him that much, but I've been favorably impressed with what I've seen. The whole family seems very nice."

"Fleur's too young to have a boyfriend."

"She already had a boyfriend, back in Anchorage. Did you not know?"

"What? When? Are they still in contact?"

"They broke up toward the end of the school

year. According to Fleur, it was because Owen was cheating with her friend Brooklyn. So now Owen and Brooklyn are together and Fleur isn't speaking to either of them. I don't know if Fleur necessarily sees Mark as a potential boyfriend, but if she does, I would consider him an upgrade."

"Why didn't she tell me about the boyfriend in Anchorage?"

"Probably the same reason she didn't tell you about missing the assignments. She didn't want to hear your reaction. You've got to be careful. Teenagers are feeling their way, and sometimes they don't make the best choices, including their choice of friends. But if you override them, they dig in their heels. It's more effective to gently guide them toward better decisions. Don't you remember what it was like to be fourteen?"

"That's exactly why I'm worried."

Gen laughed. "Well, she's not going to get into too much trouble in a pizza parlor with the Sullivans. Here they come. Smile." She moved back to her chair on the other end of the row as the girls returned.

Caleb might not have smiled, but at least he didn't immediately demand Fleur confess every detail about this ex-boyfriend in Anchorage. That would most definitely count against him when Fleur made up her mind whether to live with her mom or him this school year. They were here to celebrate Independence Day and enjoy the parade. Spending time together doing fun things would help strengthen their bond, and maybe then Fleur would trust him with the details of her life. He hoped.

Music interrupted his thoughts, and he turned to see the flag bearer coming toward them at the head of the parade, followed by a high school band playing a Sousa march. Everyone stood as the color guard passed by, followed by the drum major and drummers, including a girl who couldn't have been any taller than Fleur beating a huge bass drum as she marched along the parade route. Then came a fire truck, with firefighters throwing candy for the kids. From the way Evie, Maya and even Fleur pounced on the wrapped hard candies, you'd have thought they were gold sovereigns. Gen got up to help settle a dispute over a particular butterscotch.

"Gen! I was hoping I'd see you here." It was Jolene, dragging a younger man through the crowd. "I wanted to introduce you to my nephew, Orson." Oh, great. Gen had already told Jolene she wasn't interested in dating her nephew, but Jolene was never one to take no for an answer. "Orson, this is Gen Rockford, the woman I was telling you about."

"Hi, Jolene." Gen stepped onto the curb to meet them. "Hello, Orson."

"Gen." He offered his hand. Gen shook it and then seemed to have to tug to get her hand back. "Aunt Jo tells me you're doing a fantastic job with the co-op marketing, but she didn't tell me you were so beautiful."

Caleb supposed the man's smile wasn't really reminiscent of the big bad wolf, but it looked that way to him. Orson stepped closer to Gen, moving into her personal space. "I wonder if we might have lunch together after the parade and get to know each other a little better."

"That's nice of you, Orson, but I already have plans." Gen's smile had just the right amount of regret but firmness.

"Then how about tomorrow, or later this week?"

"I'm afraid I'm not dating right now."

"Neither am I, but I was hoping to change that." Orson laughed at his own joke. "How about I give you my number— "

Caleb couldn't take any more. He came around to stand beside Gen, slipped his arm around her waist and gave Orson a back-off stare. "That won't be necessary, Orson. She said no."

"Oh. Oh!" Orson finally took a step backward. "I didn't—that is—uh, it was nice to meet you, Gen. Aunt Jo, we'd better get back before we lose our spots." He practically dived into the crowd.

Gen called her goodbyes. She looked down at the arm around her waist and back up at Caleb, chuckling. "Taking this alpha wolf thing seriously?"

At least she wasn't calling him a goose again. "I just want you to enjoy the parade without having to deal with Orson and his ilk." Besides, it felt good, like his arm belonged there, around her waist. He noticed she wasn't in any hurry to move away from him, either.

"Gen!" This time it was Clancy Latham pushing through the crowd. "I was hoping to catch you here." He licked his lip in a nervous gesture Caleb recognized.

What was going on today? Yes, Gen looked great in that dress, but really, was every single man in the Mat-Su Valley going to ask her out? "She's not working today, Clancy. It's a holiday."

"This isn't about work. I wanted to ask Gen—" And then he noticed Caleb's arm still around her waist and even Clancy got the message. "Never mind. Enjoy the parade. See you at the next board meeting, Caleb."

"Bye, Clancy," Gen replied. "I'll be out next week to take pictures of your farm." When Gen looked at Caleb, the little lines at the corners of her eyes crinkled in amusement. "Now you've done it. The whole co-op board will hear that I'm fraternizing with the chairman."

He shrugged. "Nobody pays attention to anything Clancy says."

"What about Jolene?"

"Her, either." But he didn't want their daughters getting any ideas. He reluctantly removed his arm and glanced back toward the street. Fortunately, the girls were preoccupied watching a float being pulled by a pair of Clydesdales and hadn't noticed their interaction.

"Mommy, it's Thor!" Evie called.

As the enormous horses passed and the float came into view, Caleb spotted Francine perched on one side of the float with Thor sitting regally beside her. Caleb had forgotten that the Easy Living Senior Apartments in Palmer always entered a float. Francine saw Fleur and blew a kiss, and then threw some trinkets at the girls' feet. They scrambled to gather them up. Thor barked a greeting as they pulled on down the street.

The two little girls ran to Gen. "Look, Mommy!" Maya held up tiny plastic bottles. "More bubbles!" She added the bubbles to the candy and beads already stashed in her pockets and gave a happy sigh. "Today is the best day ever!"

Caleb couldn't disagree.

THE NEXT SATURDAY might have been custom-made for a canoe trip, with only the slightest breeze stirring the air. Caleb balanced the portage yoke of the second canoe on his shoulders, carried it to the shoreline and rested it next to its twin.

Female voices and laughter reached his ears before he spotted Fleur and the two little girls hurrying down the trail. Thor was off being a therapy dog today, which was just as well because he would have made a nuisance of himself, jumping in and out of the canoe.

Evie ran for the rack of life preservers and selected the one she'd worn before. "We've got sunscreen and bug spray and jackets," she told Caleb, "and Mommy's bringing the food."

"Sounds like you're well prepared," Caleb said. "Have you and Maya ridden in a canoe before?"

Maya nodded. "We rode in a boat and saw ducks and a beaver."

"That was a paddleboat," Evie corrected her sister. "We've never been in a canoe. But Mommy has!"

"It's been a long time, though." Gen had followed them down the path, carrying a cooler and a tote bag. "Hope I still remember how. How are the peonies coming along?"

"They're looking good." He'd checked again this morning, on the way to the lake. "The Kathryn's Hearts are almost to marshmallow stage, but not quite. I've scheduled a crew to start cutting on Monday."

"How big a crew?"

"Five. A mushing family near here, two parents and three teens who have been harvesting for me for the past three years. It's a way for them to make a little extra money. Here, let me take those." Caleb packed the cooler into the middle of one canoe. "And don't worry. Canoeing is like riding a bike. After a few strokes with the paddle, you'll remember. Do you want to take Fleur with you to help paddle while I take Evie and Maya in my canoe?"

Gen looked at her girls doubtfully. "I'd better keep the girls with me. They're in kind of a mood this morning."

"Okay. It's not all that far." After checking to make sure everyone had a life jacket properly buckled Caleb pushed the first canoe into the water and pulled it up next to the dock. "Time to get in. This is the hardest part of canoeing. Gen, you're first."

He held the canoe while Gen stepped down from the dock and settled herself on the rear seat. He passed her a paddle. "Who's next?"

"Me!" Maya cried. "I want to ride in front."

"I want to be in front," Evie complained. "I called it at breakfast."

"Girls, we talked about this," Gen said. "It doesn't matter, because one of you will ride up front on the way there, and the other on the way back."

"Well, I'm first." Evie pushed past Maya to stand beside Caleb. "Because I called it."

"Humph." Maya crossed her arms and stuck out her lip.

Caleb got Evie settled on the front seat. When it was Maya's turn, she skipped over to the edge of the dock. If Caleb hadn't grabbed her, she would have jumped directly into the canoe like it was a trampoline. "Hey, slow down there. Canoes are tippy. First rule of canoeing—stay low and don't stand up."

"Okay." Maya let him lift her down onto the middle seat of the canoe. Evie turned around and stuck out her tongue at her sister. Caleb had considered giving the girls paddles so that they could begin to learn, but judging by Maya's expression, the paddle was more likely to be used to sweep her sister out of the boat than to propel them forward.

Instead, he tucked an extra paddle under the gunwale. "Ready to give it a try?"

"Girls, stay in your seats," Gen cautioned. "Okay, ready."

Caleb gave the canoe a push, and it glided forward out onto the smooth water of the lake. Gen gave a few experimental paddles, pushing the canoe forward but turning toward port. "Try a j-stroke," he called. "Push outward at the end of the stroke to straighten your heading."

"Oh, now I remember. That is better," Gen called back.

It only took a minute for Caleb and Fleur to climb into the second canoe and join them on the lake. Caleb called, "Let's get this adventure started. Follow me!" He and Fleur paddled the canoe out of the little cove where their dock was and into the main lake.

When he looked back a few minutes later, Gen was paddling like mad to try to catch up. "Slow down," he told Fleur. "We're losing them. Let's let them paddle beside us instead of going single file."

It was about two miles by water to the trailhead, and a half-mile walk to get to the waterfall. Alone, it would take him about forty minutes to get there, so he'd figured on an hour with the group. But that was when he'd assumed Gen and Fleur would be paddling together. With Gen paddling alone and unpracticed, he mentally doubled that estimate. It was fortunate the good weather was expected to continue all day, because it looked like they were going to be out for a while.

"Oh, look." Fleur pointed at the shoreline. Two red fox kits looked over at them. A third furry face peered at them through a bush. As Gen caught up, Fleur put her finger to her lips and pointed at the foxes.

Evie looked over and gasped. "They're so cute," she whispered.

"I can't see," Maya complained. "What is it?"

"Baby foxes." This time the whisper was louder. The foxes were looking in their direction, as curious about the people as the humans were about the foxes.

"I can't see them. Move, Evie."

"I can't move—we're in a boat." Evie had completely given up on whispering.

"But I wanna see." Maya got up from her seat.

"Just a sec. I'll move the canoe—" Gen started to say, but it was too late. Maya was already trying to push past Evie, who stood up to push back, and before Gen could react, the canoe was upside down in the lake, and the three of them bobbed in the water. The noise sent the fox kits running.

Caleb paddled closer. "Everybody okay?"

Both girls nodded. Gen pushed her wet hair from her eyes. "This is why Caleb said not to stand up in a canoe."

Maya had the grace to look repentant, at least temporarily. Evie just looked mad. Caleb paddled closer, flipped the empty canoe upright again and returned the paddles to the boat.

Gen eyed the canoe warily. "How do we get back in?"

"Easiest to swim to the shore. I'll bring the boat." He grabbed the bowline. They were only about ten yards from the shore, where a gravel beach would make a good landing spot. The water was about fifteen feet deep where they were right now, but it looked like it got shallow quickly.

"Come on, girls. Head for the shore," Gen urged. Both girls obeyed, but Evie angled left while Maya veered right. Gen followed Maya.

Caleb paddled in Evie's direction, intending to follow her to the shoreline. Suddenly, she screamed. "Alligator!"

"There are no alligators, Evie!" Gen didn't yell, but her voice lacked its usual patience.

Another screech. "It's touching my foot! It's going to eat me! Help!"

"Fleur, lean left." Caleb reached out to the right, grabbed the strap on the top of Evie's life jacket and hauled her into the canoe in front of him.

As soon as her knees contacted the bottom of the boat, she twisted around and threw her arms around Caleb's waist, sobbing. "Th-thank you."

"Shh, it's okay." He patted her wet hair. "Nothing is going to get you. There are no alligators. I promise."

"B-but something t-touched my foot!"

Gen, who had reached the shoreline along with Maya, held up a branch of pondweed. "This is what touched your foot, Evie," she called. "It's just a plant."

Evie glanced over but she didn't look convinced. "I don't want to swim where stuff touches me."

"Well, nobody told you to swim here," Fleur pointed out. "If you'd stayed sitting like my dad said, you'd still be in the canoe."

Evie sniffed and glared at Maya, who was standing on the shoreline. She called out, "I don't want to be in a canoe with Maya any-more. She tipped it over."

"Did not! You're the one who pushed me—"

"Nuh-uh. I—"

"Enough!" Gen's face looked like thunder. "What's done is done. We're all okay, there are no alligators and it's a warm day so we'll be dry soon enough. We're going to get back in that canoe, and we're going to find this waterfall, and we're going to have a nice picnic. Is that clear?"

Everyone shut their mouths and nodded, in-cluding Caleb. He paddled to the shoreline, pulling the empty canoe with him. "Your mom's right. We need to keep moving if we're going to get to the waterfall by lunchtime." Once he'd beached his canoe, he got out and pulled the empty one onto the shore. "But maybe Evie should ride with me, and Fleur can ride with you and Maya and help paddle. Would that be okay?"

Gen looked at the four of them, who were all staring at her in anticipation of her next word. She opened her mouth, but instead of answering, she burst into laughter. "That..." She was laughing so hard she could barely get the words out. "That would be great!"

THE WATERFALL WASN'T particularly tall, but it was pretty, and the water cascading over the rocks made a relaxing soundtrack for their picnic. Several huge ferns clustered around the pool at the bottom of the falls, and a couple of good-size rocks and a fallen log in the adjoining meadow provided seating. Gen reached into the cooler for the grapes she'd packed and sat back down. Fleur passed around the tin of chocolate chip cookies now that everyone had finished their sandwiches. Evie and Maya, unusually cooperative since their dunking, were busy sorting through the pretty river stones they'd collected from the creek that ran parallel to the trail.

Caleb lay stretched out on the grass at Gen's feet with his eyes closed, soaking in the sun. He was probably exhausted from his rescue duties. Gen smiled, thinking of how reassuring he'd been with Evie when she was convinced an alligator was after her. He was a good dad, whether or not the kids in question were his.

Fleur put the lid on the cookie tin and set it on the cooler. "Who wants to take the trail to the top of the falls with me?"

"Me!" Maya jumped up.

"Me, too." Evie finished her cookie as she climbed to her feet.

Gen had already confirmed that the trail and overlook were safe. "Fine, but listen to Fleur and don't get too close to the edge."

"Okay." Off they scrambled through the woods.

Gen decided to take advantage of this unexpected moment alone. She nudged Caleb's shoulder with her toe. "Hey there. Want some grapes?" She dangled the bunch over his mouth.

He opened his eyes and gave her a lazy smile before biting off a grape. "Mmm, good. But you know what I'd really like?"

"A cookie?"

"Guess again." He raised himself to his elbows, and his eyes went to her mouth.

Gen suddenly realized she hadn't combed her hair since getting dunked in the lake. And when she was putting on makeup this morning—because she wanted to look good even though they were going out on the lake—had she chosen waterproof mascara or the regular kind? It was quite possible she was looking like an extra in a zombie movie about now. But if she was, Caleb must have a fondness for zombies, because he tilted his head closer.

She leaned down, and their lips met. Just a little kiss, quick and simple. But when they kissed, everything seemed better. Brighter. Warmer. Happier.

"Sweet." He grinned. "May I have seconds?"

"Not right now. Our daughters will be

reaching the overlook beside the waterfall anytime now."

"Later?"

"We'll see." She winked before gathering up the wrappings and leftovers from their picnic. "I imagine the girls will be tired tonight after such an exciting day and be ready for bed early."

"And on such a warm day, you'll probably want to sit out on your porch this evening, just to cool off."

She smiled. "Quite likely."

"Mommy, up here!" The three girls stood above them, waving.

"Look at you!" Gen grabbed her cell phone. "Stand right there. I want a picture so we can remember this day forever."

Gen took several shots, some with the whole waterfall and others zoomed in on the three girls, who, with Fleur's encouragement, were hamming it up. Once they'd finished their exploration and returned to the meadow, it was time to go. The girls skipped ahead, the bear bells Caleb had attached to their wrists jingling merrily. Caleb and Gen carried the mostly empty cooler swinging between them.

When they got to the shoreline, they set the cooler down and Gen stretched her back.

"Look how smooth the water looks," she commented.

Fleur turned. "Let's skip rocks!"

"What does that mean?" Evie asked.

"We find a flat rock, like…" Fleur searched among the pebbles at the edge of the creek bed. Most were more egg-shaped than flat, but eventually, she found what she needed. "This one!" She pulled her arm back and sent the rock flying across the lake where it bounced on the water once, twice and then sank into the lake.

Evie bounced with excitement. "I want to try it!"

"Me, too." Maya ran to Fleur.

"We need to find more flat rocks. Look around."

Gen and Caleb went to help. Flat rocks weren't easy to come by and soon the group had drifted apart as they searched different areas. Gen had collected two when she heard Maya gasp. "Aw."

Gen turned to see a bear cub prowling around the cooler they'd left at the edge of the trailhead. She froze. Fortunately, Caleb didn't. "Everyone in the canoes."

"But I want to skip rocks!" Evie protested.

"Look at the baby bear. She's so cute!" Maya took a step that direction.

Caleb scooped Maya up with one arm, Evie with the other, and carried them to the canoes. "Fleur. Gen. Now!"

He plunked the two girls into one canoe, shoved it farther into the water and climbed in the back. "Put on your life jackets," he ordered as he paddled the canoe away from the shore.

Meanwhile Fleur and Gen piled into the other canoe and paddled hard. Once they were well into the lake, they turned to look toward the shore.

"Why can't we stay and watch the baby bear?" Maya wanted to know.

"Because bear cubs seldom wander far from..." Before Caleb could finish the sentence, a full-grown black bear burst out of the woods and ran toward them, sending up a plume of water in her wake. Once she was up to her shoulders in the water, she stood on her back legs and bared her teeth, making it clear she didn't want them coming back.

Maya and Evie stared at the bear with awe. A second cub ambled out of the woods, and together the siblings made short work of ripping the lid off the cooler to get at the grapes, sandwich crusts and leftover cookies. After giving the canoe party a parting grunt, their mother went to join them.

"What about the cooler?" Evie asked Caleb.

"I'm afraid the cooler is toast."

"But we can't leave it there." Evie looked horrified. "That's littering!"

"I'll come back for it," Caleb reassured her. And knowing him, he probably would, if only because he'd promised.

A safe distance from the shore, Gen and Caleb parked the canoes side by side so they could all watch the bears. Once they'd eaten everything, the two cubs turned the cooler into a toy, batting it around and pouncing on it as it rolled down the hill. Gen was glad it was a cheap one she'd picked up at the discount store and not one of her brother's high-dollar beauties.

Caleb gave Gen a rueful smile. "Well, so far on this little outing you've been dumped into the lake and had bears steal your picnic basket. I think I'll hang up my hat as a tour guide."

She laughed. "None of that was your fault, and you kept us safe. I'd give you four stars, five if you teach the girls how to skip rocks at home later. Maybe you should branch off into adventure tourism."

"I think I'll stick to farming."

Gen reached her hand across the water and Caleb grasped it. "Thank you for bringing us out today," she told him. "This will be an adventure the girls will remember all their lives." She squeezed his hand. "And so will I."

CHAPTER TWELVE

THE HARVESTERS STARTED EARLY, but the sun had gone to work earlier, driving off the last of the dampness from yesterday's rain and leaving the peony buds dry and in perfect condition. At least that was what Caleb said in a short video clip a few minutes ago when Gen had come out to gather material for the co-op's social media this week. Fleur and the rest of the crew were hard at work, moving down the rows, clipping the long stems and laying them gently onto garden carts. Gen snapped dozens of photos, loving the way the morning sun lit the faces of the workers. Even though the buds weren't releasing their perfume, the scent of leaves and sun-warmed earth was almost intoxicating.

Later this morning Gen's mom would be driving from Anchorage to stay for a couple weeks so that Fleur would be free to help with the harvest. She and her granddaughters had spent much of Sunday afternoon making plans by phone for craft projects and trips to the Frosty Moose for ice cream.

Gen would have liked to stay and watch longer, but orders were coming in fast, and she needed to get them processed. Once Mom arrived, Gen would be heading over to some of the other farms to take more harvest photos. She couldn't resist one last look at Caleb, though, the muscles in his arms bunching as he pulled a heavy garden cart farther down the row. Maybe he hadn't inherited his parents' green thumbs through his genes, but he'd certainly absorbed a love of growing things. Or perhaps he'd inherited it from Vickie. That secret continued to gnaw at Gen's conscience. She hated keeping it from Caleb, but she'd promised Vickie.

Saturday evening, when Caleb had stopped by after the girls were asleep, Gen had managed to work in another suggestion that he might want to find out about his birth parents, but he hadn't shown the least bit of interest. Of course, they'd both been a little distracted…

Once he'd parked the cart, Caleb turned her direction. She waved, and he waved back before pulling out the new secateurs Vickie had given him and beginning to cut peonies. Gen called to Maya and Evie, who had been riding their bikes up and down the drive. "Grandma will be here soon. We'd better go home and get some breakfast."

They hadn't even finished their cereal when Gen's mom arrived. The girls rushed to the porch to greet her. Gen followed, giving her mother a warm hug. "Thanks so much for doing this."

"For spending time with my granddaughters? I should be thanking you."

While Maya and Evie ushered Mom inside, both talking at once, Gen grabbed the two bags in the trunk of Mom's car. The small one, Gen knew from experience, would be filled with yarns, needles and whatever embroidery project Mom was currently working on. The other would have treats and craft supplies for the girls, tucked in among the basic necessities of clothes and toiletries. Mom had her priorities.

Mom perched on the fireplace hearth now, stroking the two kittens in her lap, while Evie and Maya regaled her with cute kitten stories. "Lacey can't hear," Maya was telling her, "because she has blue eyes."

"Oh?" Mom looked skeptical.

"Apparently, it's a linked gene thing," Gen explained. "We looked it up after Vickie mentioned it. Something like seventy percent of white cats with blue eyes are deaf."

"It doesn't seem to slow her down." Mom

laughed as the white kitten batted at a reflection caused when light from the window bounced off the metal brace on her leg. Mom didn't let that slow her down much, either. A full day with Evie and Maya could leave anyone exhausted, but Mom handled them with ease.

"Well, if you're all set, I'll get to work. Lots of brides seem to want Alaska peonies this summer."

"Who wouldn't? They're absolutely gorgeous. We'll be fine, won't we, girls?"

Both girls nodded, so caught up with their grandmother they hardly gave Gen a second glance when she pulled out her laptop and moved to the kitchen island.

Gen spent the next few hours processing the orders, checking inventory and assigning shipments to the various members of the co-op before moving to email questions. Even though they charged a premium for coral peonies, the preorder inventory had been sold out since early summer. Still, several customers had written hopeful letters asking to be contacted if the co-op had more to sell.

With demand this high for the existing coral varieties, Gen could only imagine how popular Caleb's new coral would be. Right now the co-op sold a limited supply of Dawn Dreams, a salmon-colored semidouble with a yellow center, and Coral Globe, a bomb-shaped coral with peach tones. Both were gorgeous, but in Gen's opinion, neither could hold a candle to Caleb's new variety with its full head of fluffy petals in a rich shade of coral with flecks of deep red. It was a shame he couldn't sell the flowers until trials finished.

Mom and the girls came in from the backyard, where, judging from the colorful smears on their hands and the old shirts they wore, they'd been painting. "We've volunteered to make lunch for the harvest crew," Mom announced. "Do you have enough food, or should we run into town and pick up more?"

"What a great idea," Gen replied. "I have some extra loaves of sourdough bread in the freezer, and I stocked up on turkey and ham so we should at least have enough for a day or two."

"Good. Girls, go wash your hands and let's get started."

Mom had the lunch preparations and the two girls well in hand, so Gen continued to work until it was time to leave for her appointment at the Sullivans' farm to get more harvest photos.

All six Sullivans were hard at work, along with three other teenagers, who, Janet explained, were cousins from Palmer. They all talked and laughed as they moved down the rows, but their hands never stopped cutting and gathering the flowers. The co-op always got lots of engagement on social media when she posted action shots from the peony farms, and the photogenic Sullivan kids were better than any models.

After getting some great shots, she had returned to the minivan to drive to the next farm when the phone rang. Larry? It figured when her ex finally remembered to call, it would be when she was in the middle of her workday. "Hi, Larry. The girls aren't with me right now."

"That's okay. I wanted to talk to you. I'm taking a week of vacation at the end of July, and I thought I'd spend it with the girls."

"That's great!" She just hoped he didn't expect her to drop everything and fly the girls to Florida. She'd done that last summer, staying at a rental in the same complex as Larry's apartment. Only he hadn't taken off work during the week and had spent much of Saturday golfing, so it ended up with Gen entertaining the girls at the pool and nearby park all week so that they could spend an hour or two with their dad every day. She'd mentioned to Larry long ago that she wouldn't be free to travel this summer, but he'd likely forgotten.

"I was looking into flights, but it's really expensive to fly the girls from Alaska."

"Well, it is the prime tourist season, and you've waited until the last minute to look for tickets."

"Besides, there's the extra cost to the airline for unaccompanied minors. Unless you could get off work to travel with them," he suggested hopefully.

"I can't," Gen answered firmly. "And we can't send them unaccompanied." Technically, they could, since both girls were over five, but she wasn't about to put her two daughters on a plane trip involving three connecting flights without a responsible adult along. "You'll have to hire someone to be with the girls or fly up and take them yourself."

"I suppose I could fly up and see them in Alaska." Something in his tone made Gen suspect this was his plan all along. "Then it would just be one ticket."

"That would work. Alaska's much more pleasant in the summer than Florida."

"Great. So you'll pick me up at the airport in Anchorage on the twenty-fifth and I can stay with you in—what's the name of this town where you're staying? Sycamore?"

"Willow. And no, there's no guest room in the cabin where we're staying." There was the surprisingly comfortable foldout couch, where Gen was sleeping while Mom stayed over, but Gen needed her ex in her house like she needed a broken leg.

"Well, I looked at hotels and I can't afford to do that and foot the bill for an airline ticket."

Gen stifled a sigh. Larry never seemed to worry about the cost of his country club membership, or of those frequent golfing resort weekends.

When she didn't answer, Larry hedged, "You know, if you don't have room for me, we could just skip it this summer. Maybe you can bring the girls for Christmas."

"No." Come Christmas, it would be another excuse. She didn't want her girls growing up believing their father had no interest in their lives. Even if it was somewhat true. "The girls need to see their dad."

"Well, maybe you should have considered that before you moved our daughters across the country."

Gen clamped her jaw together to avoid reminding him of how he'd quit his job, moved in with his girlfriend and not bothered to visit the girls in the four months it took them to push through the divorce and sell their heavily mortgaged home. How she'd had to move in with her brother in Anchorage because Larry had been dabbling in stand-up comedy and refused to pay child support for the first several months after their divorce. "As you may recall, I didn't have much of a choice." She could elaborate, but refighting old battles wouldn't solve this problem.

Instead, she suggested, "Let me check around. Maybe I can find a place for you to stay with the girls."

"All right." He was suddenly agreeable again. "Oh, say. Doesn't your cousin have some little place out in the sticks somewhere?"

That *little place out in the sticks* was a luxury backcountry lodge near Seward. Her cousin Dane and his wife, Brooke, would certainly host Larry and the girls there if she asked, assuming they had room. Had a free stay been Larry's objective all along? Probably. And while she hated to reward Larry's manipulations, she would feel better knowing the girls were around family. "Rockford Backcountry Lodge is usually booked up, but I'll see if they have any room."

"Great. Let me know sooner than later, because I need to buy the airline ticket."

"Right. I'll let you know. Bye, Larry." She ended the call and shook her head. Why? Why had she ever believed Larry was the man she should marry, much less have children with? Anyone could see the man was completely self-centered, and yet she'd convinced herself that he loved her. And even after two years of a marriage in which she felt like an afterthought, she'd convinced herself he would change once they had children. But of course, he hadn't.

One would think that she, a psychology major, could have recognized a narcissistic personality from the beginning, but somehow, she'd ignored the signs. Was she doing it again? Not that Caleb was a narcissist—far from it— but he was settled on the farm and in his life. Gen had spent the past two years working hard to qualify as a school counselor in the Anchorage School District. Their lives weren't compatible. And yet, she could hardly wait to see him again, to get a few minutes alone with him.

Maybe that was okay. Maybe, as long as they both recognized that this was a temporary relationship, they could enjoy one another's company without worrying about the future. She hoped so. Because, if he happened to drop by that evening to sit beside her on the front steps, she wasn't going to turn him away.

AT THE END of his tenth day of harvest, Caleb felt weary all the way to his hair. He stepped into his kitchen, dropped a few peonies into the sink, snagged a piece of cold pizza from the box on the kitchen counter and took a bite. Ambrosia. He supposed he could pop it into the microwave to warm up and it would be even better, but he couldn't wait, wolfing it down as he climbed the stairs. After a long day in the fields, nothing felt better than a warm shower.

Once he'd washed the day's dirt from his skin and pulled on clean jeans and a non-faded T-shirt, he headed back to the kitchen. This time he took thirty seconds to heat up a slice while he nibbled on a carrot and poured a glass of milk. Once the microwave dinged, he grabbed his second slice and wandered into the living room, where Fleur was ignoring some comedy on television while smiling at her phone. She'd been doing that a lot lately. He suspected it had something to do with Mark Sullivan. He still wasn't too sure how he felt about this budding relationship between Fleur and Mark, but he had to admit, ever since she'd begun attending their math sessions, her attitude had improved dramatically. He'd had to leave off harvesting early on the last two Thursdays but seeing Fleur's steady progress on getting her assignments done was worth it.

He swallowed his first bite. "I saw the FedEx

truck earlier. You got all the shipments out?" It was their first shipment of the year, and he'd sent Fleur to handle it while he stayed with the crew to finish cutting pinks. They'd worked two hours past their usual quitting time, but they'd finished the job.

Fleur nodded and ticked off on her fingers. "Three boxes to that florist in California, all triple A Mary Lous. Four other assorted boxes. And yes—I updated the inventory on the computer."

"Excellent. Thanks." He waved the remaining part of his pizza slice. "And thanks for ordering dinner."

"No prob. Did you finish the Peggy's Pinks?"

"All done. That's it for the reds, corals and pinks. Only have the whites to go." He finished the last bite of the slice. "Couldn't have done it without you. You've been great."

"Yeah?" She grinned. "Does this mean I get a bonus come payday?"

"Possibly." Production was up this year and demand was strong. He might just give the whole crew a bonus. He gulped down the glass of milk. "Leave the pizza out. I'll finish it off after I take Thor for a walk."

"Okay. Tell Gen I got an A on that history paper she helped me with. One more math assignment, and I'll be done."

Caleb, who had been heading toward the kitchen, stopped and looked back. "What makes you think I'll see Gen?"

Fleur rolled her eyes. "Oh, come on, Dad. Like you and Thor don't get enough exercise in a day and have to go for a walk every evening? Do you think I'm oblivious?"

Yes, he realized, that was exactly what he'd thought. "Gen and I are just friends."

Fleur chuckled. "If you say so."

"I do." It didn't sound convincing, even to his ears.

"Whatever." Fleur went back to her phone, still smirking.

He continued into the kitchen and set his glass in the sink. This was a complication he didn't need. Fleur wasn't supposed to realize he and Gen were...whatever it was they were. They'd been careful not to act like anything more than friends around their families. That way, no false expectations were set, and nobody got hurt. But now Fleur had figured it out. And Debbie, Gen's mom, who had been staying with them for the past two weeks, must at least have suspicions, since every time he stopped by in the evenings Debbie would find some excuse to go inside and leave Gen and him alone together.

Did it matter that Fleur knew? She was fourteen. She'd already seen her parents divorce and her mother go through at least two other relationships before she started dating the man she was about to marry. Presumably, Fleur understood that not all relationships were forever.

All Caleb knew was that after working for fourteen hours in the fields, what he wanted more than anything else was to sit on the porch next to Gen and let the peace that seemed to surround her seep into his soul. He could worry about the rest later. He grabbed the peonies he'd left in the sink, whistled for the dog and headed for the cabin.

As he drew closer, he spotted Gen and her mother outside in the front garden, admiring the golden-yellow trilliums floating like balloons on their long stems above a bed of cool blue hardy geraniums. His mom would be pleased to know her flowers still provided so much pleasure even after she was gone. Debbie bent down and pulled up some chickweed.

"You don't need to do that, Debbie." Caleb let himself in the gate. "You're already watching two energetic girls and making the harvesters lunch every day. The turkey wraps today were delicious, by the way." When Debbie had offered to make lunch for them the first day, Caleb hadn't realized she was volunteering for the entire harvest. He'd considered telling her it was too much, but Gen said her mother loved feeding crowds. "We're getting spoiled."

"The girls and I have enjoyed being part of the harvest."

"Speaking of the harvest, how is it going?" Gen asked him.

"We got all the pinks in today. Only the whites are still in the field. Here, I brought you some peonies. This is a mix of reds and pinks. They should open in about two days." He handed over the cluster of stems to Debbie.

"Goodnight, Mom." Gen waited until the door closed behind her mother to step closer and greet Caleb with a kiss. "Hi there."

"Come sit down. You must be exhausted. I saw you and the crew still out well past eight."

"We decided to press on and get it done." He settled on the bench in the garden next to a blooming rugosa rose. "The Johansens have a family wedding and the white peonies are still in tight bud and will keep for a couple days, so we're taking tomorrow off. Which works out well, because it's supposed to rain."

Gen sat beside him and reached for his hand.

She turned it over to see the palm, running her fingers over the calluses. "You work so hard. But you love it, don't you?"

"I do." He closed his eyes as Gen massaged the ball of his hand with her thumb. If he were one of the kittens, he would be purring. "I might just sit here and let you keep doing that for the rest of my life."

She chuckled and continued rubbing. The sweet scent of the pink roses drifted their direction, mingling with the clean smell that clung to Gen's hair. There it was, that bone-deep sense of peace he only seemed to find when he was with her. His phone chimed with a text. He almost ignored it, but fathers of teenage daughters were never off duty.

He pulled out his phone and read the text. "Oh, shoot!" He got to his feet.

"What? Is it Fleur?" Gen asked.

"No, it's a general text to all the co-op members from Vickie. The weather service has predicted hail tomorrow."

"Hail?"

"Yeah. Early evening. We could lose the whole crop of whites."

Gen's eyes opened wide. "And whites are the biggest sellers for weddings."

"Exactly." Caleb scrolled through his contacts. "I need to call—oh, shoot! The Johansens will be in Talkeetna tomorrow." He pocketed the phone. "Well, Fleur and I will just have to get as many out of the field as we can."

"I'll help," Gen offered.

He hated to impose, but he would need all the hands he could get. "Thanks."

"And I'll make some calls. Maybe I can find some more people."

"Sure. I appreciate it." But he was only half listening, already planning which rows he would harvest first. The most southern area tended to have the highest bud counts. And it was unlikely Gen would find any extra workers, since all the other farmers were in the same boat. "I'd better head home. Get an early start tomorrow." When the sun came up around five, he planned to already be harvesting.

"I understand. Try to get some sleep." She rose to her tiptoes and kissed him.

"I will. See you in the morning."

CHAPTER THIRTEEN

CALEB HAD FILLED a garden cart with Glee buds and was dragging it to the cold room when Gen reported for duty. Caleb looked at his watch. Only six fifteen. He'd told Fleur she didn't need to be there until six thirty, figuring she'd be more productive with a little more sleep. Gen looked prepared, wearing gardening gloves and carrying a rain jacket. The sun was shining in the northeast, but clouds were already building to the west.

"Good morning," Gen greeted him. "Tell me what to do."

"Come with me." He parked the cart in front of the cold room and led Gen on to the equipment room in the barn. "Choose a pair of clippers that feel good in your hands and take one of these sticks." He'd precut guides for the harvesters. "These are twenty-two inches long, the stem length we promise. Then choose a row, cut the flowers and pile them on the cart. I've already parked garden carts in the rows I want to start with."

"Do I cut all the buds?"

"Generally, yes. If you see any tiny buds or buds that aren't showing color yet, you can leave them. Cut everything else. We'll grade them for size later. When your cart is full, call me and I'll take them to the cold room."

"Sounds good. I'll get started."

"Gen." He waited until she looked at him. "Thank you. Your help means a lot."

She flashed a grin. "You ain't seen nothing yet." She turned and reached for a pair of clippers.

He returned to transfer the peonies he'd cut into five-gallon buckets, marking each bucket with the variety. The buckets went onto shelves in the cold room, designed to hold the buds at thirty-four degrees, only two degrees above freezing. When he returned to the field, Gen was already at work in the row next to his. He stopped to watch for a moment and then, satisfied she'd understood his directions, went back to work on his own row.

He'd half filled another cart before Fleur wandered out, fifteen minutes late but ready to work. Shortly after, an unfamiliar SUV rolled up the drive and went on to park at the cabin. Thor ran to greet the three men and two women walking back toward them. Caleb recognized Gen's brother, his wife and Gen's uncle, whom he'd met at Gen's party. When Gen had mentioned making calls, he'd assumed she meant calling locals who had indicated they might want a few hours of work, but it appeared she'd called in family instead. Gen left the field to greet them and took them to the barn. When they returned, they all wore gloves and carried clippers and measuring sticks.

"Caleb, you remember Tanner, Natalie and Uncle Russ, and this is my cousin Dane, and his wife, Brooke. Where do you want them to start?"

"Wow, hi. I really appreciate this. You can take these five rows." He pointed them toward the first rows of Snowfalls. "I'll get some more carts." He got them set up and then took the stems Gen and Fleur had cut to the cold room. He was still transferring them to buckets when Debbie showed up, pushing a sleeping toddler in a big-wheeled stroller. Gen's girls were with her, on their bikes.

"Is this task something I could do while I watch the kiddos?" Debbie asked after greeting him. "Or would we be of more help elsewhere?" Caleb's eyes flickered to the brace on her leg, but when they returned to her face, her smile was chiding. "Don't worry about me. When I get too tired, I'll sit. Until then, put me to work."

"All right. Flowers go in these buckets." He pointed to the stack beside the cold room door. "Don't pack them too tightly—we don't want any damage. Then put the buckets in the cold room. The shelves are marked by variety, but I like to mark the buckets, too, in case something gets misplaced. The ones in this cart are all Glee, but the ones Tanner and the rest are cutting now are called Snowfall."

"Do I put water in the buckets?"

"No, the cold keeps the buds in suspense—they don't need water. Thanks, Debbie. This will be a huge help. Where did the baby come from, by the way?" He smiled at the sleeping toddler.

"Steller belongs to Dane and Brooke. She just fell asleep, so I've probably got an hour before she'll wake up and demand my attention."

"She's cute. I've never met a Steller before."

"She's named after Georg Steller."

"Oh, as in Steller jays and Steller sea lions?"

"Exactly." Debbie smiled. "I've got this. Go do what you need to do."

He returned to the field and looked up. No rain yet, but dark clouds were building, and the air had that heavy feel. With a full crew, even an inexperienced one, they had a fair shot of harvesting a good percentage of the whites before the hail hit this afternoon. Gen and her family just might save his crop.

When he took the next cart to the cold room, Debbie was still there, putting away a load of Snowfalls. She'd spread a blanket on the ground nearby, where Evie and Maya played with Steller, stacking alphabet blocks into towers and giggling when she knocked them over. "These are Glee?" Debbie indicated the cart.

"Yes. Thanks, Debbie."

"Here, you can take this cart back with you." She removed the last armful of Snowfalls and placed them in a bucket. Two more unfamiliar cars crawled up the drive.

"Now, who could that be?" Caleb wondered.

"I imagine it's some of Gen's friends from Anchorage. She knew of a few teachers who were taking the summer off. And I called a couple of dedicated gardeners I know who were thrilled at the chance to visit a real flower farm. They should arrive soon."

Caleb blinked. Debbie just smiled and began unloading the stems he'd brought. Caleb noticed a few crooked stems they wouldn't be able to ship as premium. "Say, Debbie. You see these bent stems?"

"Uh-huh."

"If you want, you can set those aside in a separate bucket and give them to the helpers to take home with them. In fact, there are a couple buckets of pinks and reds labeled 'do not ship' at the back of the shelves inside. You can give those away as well."

"Wonderful. They'll love that."

Gen waved to them as she made her way out of the field toward the newcomers. "I'll get them equipped," she called to Caleb. "Where do you want them cutting?"

"The rows just north of where you and Fleur are working would be great."

Caleb lost track of the number of people who came and went. There may have been as many as twenty people working the fields at some times. Some only stayed for an hour or two, others for longer. A pregnant woman and another with a baby in a backpack set out a spread of sandwiches, chips and fruit under the eaves of the cold room, so that the harvesters could grab food at their convenience.

At some point Debbie took the kids back to the cabin and Gen took over moving the flowers to the cold room. The first sprinkles hit about three, but the workers just flipped up their hoods and kept cutting. At four thirty Caleb heard the first rumble of thunder in the distance. By five the extra helpers had taken their bouquets and gone, but Gen's family and Fleur were still working in the fields. A flash of lightning, followed by thunder only ten seconds later, convinced him the storm was too close for comfort.

He gave a sharp whistle, and everyone stopped and looked toward him. "Time to wrap it up. Take whatever you have on the cart to the cold room. I don't want anyone in the fields when the lightning gets here. Hurry!"

Once they'd processed all the buds and put the carts away in the barn, Caleb stepped forward.

"Thank you, everyone, for all your work. I so appreciate that you came all the way out here. I can't find the words—" A flash of lightning followed by a boom of thunder interrupted his speech.

Gen chuckled. "Why don't you look for those words once we're all inside? Mom says she has a big pot of chili in the slow cooker at the cabin. Let's head that direction while we wait out the storm."

"This was so much fun!" Brooke told Caleb as they walked toward the cabin. "Dane and I were on a supply run to Anchorage when Gen called last night. I've always wanted to see how a flower farm worked, so we decided to take another day. I'm glad we did. You know, with the cabin you have, you could set up a guest farm program if you wanted to."

"What is a guest farm?" Caleb asked.

"It's like a dude ranch. A working farm, but with accommodations for guests who want to see a real working farm firsthand and perhaps participate in some of the chores like we did today."

"People pay to do farmwork?"

"Exactly!" Brooke beamed. The rain grew heavier, and a gust of wind swept leaves from the lilacs lining the driveway and swirled them around. They all walked faster. Caleb fell to the rear, so that he could keep an eye on everyone.

Gen dropped back to walk beside him. "Brooke knows what she's talking about," Gen told him. "She and Dane own a remote lodge near Seward, and before that she was manager at a resort in Fairbanks."

"I just can't imagine someone paying for the privilege of working on a farm."

"You would." She reached for his hand. "Admit it. If you were working at some job in the city, you'd thankfully spend your vacation budget for a chance to get your hands in the dirt."

"I probably would." He squeezed her hand. "Thank you. You may very well have saved the crop and the farm's reputation."

"All I did was make a few calls."

"You did a lot more than that."

At the cabin, the wind tugged at the corners of landscape cloth someone had stretched over much of the flower garden. "What's this?" Caleb asked.

"Mom said she and the girls were going to try to save some of the flowers. They found fence posts and landscape fabric in your garden shed. Hope it was okay to use it," Gen told him.

"More than okay. This is above and beyond."

"Caleb!" Evie and Maya ran outside to meet them. "We made tents for your flowers."

"We wanted to save them from the hail rocks!" Maya told him.

"Hail*stones*," Evie corrected.

Something bounced off the ground a few feet away. Caleb touched the girls' backs and urged them toward the porch. "Let's get under cover, everybody. Quick!"

The first hailstones were only pea-size, but then came bigger balls of ice, some the size of the chocolate truffles Vickie made at Christmastime. The plant covers sagged as they filled with ice. Beyond the yard, in the parts of the garden that hadn't been covered, the ice battered the plants, ripping off leaves and driving stems to the ground.

Caleb set a hand on each girl's shoulder. "Thank you for all your work. It looks like your tents are going to save the plants."

"We covered the vegetables in your garden, too." Maya smirked at her sister. "Evie didn't want to do the Brussels sprouts, but Grandma covered them anyway."

Caleb exchanged smiles with Gen over Maya's head. "That's wonderful. Absolutely wonderful."

IT WAS OVER. The storm had moved on and so had Gen's family. Caleb woke early, as usual. When he left the house, Thor still snoozed on the rug beside Fleur's bed, both of them exhausted from the day before. Now, in the watery sunshine, Caleb walked the fields. The worst damage was west of the farmhouse, where some of the whites, so strong and healthy yesterday, had been beaten to the ground. Without the foliage to convert sunlight to energy for the rest of this summer, next year's yields would likely fall off, but thanks to Gen and her friends and family, this year's crop was saved. This afternoon he would walk the uncut rows and see if there were any buds worth salvaging, or if the rest was a total loss. The pinks, reds and corals that had already been cut looked a bit battered, but they still had plenty of leaves left. Amazingly, hail had missed the experimental garden entirely.

According to the group text this morning, Vickie's farm had been spared as well. She said her crew should finish cutting her whites within two or three more days. Some of the other farms in the co-op reported spotty damage, but Caleb's seemed to have gotten the worst of the storm. Thank goodness for Gen.

Without really meaning to, he'd made the journey from the fields to the cabin, but Gen wasn't on the back stoop with her early-morning coffee yet. In the front the makeshift shelters still stood, sagging but functional. Gen's mom was a wonder, unloading carts while babysitting all morning, erecting these covers to protect his mother's garden and then feeding the whole family with chili and cornbread while the storm raged around them. He could see where Gen got her energy and positive attitude.

He crossed to the vegetable garden and opened the gate to see how the vegetables had fared. There he found Gen, already at work removing the covers her mom had erected the day before. He took a moment to appreciate the graceful way she moved. The way her hair shone in the sunlight. The beautiful curve of her cheek. "Good morning."

She smiled when she saw him. "Good morning to you." She walked over and greeted him with a kiss. He could get used to this. "I thought you might be sleeping late today after all the hours you've been putting in."

"No, I was up with the birds. Habit, I guess. And I wanted to see how much damage was done."

"How much did you lose?"

"Not that much, thanks to you. I'd estimate we got eighty percent of the whites in before the storm hit. I'll need to grade and sort, but I should be able to fill my share of the preorders easily. Sounds like the other farms fared well. Did you see the group text?"

"No." She pulled out her phone. "Huh, I must have had the sound turned off." She pulled up the texts. "Oh, good, Vickie's okay and so are the Garcias. Sullivans had light damage, Clancy had already finished harvesting." She continued to scroll through while Caleb removed the rest of the coverings. The damage to the carrots, lettuce, broccoli and Brussels sprouts underneath was minimal.

"Oh!" Gen said suddenly.

"What's wrong?"

"I'm glad you mentioned this text, because apparently I missed a call from Bartlett High School in Anchorage yesterday, so they texted.

They want to know if I can interview today." She checked her watch. "Rats! It's in three hours! I've got to go call them, and then get dressed and drive to Anchorage." She was already halfway to the gate. "Mom went back to town, so I'll drop the girls off with her or Tanner while I interview. Don't worry, I'll make up the time and get all the peony orders updated later today."

"I wasn't worried." At least not about the peony orders. But this was an unwelcome reminder that in another month, Gen would be moving back to Anchorage. Back to her real life. Something he'd been trying not to think about. "Good luck on your interview."

"Thanks!" She shot a smile over her shoulder and disappeared through the gate.

Just like she would soon be disappearing from his life.

CHAPTER FOURTEEN

A FEW DAYS LATER Caleb stood in line with Fleur and Gen at a movie theater in Anchorage. The buzz of a hundred conversations filled the lobby, accompanied by the aroma of fresh popcorn. To celebrate Fleur's submitting her final assignment, Gen had suggested a trip to Anchorage for dinner and a movie. Crowds weren't Caleb's favorite thing, but Fleur deserved a reward for her hard work. Besides, Gen's two girls were with their father this week, and Caleb suspected she could use a little cheering up as well.

They'd dined on the patio beside the creek at Fleur's favorite restaurant, Arctic Roadrunner. With his stomach full of burgers and onion rings, Caleb wasn't sure he'd be able to make it through a whole movie with his eyes open, but Fleur was eager to see the latest superhero flick. Hopefully, it wouldn't sell out before they reached the front of the line.

Gen pointed at the listings. "They're still

showing that mystery set in ancient Greece. I'll have to get in and see it before it's gone."

It did look a lot more appealing than the superhero movie. "What do you think, Fleur? Want to see that one instead?"

Fleur wrinkled her nose. "Ancient Greece? Are you kidding?"

Before Caleb could answer, a girl's voice called from the other side of the foyer where they stood. "Fleur!"

"Abby!" The two girls met and hugged. A group of about five kids clustered around Fleur, chattering excitedly.

"Some of Fleur's friends from school," Gen whispered to Caleb.

Fleur looked around suspiciously. "Where's Brooklyn?"

"She's grounded," one of the boys said. "Her parents caught her sneaking out."

Fleur's face brightened at the news. "Hey, Dad, would it be okay if I saw the movie with my friends? You and Gen can watch that Greek movie instead and I could meet you in the lobby after."

"But Gen and I—" Caleb paused when Gen nudged him with her elbow.

"Fleur hasn't seen her friends all summer," she whispered. Another boy arrived and the group stepped over to greet him, leaving Caleb and Gen a few moments alone.

"But you went to all the trouble to plan this—" Caleb started to say.

"As a reward for Fleur," Gen reminded him. "That blond boy who just arrived is Owen, Fleur's old boyfriend."

The one who had cheated? "Even less reason for her to spend time with this group."

"They're not bad kids, especially when Brooklyn isn't around. Fleur shouldn't have to lose all her friends because she and Owen broke up. Let them work through this themselves."

"You really think it's a good idea?"

She shrugged. "It's a ninety-minute movie. What could happen?"

"Okay, fine." When Fleur looked back at him, Caleb gestured her closer. "Here. Take some money. It looks like your movie gets out ten minutes before ours, so wait in the lobby near the exit doors. Okay?"

"Thanks, Dad." She snatched the cash and hurried back to her friends, who moved to the back of the line.

Caleb looked at Gen. "Well, it looks like it's just us. Wow, two adults. We could even watch an R-rated movie if we wanted to."

Gen laughed. "We could, but the mystery looks better."

"Agreed." And it was. The cinematography was excellent, immersing them in the semiarid landscape of the Greek countryside, so different from Alaska, but beautiful in its own way. And the plot was probably pretty good, although once Gen leaned her head against him, Caleb found it hard to concentrate on anything else. She shivered in the air-conditioning, and he put an arm around her, his fingers on the smooth skin of her shoulder. She snuggled closer, perfectly molding herself against him. There was something about being with Gen that was simultaneously relaxing and invigorating. Pretty darn perfect.

The identity of the murderer was revealed, a complete surprise to Caleb, and the credits rolled. Before the lights went up, he took the opportunity to lean in for a kiss. Gen's response was gratifying, but the shuffle of feet and a cleared throat reminded him that they were blocking the aisle. Reluctantly, he stood and laid a hand on Gen's back, inviting her to lead the way.

They came out of the theater and blinked in the light. "That was great," Gen told him. "Thank you."

"I enjoyed it, too." They followed the rest

of the audience to the lobby. Looking around, he didn't immediately spot Fleur. They waited a few minutes for the crowd to dissipate, but still no sign of Fleur.

"I'll check the ladies' room," Gen suggested.

"Good. I'll text."

Five minutes later Gen was back. "She's not there, and I peeked into the superhero movie. It's empty."

"No answer to my text."

"Do you think she might be waiting at the truck?" Gen asked.

"Let's go see." But she wasn't there. Caleb was beginning to worry. Fleur still hadn't responded to his text. He called, but the phone went straight to voice mail.

Gen was looking across the parking lot at a scraggly row of lilacs and sand cherries. "Maybe, um, we should check the hedge."

"Why the hedge?" As he watched, two unfamiliar kids pushed between two shrubs to the other side.

She chuckled. "I forgot you didn't grow up in Anchorage. The hedge at the theater is where middle schoolers sneak off to make out."

"What?"

"Oh, come on. Didn't you do the same thing?"

"No. Well, I— This isn't about me. I specifically told Fleur to meet us in the lobby." He returned his phone to his pocket. "You wait here in case she comes."

"Caleb, don't—" But he didn't wait to hear what it was he wasn't supposed to do. He had to find his daughter.

Gen ignored his request to stay at the truck and followed him across the parking lot. Soft giggles and murmurs of conversation drifted from between the bushes. A girl about Fleur's age with black hair and a pale face appeared from a gap in the hedge, her red lips drawn back in a snarl. But Caleb ignored her as he worked his way along the hedge, looking for any sign of Fleur. He finally spotted a glimpse of the purple top she'd worn and crashed into the hedge after her. Fleur and the blond boy with her both gaped at him. From appearances, they were only talking, but who knew where it might have led? "Dad?"

"Let's go."

"But—"

"Now!"

Fleur let out a massive sigh and rolled her eyes. "Sorry, Owen."

Both kids followed Caleb out of the bushes. Behind them there was a shriek followed by a string of cursing. Caleb turned to see the black-haired girl rushing toward Fleur, but before she got close, Gen grabbed her by the arm. "Brooklyn! Stop it."

"That sneaky little—" She glared at Gen, her fists clenched. "Owen is my boyfriend. Fleur had better not be—"

"You should go home now. Otherwise, I'll have to call your parents." Gen hadn't raised her voice, but she got her point across.

"Fine." The girl shook off Gen's hand. "I'm going. But don't think I've forgotten this!" she shouted in the general direction of Fleur and Owen before she stomped off.

The boy ducked his head and mumbled, "Talk to you later, Fleur," before slipping away into the crowd of young teens that had gathered to see the drama.

Fleur wheeled around and flounced toward the truck. Caleb looked toward Gen, who gave him a wry smile. Yeah, that could have gone better.

It was a long, silent trip home.

GEN GATHERED THE stems she'd sorted and placed them in their respective buckets. She'd offered to help grade the peony buds with Caleb, mostly to give him the chance to talk about yesterday's fiasco if he wanted. So far he hadn't, but the unusual tightness in his jaw gave her a clue he wasn't thinking about peonies.

"This one's close. Is it AAA or AA?" Gen showed Caleb the peony bud that just fit through the hole of the sizing guide.

"AA. To be a triple, it can't fit through the hole at all."

"Thanks." She added it to the others. Most orders requested a mix of their largest premium blooms for bridal bouquets and wedding arches, and smaller buds for table arrangements, boutonnieres and sometimes cake decorations since peonies were edible.

"So is this repairable, or did I lose her forever?" Caleb asked suddenly.

Gen didn't pretend not to understand. "What did Fleur say when you got home?"

"Not much. Mostly just gave me the death stare. Snarled like a tiger when I grounded her for a month."

Gen raised her eyebrows. "A month? Really?"

Caleb shrugged. "I was angry."

"It's not a great idea to make those sorts of decisions when you're angry. A month seems like a pretty harsh sentence for not being in the lobby on time."

"It's meaningless anyway. Her mom's wedding is this Friday. Mallory and what's-his-name are going on their honeymoon for a week, and then they'll head off to Atlanta with Fleur. No way Fleur is staying with me now." His sigh could have softened the hardest heart, except maybe Fleur's.

"Still, what did Fleur actually do that requires grounding? So she kissed a boy—"

"She claims they were just talking."

"Good. Maybe he apologized." Gen hoped so. Owen seemed like a good kid at heart. "You could take a clue and apologize yourself."

"Apologize? For what?"

"For embarrassing her in front of her friends? That's about the worst possible thing a parent can do to a middle schooler. Sometimes it's unavoidable, but in this case—"

"What? How would you have handled it?"

"Well, if you had to go looking for her, you could have called her name and waited for her to come out instead of plunging into the bushes like Thor chasing a rabbit."

He thought it over. "Maybe I overreacted. You really think I should apologize to Fleur?"

"If you believe you were in the wrong, you should. I know it feels like you're being wishy-washy, but accepting responsibility for your actions and admitting when you're wrong models the proper way to handle a mistake. It's a learning opportunity."

He gave her an appraising glance. "You're going to be a great school counselor."

"Thank you." She'd worked hard to get her qualifications and it felt good that he had confidence in her. But at the same time she dreaded the reality of moving to Anchorage and leaving the peony farm behind. Leaving Caleb behind. Because despite his affection, he'd never indicated any desire to continue this relationship past the end of summer.

"Have you heard back on that job you interviewed for?" he asked.

"They want another interview. In fact, it's this Friday. If you want, I could drive Fleur into Anchorage for her mom's wedding when I go."

"I couldn't ask you to do that. They want her there by noon to get ready for pictures before the wedding, and she won't be done with the reception until after ten."

"No problem. My interview is at two. I can drop her off and then spend the rest of the day with my mom, do a little shopping. Better yet, Fleur and I can spend Friday night with Mom, and I'll bring her back here on Saturday morning."

"That would be great. Thanks." He put a bucket of peonies in the cold room and straightened his shoulders. "Guess if I'm going to apologize, sooner is better, right?"

"That's the spirit." Gen grinned and rose on her tiptoes to kiss him. "That's for luck. Now, go in there and face that tiger."

THE WONDERFUL AROMA of fresh coffee made by someone else lured Gen out of bed on Saturday morning. Fleur still slept in the other twin bed. After a day of all wedding, all the time, it was no wonder she needed a little extra sleep.

In the kitchen Mom was stirring batter in the blue mixing bowl that she'd been using for as long as Gen could remember. Funny how comforting little things like that could be. "Good morning. Coffee smells amazing."

Mom smiled at her. "It's a Kona blend. The neighbors gave it to me for watching their dog while they went to Hawaii. Do you want berries or maple syrup on your waffles? Never mind, I'll get out both and see what Fleur wants."

"Ooh, waffles. My favorite!"

"I know. I thought we'd have a special breakfast to celebrate your new job and apartment." Gen had received a job offer at the interview.

Afterward, she'd called Doreen's apartment manager friend, who happened to have a vacancy. She and Mom had toured it yesterday, and she'd already signed the lease.

"Thanks, Mom. That's really sweet." Gen poured a cup of coffee. "Can I do anything? Cut up the berries?"

"All done. Sit." Mom pulled out her Belgian waffle maker and plugged it in. "I'll join you in a cup. Fleur still sleeping?"

"Like a baby."

"Such a nice girl. I can't get over how beautiful she looked yesterday with her hair up. That dress really brought out the blue of her eyes."

"I know! Fleur told me the women who did their makeup showed her some tricks so that people noticed her eyes instead of her eyeliner. Caleb will be happy about that. It sounds like Fleur had a good time at the wedding."

Mom sipped her coffee. "Has she decided which parent she plans to live with this school year?" Gen had told her mom about Fleur's dilemma when she was staying at the cabin.

"Not as far as I know. We've talked about it a little, but I try not to influence her. She needs to do what is best for her. But I know it will break Caleb's heart if she moves away."

"He'll need support, for sure." There was an implied question in Mom's expression.

"He will." Gen sighed. "But I'm not sure he wants it from me."

"I thought you seemed a little melancholy for someone who just accepted a job she's been working toward for more than two years. Have you and Caleb had a spat?"

"No, nothing like that. It's just that…" Gen blew out a breath of frustration. "He hasn't said anything to make me think he wants to see me anymore once summer's over."

"Hmm. Have you asked him about it?" The waffle maker's green light clicked on, and Mom returned to stir the batter.

"Uh, no. But…" But what? Wasn't communication the basis of Gen's entire profession? Why was she so reluctant to bring up the topic with Caleb? "I guess I'm afraid he might not tell me what I want to hear."

Before Mom could answer, footsteps sounded in the hallway, and Fleur appeared, looking adorable in shorty pajamas with pandas in the print. "Morning." She yawned as she sat down at the table.

Gen smiled. "Hi there, sunshine. My mom's making sourdough waffles for us."

"Yum! We only do the kind of waffles that you put in a toaster."

Mom set a bowl of strawberries and a glass of milk in front of Fleur. "Well, then, you're in for a treat."

AFTER DROPPING FLEUR off at her house and collecting the two kittens, who had spent the night in Caleb's laundry room so they wouldn't traumatize Thor, Gen returned to the cabin. Velvet, once she'd determined the girls were not at home, approached Gen to register a loud complaint.

Gen tickled the kitten under her chin. "I know. I miss them, too. But they'll be back on Monday." Lacey rushed in, greedy for her share of affection. Gen sat cross-legged on the kitchen floor so that both kittens could cuddle in her lap. "Big news. We've got a new place. I put down a pet deposit, so you'll be welcome. It's got big south-facing windows, with nice sun puddles, and a tiny balcony where I can put up a planter box for flowers." Having spent the summer surrounded by gardens, Gen had discovered the mood-enhancing value of flowers. "I think the girls will like it." Although there was no yard, and she wasn't sure where they would park their bikes. The nearest bike trail was about two miles from the apartment building, so she would need to get a bike carrier for her car. She should look into that.

Gen shook her head. Here she was, inventing tasks to keep herself busy instead of doing the one task that would determine the shape of her future. She needed to find out exactly where she stood with Caleb. Because even though she'd been telling herself that this was only a summer thing, her heart was saying something different. It was telling her that if she was to let him go, she would regret it for the rest of her life. But what if he didn't feel the same? She gently dumped the kittens on the floor, ran a brush through her hair and stepped outside onto the porch. Time to find out.

She found Caleb coming out of the cold room, carrying four big boxes, which he placed on top of the six already awaiting pickup. "Looks like a big order today."

"Huge." He looked pleased to see her, and even more pleased when she greeted him with a kiss. But there was an unusual tension in his jaw. "Thanks for taking Fleur to the wedding for me."

"You're welcome. Did she show you pictures?"

"Oh, yeah. My little girl looks like she should be on a red carpet somewhere, doesn't she? So grown up."

"I know. She looks amazing."

"She didn't give you any indication about where she's planning to live—"

Gen shook her head. "She didn't say anything to me."

"Me, either. I think I'm back in her good graces after I apologized, but I still don't know which place she'll choose. I guess we'll find out next weekend." He closed the door to the cold room foyer. "How did your interview go?"

"Very well. They've offered me the job. I start in two weeks."

"Congratulations." His smile seemed tight. "Then you'll be pleased to know Christabel called me this morning. They arrived in Alaska a little sooner than they'd expected, and she says she can go back to work on Monday."

"Oh." Gen had thought she had a full week more to say goodbye to everyone in the co-op. But now she'd have two weeks off to move and get the girls enrolled in their new school. "Yeah, that's…that's good news."

Caleb was watching her, as if gauging her reaction. "There's no hurry to move out of the cabin, of course. You can stay as long as you like."

"Thank you. The girls will be back Monday. I've got an apartment lined up for us in

Anchorage, so I imagine we'll be packing up in the next couple of days."

"Mmm." He opened his mouth to speak, then closed it again. Paced a few steps. When he turned back, his expression was pained. "I don't know how to do this. Is this goodbye? Or do we pretend everything is normal for the next couple of days until you go? I've never been in a relationship with an expiration date."

"Does it have to?" Gen took a step closer. "Expire, I mean. Anchorage is less than two hours away, not an unreasonable distance. I have a friend from college whose husband is on an aircraft carrier somewhere. Now, that's an unreasonable distance, but they video chat almost every day and they stay close."

"Do you—" Caleb looked hopeful, but then he shook his head. "No, you think that's what you want now, but once you get into your new life, you'll forget all about me and the farm. I mean—look at you! You're smart and beautiful, with a great job. And I'm just a farmer with a few acres, trying to get by."

"What do you mean *just a farmer*? Farmers are the foundation of any community. Secondly, a profession is only part of a person's identity. You're an amazing farmer. An excellent father. An exceptional neighbor. And a wonderful man. You're generous and giving.

It's no wonder I love you!" Even as the words left her mouth, Gen wished she could call them back. She'd never even allowed herself to think those words, and yet they'd come tumbling out of her mouth. Caleb was obviously trying to let her down easy. Had she made an already awkward situation intolerable?

But rather than looking uncomfortable, Caleb was staring at her. "You love me?"

"I do," she admitted in a small voice. "I didn't mean to, but—"

"Gen." His voice sounded rusty. He pulled her into his arms and held her close against his chest so tightly she could feel his racing heart. "I love you, too."

He loved her! Little sparkles of joy ignited in her heart. Caleb loved her! She looked up to see his face, and he captured her mouth in a kiss that she felt all the way down to her toes. If he wasn't holding her upright, she would have melted into a puddle. When he pulled back from the kiss, he looked a little dazed, as though he was as surprised as she was at the turn of events. But then the doubts started creeping in. She could read them crossing his face as easily as if they were subtitles.

He stepped back. "But does this change anything? I know from experience, and so do you, that love isn't always enough. And it's not only us to consider. If things don't work out, Evie and Maya could get hurt, too. And I have Fl—" He paused, and Gen knew he was remembering Fleur might not be living with him much longer. But that was all the more reason for them not to give up on their relationship.

"Yes, all that is true. You and I have both been hurt and betrayed in the past, and that makes it harder. But we can take it slow. Feel our way until we've figured out what works for us. Or doesn't—there's always that risk. But what we have together is special. We shouldn't let the past dictate our future."

He thought about that. "I want..." He stopped.

"What? What do you want?"

"I want to believe. In you. In us. In the possibility we could be together. That I can put my trust in you. Don't get me wrong—I trust you to be honest with me. And that's not easy for me." He chuckled uneasily. "You know how I feel about secrets and lies."

"I do know." Gen's conscience pricked. She was keeping a secret from him, a big one. But it wasn't her secret. "Although in my job people share their private lives with me. I can't betray a confidence. Even to you."

"No, of course. That's different. But I mean in our personal lives. If you're having doubts, if you change your mind about us, I want to know. I can't be blindsided again."

"Don't forget, I also know what it's like to be lied to." Gen touched his face. "I would never do that to you."

"I know you wouldn't." He looked deep into her eyes. "Then, yes. Let's see where this relationship leads. Because so far, I've liked everywhere it's taken me."

"I'm glad." She leaned in for another kiss.

"So does that mean, I guess, we're officially... What are we?" He grinned. "Dating?"

"Dating sounds good."

"Then maybe we should go on an actual date. One that doesn't end with a surly teenager in the backseat. Tomorrow evening?"

"I'd like that."

His phone rang, but he ignored it and kissed her again. She nudged him. "It could be Fleur."

He pulled out his phone and checked. "No, it's a guy I went to high school with. He's an EMT now. Strange, I haven't heard from him in years. Anyway, he can leave a message." He was about to decline the call when Gen's phone rang.

She laughed. "Sorry. It's Larry's number. Probably my girls calling. I won't be long."

"Okay, then I'll take this." He answered his

phone. "Hi, Brad. Haven't heard from you in a while."

Gen walked a few paces away and listened to Evie and Maya's latest adventures. It seemed Dane had taken them all fishing, and Larry had fallen into the creek. Gen didn't say so, but the mental image of Larry thrashing around in icy water made her want to laugh. "I'm glad you're having a good time," she told the girls. "Velvet and Lacey miss you."

"Are you playing with them?" Evie demanded. "They get bored if nobody plays with them."

"I am, I promise. But they'll be glad when you're back." She decided to wait to tell them about the new apartment in person. "Be good for your dad. I love you both."

"I love you," the girls sang in unison. "Bye, Mommy."

"Bye." Gen turned back to Caleb, intending to tell him about Larry's misadventures, but her smile faded when she saw him standing with his feet apart, the color draining from his face as he talked to someone. "But…okay, I understand. Thank you." He ended the call.

"What is it? Is something wrong with Fleur?"

"No. It's Vickie. She's been in an accident."

CHAPTER FIFTEEN

IT FELT WEIRD digging through Vickie's desk while she lay alone in a hospital bed, but the staff there was adamant. Family only. As far as Caleb knew, Vickie's brother was the only family she had left. Finally, he discovered an old address book stuffed in the back of the drawer and managed to find the brother's phone number. Caleb just hoped it hadn't changed in the past twenty years or so.

Thank goodness his old pal Brad had been willing to bend the rules or Caleb might not have known about Vickie's injury for days. Brad had only called because Vickie, while they were getting her out from under the ATV that had tipped on top of her, kept fretting that people were counting on those flowers to be shipped out today. Brad said once he'd promised to alert Caleb, Vickie had calmed down, but on the way to the hospital in Wasilla, she'd lost consciousness. Brad suspected internal bleeding. And that was all Caleb had been able to find out.

To his relief the phone rang through to the number listed in Vickie's book. It went to voice mail, but at least the name in the recording matched the brother's name. He left a message with the basic facts, the phone number of the hospital and his own phone number. "Please call me back when you get this." Then he returned to Vickie's cold room, where Gen and Fleur were busy packing flowers.

"I left a message with her brother," he told them. "Hopefully, he'll call the hospital and then call us back with an update on Vickie's condition."

"You should be with her," Gen urged.

"It wouldn't do any good," Caleb argued. "They've already told me only family can get in to see her."

"But you are family!" Gen exclaimed. "I mean, you and Fleur are infinitely closer to family than a brother Vickie has barely spoken to in forty years."

"How do you know she hasn't talked to her brother in forty years?" Caleb knew Vickie and her brother weren't close, but he didn't realize they were estranged. Now he wondered if the brother would even respond to his call.

"She mentioned it once. You should go. Tell them you're her son."

Caleb considered it for a minute. Would it

work? But then he saw Fleur watching him. "No. I won't lie."

"It's not—" Gen started to say, but Caleb cut her off.

"We'll figure something out. In the meantime, we can be of more help here." He double-checked the contents of the box Fleur had packed, stuck a Susitna Peony Cooperative sticker to the tissue paper, added cold packs and closed the lid. "Is that the last one?"

"Yes." Fleur peeled the backing from the shipping label and attached it to the outside of the box.

The sound of an approaching truck meant they'd barely finished in time. Mike Chapel, another local Caleb had known since fifth grade, was driving the truck today. "Hi, Caleb. Ladies. Sorry to hear about Vickie."

"What did you hear?" Caleb handed over two of the boxes and waited for Mike to scan them and put them in his truck. "I can't get any updates."

"My sister works in the ER, and she told me about it. Sounds pretty serious." Mike scanned two more packages. "They're taking her for surgery to stop internal bleeding. She says Vickie's blood type is AB negative, so they're getting that lined up."

"That's my blood type," Caleb told him.

"In that case you might want to hustle over and donate some blood. I don't know how all this works, but my sis says only one percent of the population is AB negative." He scanned the last box and closed his truck. "Anyway, hope she recovers. Vickie's one of the good ones." He got into his truck and drove away.

Caleb stood rooted in the spot. Vickie was AB negative. Just like him. And she'd once mentioned that she spent a summer in Alaska when she was in college. He did the math, and yes, that would have been just about the time he was born. Was it possible? "Could Vickie be…?" He looked at Gen, who had just been urging him to tell the hospital staff that he was Vickie's son. She swallowed and gave a little nod. "You knew?"

Gen's voice was soft, but her response was clear. "Yes, I knew."

Another secret. And this one from Gen, one of two women in the world he'd believed he could trust. The other was about to go into surgery. And they'd both been lying to him all along. "When did— How could— Never mind. It doesn't matter. I have to get to the hospital. Get in the truck. I'll drop you both at the farm on my way."

"What's going on?" Fleur looked baffled.

"Ask Gen," Caleb told Fleur, and even to

his own ears, his voice sounded harsh. "Apparently, she has all the answers. She can explain it to you while she's packing."

Fleur frowned. "Packing?"

"Yeah. Christabel's coming back to work on Monday. It's time for Gen to move on."

IT WAS A long night. Vickie was already in surgery when Caleb had arrived, and fortunately, no one seemed inclined to demand proof that he was, indeed, her son. After hearing she would be at least another hour, he'd nipped over to the blood bank to donate before returning to the waiting room at the hospital. Maybe it was superstition, but at least he felt like he was doing something constructive to help Vickie.

Fifty-five minutes had ticked by after he'd returned, three thousand three hundred seconds, and he'd counted every one of them. His anger at Vickie's deception warred with terror that he might lose her. Forever. Without ever telling her how much her presence in his life had meant to him. Ironically, Gen probably would have been useful at helping him sort out his feelings—if so many of them weren't directed toward her. Because once again, someone he cared for had let him down. Lies and secrets. How he hated them.

Finally, he was informed that Vickie was in recovery. The doctor was cautiously optimistic. Caleb was only allowed to be with Vickie a few minutes each hour, but he'd been holding her hand when she woke from the anesthesia. She'd smiled and whispered his name before falling asleep again.

He spent the night in a different waiting room, one with gray tiles on the floor and a muted television flickering in the corner, waiting to be called for his five-minute hourly visits. Various medical people came and went, and at some point he must have dozed off, because he awoke to a nurse shaking his shoulder. "Hey, I'm Tony. You're Vickie's son, right?"

"Yes." It was surprisingly easy to say.

"Good news. The doctor just saw her and we're moving her from intensive care to a regular room. Room 243. You'll be able to stay in the room with her. You can meet her there in about an hour and a half. Go get some breakfast."

"Okay. Thanks." Caleb decided to head home for a shower, and to check on Fleur. According to her text she was fine, but he wanted to make sure. At some point he'd need a few hours to get his and Vickie's peony orders out—no, wait. Today was Sunday. Nothing would be scheduled to ship today.

The house was empty. Not even Thor was there to greet him. Only a note on the kitchen table in Gen's handwriting saying Thor and Fleur would be spending the night with her at the cabin. A surge of annoyance flared. What made Gen think she could make decisions about where his daughter should spend the night? But on reflection, he realized it was good that Fleur hadn't been alone. He'd texted her when Vickie came out of surgery, but she had to be worried, not to mention shocked at learning Vickie was her biological grandmother.

He should have been the one to break the news to Fleur, not pawned that conversation off on Gen in a moment of frustration. But then, Gen apparently knew the whole story, one she hadn't seen fit to share with him.

He sent another text to Fleur, updating her on Vickie's condition and saying he'd be back later to take her for a visit if the hospital allowed it. He considered texting Gen, but what was there to say? He jumped in the shower, pulled on clean clothes and returned to the hospital. Vickie was asleep when he arrived, but she looked stronger, with color in her cheeks.

The tray on the table near the door indicated she'd eaten something while he was gone.

About an hour later Vickie woke with a start. Caleb, who had been sitting by the window, came to her bed. "Good morning."

"Caleb." She smiled. "The nurse told me my son would be back soon, and I wasn't sure…" She coughed, and Caleb filled a cup of water from a nearby pitcher and handed it to her. "Thank you." She drank the water and set the cup down. "You were there last night, weren't you? Or did I dream that?" Her voice was stronger now.

"No, I was there." Caleb refilled the cup. "What happened to you? Brad says you rolled an ATV over. I can't imagine you were doing wheelies out there."

"I was putting the carts away before I packed the boxes for shipment, going slow over that drainage ditch, and then this suicidal squirrel ran in front of me. No doubt the same little demon that cleans out my birdfeeders. I swerved, and the four-wheeler rolled and caught me underneath. Fortunately, I had my phone, but for some reason I couldn't get the fingerprint reader to work and I couldn't for the life of me remember the security code. But it let me call 911."

"Good thing you did. As I'm sure the doctor

told you, you're a spleen lighter and they had to pump a fair quantity of blood into you. AB negative, same type as me." He met her eyes. "Guess it's genetic."

She paled instantly. "How did—"

"When I heard we have the same blood type, something clicked. And then I saw Gen's face—"

"I thought Gen must have told you," Vickie said.

"No, Gen kept your secret. But ever since I found out I was adopted—"

"You knew?"

"Oh, so Gen kept my secrets from you as well. She's a regular vault, that one." He must have sounded bitter because Vickie's eyes widened.

"Oh, Caleb. You can't blame Gen. I made her promise—"

"I don't want to talk about Gen. I want to know about you. Can you tell me your story? Our story?"

"Of course. I've wanted to tell you for so long." She smiled. "Better pull up a chair. It might take a while."

He sat down beside her bed. "Okay, I'm ready."

"Where to start?" She took a deep breath. "I guess first, you have to understand my parents. They were—well, not exactly strict. *Demanding* would be a better word. My older brother and I were expected to meet certain standards, and there was no grace if we didn't. Which was why I chose to attend college on the opposite coast."

"Where did you go to college?"

"Washington. Anyway, autumn of my sophomore year, I accepted a date with this attractive man with a dangerous vibe. My parents would have been appalled, which of course was much of the appeal. It didn't last long, just a few intense weeks, before his behavior started to worry me. He wanted to know where I was all the time. When I was working on a group project, he insisted on driving me to the group meets and picking me up. And then, after dating less than a month, he was pressuring me to move out of the rental house I shared with three other women and in with him. When I told him no, he grabbed my arm hard enough to leave bruises. That was the final straw, and I broke up with him."

"I'm sorry."

"Thanks, but of course it wasn't that easy. He came back. At first, he was apologetic. Brought me a gift, told me it would never happen again. Then came the arguments and the threats. He started harassing my roommates. My tires were slashed, twice. I got a restraining order. Even then I would occasionally catch him on campus or in my neighborhood, watching me. And then I discovered I was pregnant."

He could only imagine how panicked she must have been. His biological father—an abuser. Well, he'd asked for the truth, and there it was. "What happened next?"

"I couldn't go home. My parents would have been mortified to have an unmarried, pregnant daughter hanging around. Besides, he knew where my family lived, and I couldn't take a chance on him following me there. One of my roommates had an aunt who owned a bed-and-breakfast in Wasilla, and the aunt agreed to let me live there and work for her. So at Christmas break, I announced to my parents that I was taking a semester off to work in Alaska. Of course, that sparked loads of drama, but in the end, I left for Alaska and my family basically disowned me."

"How did the aunt at the B&B work out?"

"Oh, Dot was wonderful, such a kind lady. She worked hard and she worked me hard, but she watched out for me, too. Taught me to cook and made sure I ate my vegetables, got to my doctor's appointments, took my vitamins. She had six rooms in the main house plus a dozen seasonal cabins, so there was plenty to keep us busy."

"She sounds nice." Actually, she sounded a lot like Vickie. It made sense that she would have taken the woman who helped her as a role model.

"She was. Is. She's ninety now, living in Tulsa with her daughter. She still sends me a Christmas card every year." A brief smile passed her lips. "Anyway, June came and you were born. I'd made up my mind that adoption was the only way to keep you safe. I told them I didn't know who the father was, so they wouldn't need his permission. Because if he'd ever found out I'd given birth to his child..." She shuddered. "But letting the social worker walk out of that room with you was the hardest thing I've ever done."

Vickie sipped her water before continuing. "They told me I had ten days to change my mind. I almost did. I was terrified that you might end up with parents like mine. That's when Dot confessed to me that she'd overheard that the baby was going to two teachers who taught in the bush and spent summers in Willow. Dot happened to know the woman who headed up the Willow Food Bank, and she knew your parents because of all the garden produce they donated every summer. They assured me that you would grow up well loved." She smiled. "They were right."

"Yes." He couldn't have asked for better parents. "But what happened to you after that?"

"I worked for Dot for the rest of the summer. She helped me get myself declared independent from my parents so that I could qualify for student loans and finish my education. Eventually, I married a good man ten years older than me. He'd had a vasectomy. After we'd been together for a few years, I came to realize how much I wanted children. Alan agreed, and he was going to have the vasectomy reversed, but during some of the presurgical medical testing, they discovered a heart defect. In all likelihood, he wouldn't live long enough to see a child grow up. He died six years later."

"I'm sorry. Is that when you came to Alaska?"

"No. I carried on for another nine years, but all that time I was thinking of you, wondering if you were happy. Finally, I sold the house and my business and moved to Alaska."

She smiled. "I remember I still had a living room full of packing boxes when Jade and Bram stopped by with a strawberry-rhubarb pie to welcome me. I almost didn't have the courage to tell them why I was there, and when I did, Jade was horrified. She begged me to go away because you didn't know you were adopted. It had never occurred to me that you wouldn't know."

"That's what I don't understand. It seems completely out of character. Why did they keep this secret from me?"

"It's simple, really. When they adopted you, they were still trying to conceive, and they didn't want you to feel different. You see, one of your mother's students was adopted into a family with two biological children and he always felt like he was second-best. Your mom wanted to make sure that never happened with you. By the time they'd accepted that she would never be pregnant, you were a teenager and they felt it would have done more harm than good to tell you at that point."

"Obviously, you didn't go away."

"No. Jade was upset, but Bram convinced her they needed to hear me out. Once I understood her reasoning, I promised never to tell you. In exchange, they agreed to let me spend time around you and your family. Over time, as we learned to trust each other, we grew to be friends."

"How about after they died? Why didn't you tell me then?"

"How could I? You were devastated. You had just lost both of your parents. The last thing you needed was another blow. Besides, I'd promised, and if anything, that promise became more binding after their deaths, because they would never have the chance to explain." She let out a breath. "How did you find out anyway?"

"I found my adoption certificate in the bottom of a box of photos in the cabin."

"Oh dear. I thought once you'd gone through all the papers in the filing cabinet at the house, we were safe. It never occurred to me that they might have stashed that certificate in the cabin." She reached for his hand. "But maybe it was meant to be. I've wanted to tell you for ages, but I felt like I owed it to them to keep the secret. Your parents loved you so very much."

"Yes, they did. And then after they were gone, you stepped into the role."

"I did what I could, but I know it wasn't the same. Many times, especially when you were going through your divorce, I wished Jade and Bram could have been there for you."

"They were," Caleb said quietly. "I felt their

presence there on the farm. Especially when I'd work in the vegetable garden."

"They would be proud of you and all you've accomplished." Vickie squeezed his hand. "And so am I."

CHAPTER SIXTEEN

"MOMMY, I CAN'T reach the book Aunt Natalie gave me," Maya called.

Gen looked into the girls' new bedroom just in time to spot the danger. "Do not climb on that bookshelf! Ever! It could fall and crush you." Gen retrieved the book for Maya and added a trip to the hardware store for an anti-tip anchor to her growing to-do list. When she'd spotted the tall bookshelf at a garage sale this weekend, she hadn't considered that Maya might use it as a climbing apparatus.

Maya came to lean against Gen's leg. "Is Fleur coming later? I want to show her my new book."

"No, sweetie. I told you. I'll be with you full-time this week, and next week while I'm working before your school starts, Grandma will be staying with you. Fleur is still in Willow." At least for now. Fleur's mother was due back at the end of the week. As far as Gen knew, Fleur hadn't given Caleb any indication of her decision. Not that Caleb would share that news with her. He hadn't spoken a word to her since dropping her off at the farm on his way to the hospital.

At least she knew Vickie was going to be okay, based on reports from other co-op members. But she had no idea if Caleb was okay, or even if he'd told Vickie he knew about the adoption. But of course he would. He didn't believe in keeping secrets. And he would never forgive Gen for keeping this one from him.

Evie came in from where she'd been playing with the kittens in Gen's bedroom. "Can we ride bikes now?"

"No. I need to finish wiping down the kitchen cabinets first and unpack a few boxes. We can go to the park this afternoon."

Evie crossed to look out the sliding glass door to the balcony. "I wish we were at the farm, so we could play in the yard."

Gen did, too, but saying so wouldn't help. "Let's visit Valley of the Moon Park this afternoon. The one with the rocket ship slides, remember?"

"Okay." Evie agreed without her usual enthusiasm. But then, they were all in limbo, caught between their summer on the farm and the school year. Once school started and they got into their routine, they'd be fine.

Someone knocked, and both girls ran to the

door. "Wait. Let me check first," Gen ordered. Through the peephole, she spotted her mother, balancing a huge box, with two bags hanging from her arms. She opened the door quickly. "Hi. Let me take that."

"Thanks." Mom handed over the box and turned to smile at her granddaughters. "And how are Evie and Maya today?"

"We're going to Valley of the Moon, but not until this afternoon," Maya told her.

"Velvet keeps hiding under the bed," Evie reported. "She's scared of our new apartment."

"I'm sure it won't take too long for her to settle in." Mom carried the two tote bags to the kitchen peninsula. "I had duplicates of a few things in my kitchen, so I brought them for you."

"Thank you." Gen had sold or donated all the furniture and kitchenware from the house in Florida rather than try to move it across the country. Since then, she'd been living in Tanner's house and then at the furnished cabin at the farm, so she was starting from scratch in this apartment. She'd found the basics of furniture, dishes and a few kitchen gadgets at garage sales and thrift stores, but she was going to need a lot more. She opened the box and pulled out a set of baking sheets, measuring cups and spoons, and nesting mixing bowls.

One of the bowls still had a price sticker on the bottom. Gen chuckled and glanced at her mother, who didn't look the least repentant. "There's more in the car. I brought some of your grandmother's quilts."

"Thanks, Mom. You're the best." Gen leaned over and kissed her mother's cheek.

"Tanner says this afternoon he'll pick up the new mattresses you bought. Oh, and come see what I have here." Mom reached into one of the totes and pulled out a collection of cat toys.

Evie squeezed the toy mouse, making it squeak. "Velvet will love this!"

"Lacey should get to try it first." The argument continued even as they headed toward Gen's bedroom to play with the kittens.

"Uh, girls? Aren't you forgetting something?" Gen called.

"Oh. Thanks, Grandma." They ran back to give hugs, and then took off again.

"That was nice of you." Gen finished wiping down another cabinet.

"I figured the kittens needed a housewarming present, too. I also got some puzzles for the girls, but we'll wait to give them later." Mom reached into the dishwasher and handed her a stack of plates to put away. "So, I was wondering how you left things at the farm."

"We cleaned everything out of the cabin and

left it in good shape," Gen answered, deliberately misunderstanding.

But Mom wouldn't let her get away with that. "You know what I mean. How did you leave it with Caleb?"

Gen tried to keep her response matter-of-fact, but there was a little hitch in her voice when she announced, "It's over."

"Oh, I'm sorry, sweetheart. After seeing the two of you together, I thought—"

"So did I. And it almost worked out. But then we got word about Vickie." She'd told her family about Vickie's accident.

"That was terrible. But why should that change anything between you and Caleb?"

"Because," Gen said on a fortifying breath, "that's when he found out I've been lying to him." Gen hesitated, but she was tired of keeping secrets. She shared the whole story.

When she was done, her mother gave her a hug. "I'm so sorry, Gen. But I truly don't see what else you could have done. Surely, Caleb can see that it wasn't your secret to tell."

Gen shook her head. "He only sees the lie. And that's the one thing he won't tolerate."

"Then he's a fool," Mom declared. "Because you are the best thing that ever happened to that man. If he can't see that, he doesn't deserve you."

THOR SNIFFLED ALONG the row in the experimental garden, trudging ahead of Caleb. Soon, Caleb would go and pack up his orders for the day and then head over to Vickie's farm to do hers. Vickie had been discharged, but he'd insisted she stay with him until she'd completely recovered. Fleur had accepted Vickie as her grandmother easily, as though on some level, she'd known it all along.

The coral buds on JF-143C had swollen to the size of golf balls. In another couple of days they would burst into enormous clouds of petals. The late blooming time, almost two weeks later than the main crop, was another selling point for the variety, both for commercial growers who could space out the harvest, and for gardeners who wanted to extend the peony season.

At the end of the garden, inside the temporary greenhouse he'd erected to simulate a warmer climate, he'd already clipped the spent blossoms from the bushes to encourage the foliage to grow stronger, but he needed to check the plants. He stepped forward and was instantly transported back to when he'd shown Gen the new coral. When he'd kissed her. When everything had seemed full of promise.

Had he been wrong to turn on Gen the way he had? Yes, he'd been angry that she'd kept the secret that Vickie was his birth mother. But it was Vickie's secret, and once Vickie had explained her reasons, he'd forgiven her. The more he thought about it, the more he realized Gen had been in an impossible situation. But maybe it was for the best. Gen had a life planned out. She'd earned a master's degree and had a job at a high school in Anchorage. That was the life she'd chosen. Before he got the call about Vickie, they had agreed to continue the relationship, but could a relationship really survive for long when the people involved were living in different places? His experience with Mallory said no.

Caleb's phone rang, and as if she'd heard his thought, Mallory's name popped up. She and her new husband were scheduled to have returned to Anchorage last night. Before he could even say hello, Mallory announced, "Well, you win this round."

"What are you talking about?"

"Fleur called me this morning to say she'd be spending the school year with you." Mallory gave a wry chuckle. "I guess an equestrian program doesn't measure up against going to school with one of the cute Sullivan boys. Nicely played, Caleb."

Fleur was staying? "I didn't—"

"No? Then you got lucky. Or maybe your

girlfriend was pulling strings from behind the curtain."

"There's no girlfriend."

"No? From the way Fleur talked about Gen when we were getting ready for the wedding, I thought—"

"No." Caleb didn't want to talk about Gen, especially not with Mallory.

"Of course, a new grandmother might be part of Fleur's reason for staying as well. You were adopted and Vickie is your birth mother? Seriously?"

"I know. It's unbelievable."

"No kidding. But I do feel a little better leaving Fleur with you now that I know Vickie will be there for things like bra shopping and girlie stuff."

Caleb hadn't even considered that angle. "Yeah, Vickie will be good at that."

"So any chance I can have Fleur with me until school starts next week? I'd like to do some school shopping together, stuff like that."

"Of course." He cleared his throat. "Mallory, I'm sorry. I mean, I'm glad Fleur is staying with me, but I know you love her and miss her."

"So much." She sighed. "But I plan to be around a lot. You know Charles works for an airline."

"No, I didn't realize."

"He does. And that means I can fly standby for free, so I'll be coming up to see Fleur whenever I can grab a few days."

"That's good. If you want, you can stay in the cabin when you come."

"Really?" She sounded shocked at his offer, and it brought home to Caleb how adversarial their relationship had been. "You'll let me stay on the farm?"

"Why not? The cabin's empty." He'd gone through it two days ago, but it seemed cold and barren without Gen and the girls filling it with noise and love. "It will be easier for you and Fleur to spend time together there than if you have to stay in town."

"Thank you, Caleb. And I mean that. It means a lot to me that you want me to spend time with Fleur." She paused for a moment. "I'm sorry I didn't tell you about Fleur's grades dropping. I shouldn't have shut you out."

"No. But I'm beginning to see your point about how, ultimately, Fleur has to be responsible. She did well this summer on her assignments, even while babysitting part-time."

Mallory laughed. "Gen's girls sound like quite a pair. Fleur loved babysitting them."

"She did." He missed those girls. Missed seeing them riding their bikes up and down the drive. Missed their giggles, and even their bickering. Almost as much as he missed their mother. But there was no point in letting his mind go there. "I'll keep you up-to-date on Fleur's school stuff. Maybe you can be here for parent-teacher conferences and that kind of thing, or if not, we can video chat."

"That will be good. You know, I'm starting to think this will work out."

"Yeah?"

"Yeah. You're a lot more flexible." She chuckled. "It's almost like you've been spending time with a counselor or something."

"Mallory..." he said in a warning voice.

"Okay. But seriously. I like Gen, as a counselor and as a person. Fleur does, too. I don't know what happened between the two of you—"

"And you never will."

"Whatever. But, Caleb, don't let a good thing slip away over something trivial. If it's just that Gen lives in Anchorage or that she has a master's degree or something—"

"It's not."

"Okay. I'll leave it there, then. I only want you to be happy." She sounded sincere. Maybe marriage had mellowed her.

"Thank you. And speaking of happiness,

congratulations on your marriage. Hope the honeymoon went well."

"Very. Thailand was beautiful. If you ever find yourself planning a honeymoon, I highly recommend it."

"Unlikely."

"All right, then. I'll make plans with Fleur and have her back the day before school starts. Take care of yourself, Caleb."

"You, too." He ended the call and took a moment to breathe. He wasn't going to lose his daughter. And now he had a mother, too. A grandmother for Fleur. Family. It had all worked out better than he could have hoped.

And that hollow ache inside his chest? It would go away. In time.

"I WANT TO take German instead of Spanish third period." The student at Gen's desk didn't waste any time on chitchat. Which was good since she had a whole line of students outside wanting to change their class schedules.

"Let me check if there's room in that class." The odds weren't good since just an hour ago Gen had transferred a girl into the last available slot, but it was possible someone had moved out in the meantime. "No, sorry, it looks like German is completely full."

"But I need out of Spanish. I only signed

BETH CARPENTER

up for it last spring because my girlfriend was taking it, but we broke up over the summer."

Gen could sympathize. At least she didn't have to sit in the same classroom as Caleb every day, thinking about what might have been if only... She pushed the thought away and focused on her job, checking the computer for more classes. "I could get you into German fifth period, but that would mean I'd have to change your PE to third period basketball."

"No, all my friends are in flag football fifth period."

"Well, looks like you're stuck. You can check back later this week to see if any slots open in third period German, but I doubt they will. I'm sorry."

He grunted an acknowledgment, grabbed his books and headed out.

Gen stepped to the door and checked the list. "Purington? Jill Purington?"

"Here." A blonde girl got up from her chair.

Gen was responsible for students with last names beginning with $O-Z$, which she found amusing since she'd once read that L. Frank Baum had invented the name of his magical kingdom of Oz based on the label on a file cabinet. It seemed appropriate, since Gen, like the heroine of his story, felt like she'd been uprooted and swept from the farm into a strange new land. Only in Gen's case, the farm had been full of color and light, and it was the new land that felt brown and drab.

That wasn't a fair analysis. Her job was a bit hectic on the first day of school, as the students all seemed to have changed their minds about what they wanted to study this year, but it was good working with them all the same. It would be rewarding to put that theory she'd been studying for the past two years to practical use. Her coworkers and principal seemed nice. Evie and Maya liked their teachers. Even the kittens seemed to have settled happily into the new apartment, and especially enjoyed the wide window ledge in the living room, where they could watch the world go by.

But something was missing. Not something. Someone. At least a dozen times a day, something would happen and her instinctive reaction would be to share it with Caleb. Like the Oz thing—Caleb would get a kick out of that. If he was speaking to her.

Should she try to contact him? Everything had happened so fast she never even had the chance to tell Caleb she was sorry. She'd known how he felt about lies and secrets, but she'd kept this one anyway. She'd messed up. But wasn't she always telling students that messing up was part of learning and growing? To own the mistake, apologize and then do better next time? Maybe she should take her own advice.

"Ms. Rockford?"

"Oh, sorry, Jill." Gen smiled at the student across from her. Gen had worked hard to get this job, and she owed it to herself as well as to the students to give them her full attention. "What can I help you with today?"

DEW STILL CLUNG to the unfurling coral petals of the JF-143C peonies in the experimental garden when Caleb walked through on Saturday morning. He reached for his ever-present secateurs, the ones Vickie had given him, and cut a half dozen stems. Vickie had reached that point in her recovery when she was getting restless. A few flowers might cheer her up. He slipped in the back door and stopped in the laundry room to collect a vase. Through the open door, he could hear Fleur's voice.

"…new boots are so cool. I'll send you a picture." There was a pause and he realized Fleur must be talking on her phone. She laughed. "The lockers are twice as big, so I don't think it's going to be a problem. You know it's a combination junior high and high school, right? Yeah, Mark and his brother Matthew are both going there this year." Another pause while he reached for the vase on the top shelf of the cabinet over the washer. "Dad's okay. Kinda grumpy, but whatever. I'm so glad I'm not in Atlanta. Mom says it's like a steam sauna there right now."

So she wasn't talking to her mother. Caleb nodded a greeting as he moved into the kitchen and took the vase to fill at the sink. A faint look of guilt flashed across Fleur's face, followed by one of defiance. "Dad just walked in. Okay, I will. Bye." She ended the call and raised her chin a fraction when she turned to Caleb. "Gen says hello."

The quick stab of regret hardly hurt at all. At least that was what Caleb told himself, as he tried to maintain a neutral expression. "That's nice."

"I was only calling her to tell her how Vickie's doing and about school and everything," Fleur said quickly.

Caleb popped peony stems into the vase and set it on the kitchen table. They would be fully open in a few hours in the warm room. "You don't have to explain. I don't mind if you call Gen. I know she's your friend." Now he'd become the liar. Because the truth was, he was jealous. Jealous that his daughter was free to talk to Gen when he'd effectively cut off any chance of communication.

Fleur grabbed her phone. "I'm taking a shower." As she started up the stairs, Vickie came in the front door.

"Good morning." She carried a cluster of delphiniums and monkshood from the perennial garden in the side yard. "Looks like we had the same idea. Your mother always had a house full of flowers in the summer." Vickie frowned at the peonies in the vase. "These are already opening. Is your cold room malfunctioning?"

"No, no. These aren't from the cold room. They're fresh cut from the garden."

"And just now blooming? What variety is this and why am I not growing it?" She bent forward to examine the buds more closely.

"Because it's not on the market yet. I bred it."

"You did?" Vickie turned to him in amazement. "I had no idea you'd started a breeding program. And you have a new, late-blooming coral? That's fantastic! You should patent it."

He laughed. "I did, a few years ago. I'm in partnership with a development company now. If the trials go well this year, they'll put it into commercial production and pay me a royalty on every sale."

"Oh, Caleb, that's wonderful!" Vickie hugged

him. "When will you find out how the trials went?"

"Anytime now. I've gotten preliminary data from last spring regarding their performance as two-year-old crowns. Good overall, although they didn't thrive in the warmer parts of zones seven and eight."

"That makes sense. If you bred them here, they would have a high chilling requirement."

"Exactly. They seem to do well throughout most of the Midwest and North, though, as well as in Canada."

"Prime peony country." She beamed. "This is so exciting. Why didn't you tell me about this sooner?"

He shrugged. "I don't know. Guess I was afraid I'd jinx it." He hadn't told anyone. Apart from Gen. He wasn't sure why, except that Gen had that way about her that encouraged people to share their private ambitions and feelings. And then it hit him. He'd been keeping secrets, too. Maybe a new peony variety wasn't on the same scale as giving a baby up for adoption, but he'd confided in Gen, knowing she would be discreet. Same with finding the adoption papers. She'd encouraged him to tell Fleur, but she hadn't told anyone else. How could he expect Gen to keep his secrets but fault her for keeping Vickie's?

"What?" Vickie asked.

Caleb shook his head and returned his attention to her. "Sorry, what did you say?"

"I asked what you're thinking about. You got this look on your face..."

"Nothing. Just something I wish I'd done differently." He didn't want to discuss this with Vickie, to make her feel like she was to blame for the breakup. "Let me find a vase for those flowers you cut." He moved into the laundry room.

Vickie continued talking through the open door. "The co-op members will be so excited once you tell them. Oh, speaking of the co-op, have you read Christabel's latest email?"

"No. I haven't checked my email yet today." He handed her a pale yellow cylinder that would set off the blues and purples of the flowers she'd picked.

"Perfect." She carried it to the sink and proceeded to fill it with water and trim the stems of her flowers. "Christabel says we've already equaled last summer's sales and we still have three weeks of shipping dates in front of us She gives the sold and preorder figures for each variety."

"Already? She's on top of things." Caleb opened the laptop computer on the built-in kitchen desk and waited for it to boot up.

"I suspect that's more due to Gen's organization than Christabel's. She mentioned what a great job Gen did with the marketing and sales while she was gone. You should forward the email to Gen and thank her on behalf of the co-op board."

"Why don't you do that?" After the way he'd treated her, Gen would probably send any email from him directly to spam.

Vickie frowned at him. "Did something happen between you and Gen? I've been wondering—"

"Nothing happened." At least nothing Caleb wanted to talk about. "Gen has moved on to her real job."

"I thought..." Vickie trailed off.

Caleb had thought so, too, but then he'd gone and blown it. Told Gen he wanted her off the farm and out of his life, over something that wasn't really her fault at all. If he could do it over again...but life didn't work that way. As his mom used to say, *You can't unboil an egg.*

His email finally popped up and he saw the message from Christabel, but more important was the one above it. "Here's something from the plant development company I partnered with. It might be about the trial results." He opened the message and read it, blinked and read it again more slowly.

"Well? Don't keep me in suspense," Vickie demanded, coming to stand behind him and look over his shoulder at the computer.

"They want it. According to their trials, the third-year production was outstanding." He chuckled. "He says some of their trial growers are brokenhearted that they agreed to destroy the crowns after the trial was over and are asking how soon they can buy new ones."

"Oh, Caleb, that's incredible news! Your mom and dad would be so proud!" She squeezed his shoulders. "We should celebrate. I'll take you and Fleur out for a fancy dinner in Anchorage."

"That's not necessary." He got up from the desk and turned to face her. "Besides, the doctor said you're supposed to take it easy for at least two more weeks."

"Doctors!" Vickie rolled her eyes, looking so much like Fleur that Caleb wondered if eye-rolling was an inherited trait. "All right, then, we'll celebrate here. I'll make a cake." She held up a hand when he started to protest. "Correction—I'll sit quietly in a chair and coach Fleur on how to make a cake. The important thing is that we celebrate your accomplishment."

"Chocolate cake?"

She laughed. "Of course."

"In that case, yes. Thank you." He kissed her cheek. "They want to talk about a name for the variety. Apparently, JF-143C isn't catchy enough. They suggest Coral Cloud."

"Nice. How about Alaskan Sunset?"

"I like it, but I wonder if it might be too close to an existing variety name. Anyway, you and Fleur can think about it. In the meantime, I'll go get our shipments ready for pickup." He tucked his laptop under his arm and started out the door.

"Caleb." Vickie waited until he turned back to continue. "Thank you. For handling my shipping for me, and for letting me stay with you while I recuperate, but most of all for letting me be part of your family. You have no idea how much it means to me."

"Hey, I'm the winner in this deal. I get cake."

Her laughter followed him outside. As he made his way to the cold room, he let the news sink in. Within a few years people all over the country would be growing his peony, including, he suspected, most of the peony farms in Alaska. The dream he'd worked toward for so many years was coming true. Tonight he would celebrate with Vickie and Fleur. So why wasn't he on top of the world?

In the foyer of the cold room, he pulled up

the current orders on the computer and got out the boxes and packing materials he would need, meanwhile thinking back to other celebrations that summer. Like the Fourth of July party Gen threw at the cabin. His birthday, when Gen and the girls had joined them for cake and ice cream after Evie's dramatic bicycle crash. The picnic at the falls before they'd run into the bears. What made them all special was sharing them with Gen.

Gen was the person he'd thought of first when he saw the email. The one person he'd confided in about the trials. Without her, success seemed hollow and meaningless. But what could he do? He'd sent Gen away. Boiled the egg, spilled the milk, burned the bridge, whatever.

Was it too late? Was there any chance Gen would forgive him? Really, what did he have to lose by trying? Nothing. But if he succeeded, if Gen agreed to let him back into her life—to let him once again experience that sense of peace that only seemed to exist when he was close to her—it would mean everything.

But he would only get one chance. He had to make this good.

CHAPTER SEVENTEEN

"THE RED RIBBON is Lacey's favorite." Maya's voice drifted from the girls' room. It was Saturday, and they were enjoying a day off from school.

"Cats can't see colors," Evie replied. "It said so in a book at school."

"Okay, but this is still Lacey's favorite ribbon. Can you tie a bow for me?"

"All right. Give it here."

Gen, who was busy folding her third basket of laundry today, doubted that the kittens enjoyed bows as much as the girls did, but decided not to intervene. Both kittens had shown themselves perfectly capable of escaping if the girls' affection became overwhelming. Gen had already vacuumed and dusted the apartment, including the high shelves in the garage that no one seemed to have cleaned in the last decade. She'd scrubbed the bathroom, inventoried the refrigerator and made a tentative shopping list for tomorrow. She'd read an article about cooking a week's worth of dinners on the weekend to save time after work, but she hadn't yet decided whether she was willing to sacrifice a half day tomorrow to the project. Sunday afternoons were supposed to be family time.

Someone knocked at the door. The peephole revealed her mom. "Hi." Gen let her in and gave her a hug. "Girls, your grandmother is here."

"Grandma!" They came dashing in, both carrying kittens decked out with bows as big as their heads.

"Hi there. I was on the way to the craft store for more yarn, and I thought my two favorite girls might like to go along and pick out some craft we could work on at my house this afternoon." She turned to Gen. "Would that be okay with you?"

"Sounds great. I might just take a long soak in the tub."

"Oh no, don't do that. Tanner said something about dropping by this afternoon." Mom's eye traveled over the faded sweats and oversize T-shirt Gen had put on that morning before she'd started cleaning. "You might want to change clothes."

Gen laughed. "Tanner has seen me in sweats before."

"At least wash your face. You have a smudge right…" Mom pointed to her cheek.

"All right. When will you have the girls back?"

"I don't know. Why don't you dress up and we can go out for dinner tonight? We could do Italian."

Their usual Italian restaurant wasn't really a dress-up sort of place, but maybe Mom had somewhere else in mind. "Sounds delicious."

"Great. I'll give you a call later, then, and we can make plans."

"You mentioned dressing up. Do you want to take extra clothes for Evie and Maya?" They both wore leggings and tops featuring cartoon characters.

"Oh no." Mom waved her hand. "They're fine. Come on, girls. Let's hit the craft store." She ushered them out of the apartment.

Huh. Gen wasn't quite sure what that was all about, but she ducked into the bathroom and checked her reflection. Sure enough, dirt streaked across her cheek, and a cobweb was caught in her ponytail. She washed her face, took down her hair and ran a brush through it to remove any traces of cobwebs or their makers.

Now what? The house was clean, the girls were with their grandmother, and while there was plenty of work awaiting her at the school, Gen had no desire to spend her Saturday there. She realized she'd spent the past week and a half drowning herself in busywork so that she wouldn't have time for regrets.

But the what-ifs had still sneaked in. What if Gen had refused to keep Vickie's secret and insisted Vickie tell Caleb immediately? Or what if, when the thought occurred to her that Vickie might be Caleb's mother, Gen had kept her suspicions to herself? What if, that very first day, Gen had turned down Caleb's job offer? Would she be happier now?

Probably, but she still wouldn't do it. She wouldn't trade the past summer's experiences for anything. Maybe loved and lost wasn't all it was cracked up to be, but knowing Caleb was out there, growing beautiful flowers and raising a wonderful daughter—that alone was worth the pain of loss. At least that was what she tried to tell herself.

A knock sounded at the door. Mom hadn't mentioned why Tanner was coming by but knowing him it was probably to drop off something for his nieces. Gen hoped it wasn't something huge. She'd already insisted the enormous dollhouse he'd gotten the girls two Christmases ago needed to stay at his house rather than fill her new apartment's entire living room. The bicycles were taking up most of the walking space beside her minivan in her one-car garage. If Tanner had brought a life-size polar bear or something, he could just take it home again.

She opened the door without checking through the peephole, but it wasn't Tanner waiting on the other side. Instead, the doorway was filled with a mass of coral blooms so big it hid the face of the person holding them. But she knew those work boots. "Caleb!"

The flowers lowered to reveal his face, looking at her with a question in his eyes. "I have something for you. May I come in?"

"Sure." She stepped back to allow him inside. Was he bringing her flowers? Hope surged, but she tamped it down. He might just be here on co-op business. But he had brought that huge bunch of peonies. "Are these the JF-143Cs? They're even more beautiful than the ones in the greenhouse!" They were huge, each blossom the size of a salad bowl, and they filled the apartment with a heavenly scent.

"You remember the name." He seemed surprised and pleased about that.

"Of course." As though she could forget anything that important to him. "Have you heard any more from your partner about the trials?"

"Yes. I'll tell you about that. But first, where shall I put these?"

"The flowers are for me? All of them?" There had to be at least three dozen stems. Was this his way of telling her she was forgiven?

"Yes. All of them."

"Let me see what I can find. Here's one vase." A blue one that had caught her eye at a garage sale sat on one end of the fireplace mantel. She filled it with water, and Caleb stuffed it full of flowers, but it hardly made a dent in the total. Before they were done, every pitcher, mixing bowl and even teapot had been pressed into service. Flowers covered every available surface. "These are absolutely breathtaking. Thank you, Caleb."

"You're welcome. I, uh—" He looked nervous, as though he might be ready to bolt. She couldn't have that, not until he'd told her what this visit meant.

"Can I get you something to drink?" She opened the refrigerator. "Let's see. I have milk or orange juice. Or I could make tea, uh, in mugs since the teapot is otherwise occupied."

He laughed. "Thank you, but no. I don't need anything. I just— I don't know where to start."

"Let's sit down." She indicated her living

room. He sat on the couch, and she joined him there since it was the only seating in the room. She leaned forward to examine the peonies in a bowl on the coffee table. Deep coral petals made up the outer edges of the blossoms, gradually changing to rich peachy tones in the center. A few drops of deep maroon marked the heart of the flower. Each individual flower was a bouquet in itself. "Tell me about the trial results."

"My partner is happy. Other than in a few marginal areas that don't get enough winter chill, JF-143C produced well over the entire country. They want to start commercial production immediately."

"Oh, Caleb." Gen put her hand over her heart. "I'm so pleased. Congratulations!"

"Thank you. They want to change the name, of course, to something more marketable."

"What do they want to call it? Something about peaches or coral seas or alpenglow?"

"Alpenglow would be an excellent name, but I have a better one, if you agree."

"If I agree? What do I have to do with it?"

"Everything." He reached for her hand. "I want to name the peony Genevieve. After the most beautiful and loving woman I've ever known."

Gen blinked back tears. "Oh, Caleb. Does

this mean—" A sudden thought struck her. "Me, beautiful?" She laughed, looking down at her ancient sweatpants. "This is why my mom kept trying to get me to change clothes. The two of you are in cahoots!"

"Yes," he admitted. "I asked Debbie if she could take the girls so we could talk." He reached up to cup her face with his hand. "And you are beautiful, no matter what you're wearing."

"As usual, I should have listened to my mother." She leaned into his hand, reveling in the feel of his palm cupping her cheek. She'd missed it so much. "But seriously. This is your life's work. Are you sure you want to name it after me?"

"Surer than I've ever been about anything."

"Does this mean you forgive me for not telling you the truth about your birth mother?"

"There's nothing to forgive. Vickie explained why she never told me, and I've come to realize that with your integrity, you had no choice. You had to keep her secret. No, the question is, can you forgive me? I'm the one who overreacted."

There was no doubt in her mind. "Of course I forgive you."

"Are you sure? Because I'm not sure I deserve it. I wouldn't blame you if you'd changed your mind about me. It took some major groveling before your mother agreed to help me."

Gen chuckled. "Well, she is my mother, and you did hurt me. But I'm sure she agreed because she knows that I've never stopped loving you."

"Gen." He said her name like it was a precious thing. "You have no idea how relieved I am to hear that. Because I couldn't stop loving you, either. I've missed you, so much." And then he was holding her, and the world was bright again. She twined her arms about his neck, pulling him closer. Needing him. It felt so good, so right. Their lips came together.

Crash! She looked up to see Velvet perched on the windowsill, looking completely unconcerned about the blue vase now lying in three pieces on the floor, with the flowers and petals scattered everywhere. Lacey jumped up beside her and rubbed her head against Velvet's neck and then turned to blink her blue eyes at Gen, as though chiding her for displacing them from their favorite sunning spot.

Caleb laughed. "Pretty demanding for a couple of barn cats."

"Oh, they're spoiled house cats now, and they've claimed that windowsill as theirs." Gen went to the kitchen for a towel. "I'd better take care of that water before it ruins the hardwood.

It's a good thing it's a garage sale vase and not a valuable antique."

"Too bad, though. It was pretty." Caleb picked up the broken pieces so that Gen could wipe up the spill. When she was done, she took the flowers to the kitchen to transfer them to a water glass, taking a moment to admire the incredible blossoms. Genevieve. He wanted to name these flowers, his life's work, after her. Once they had been named, there was no going back. Caleb would be dealing with Genevieve peonies for the rest of his life. Now, that was a commitment. But was it enough?

When she turned, she saw Caleb standing at the table, fitting together the broken pieces of the vase. She came up behind him and laid a hand on his shoulder. "Caleb, I hate to spoil the moment, but you once said love wasn't enough. I have to know, after all this with Vickie, can you trust me? Really, deep in your heart? Or will you always wonder if I'm lying to you?"

"I trust you." He met her eyes. "Fully and completely. You've demonstrated your true character over and over. I'm just sorry it took me so long to understand that." His eyes flickered down to the table and then back to her. "This break isn't so bad. I think, once it's mended, it will be as strong as ever." From his expression, she knew they weren't really talking about the vase.

She cradled his face between her hands and brushed a kiss across his lips. "Maybe even stronger."

CHAPTER EIGHTEEN

GEN TOOK THE familiar exit in Willow, only to bounce over a pothole, jarring the pet carrier. Velvet screeched her disapproval. Even Lacey, normally silent, added an annoyed meow. Gen chuckled ruefully. After two months of making the trip every weekend, the minivan could practically drive itself from their apartment in Anchorage to the peony farm, and yet she hit that same pothole every time. It had almost become a positive, a sign they were only five minutes from the farm. Only six minutes from Caleb's arms.

"Maya's rubbing the makeup off her nose," Evie announced from the backseat.

"Am not," Maya protested, although a glance at the rearview mirror confirmed to Gen that she most certainly was. "Besides, it itches."

Gen knew she should have waited until they got to the farm to get the girls into their Halloween costumes, but Maya and Evie had wanted Fleur and Caleb to get the full effect as soon as they arrived.

"Now your dog nose is all cattywampus," Evie told Maya.

"I'm not a cat. I'm a dog!"

"No, cattywampus means crooked," Evie announced with all the authority of a second grader addressing a first grader. "My teacher says the map in our classroom is cattywampus."

They arrived at the farm. The first snow of the season covered the bare fields. After frost Caleb had cut all the peony foliage and hauled it away, to discourage any diseases that might try to gain a foothold in his crops. Now the roots rested, waiting for next year's warmth and sunlight when they would once again spring into life.

At the farmhouse an orange-and-black bow decorated the front gate, with a fake cobweb stretched in the corner of the trellis overhead, complete with a friendly-looking spider. Vickie's contribution, Gen suspected.

When Gen pulled the car to a stop, Thor was waiting. Gen and Caleb had never quite decided if Thor recognized the sound of her car from the road or was a canine psychic, but according to Caleb, Thor always stationed himself by the front gate several minutes before they arrived. Gen and the girls climbed out of the car. Gen grabbed a tissue and cleaned up the streaks of makeup on Maya's face, then dabbed a little more black onto the end of her nose. Meanwhile, Fleur and Vickie spilled out of the house and came to greet them with hugs. Although Vickie had moved back to her own home, she spent a lot of time here.

"You look fantastic!" Fleur exclaimed. "Evie, you make a perfect unicorn and, Maya, you look just like Thor!"

Both girls beamed under Fleur's praise. Gen's mom had designed and sewn the costumes for them. She'd managed to find curly brown fake fur fabric that did indeed look an awful lot like Thor's coat and sewn it into a jumpsuit for Maya, complete with a hood with long, floppy ears. Evie's costume used a soft white velour with a mane of pastel ribbons and a stuffed silver horn attached to the forehead of her hood. Both costumes were loose enough to go over a snowsuit, if necessary. Gen had added appropriate face paint.

"You two are adorable," Vickie declared.

"I need a picture of you both with Thor," Fleur decided. "Stand right here by the gate." Fleur was posing the girls for their photo when Caleb came around the corner of the house from the direction of the greenhouse.

The instant he spotted Gen, his face broke into a broad smile, and he walked faster. "I thought I heard a car." He opened his arms and Gen stepped into the warmth of his embrace. They kissed, keeping it brief since the girls were around, but it was a little taste of more to come later. Gen closed her eyes and breathed in, taking in Caleb's unique scent of earth and sky and man. The cares of the week floated away.

"Dad! Come look at Evie's and Maya's costumes," Fleur called.

With a smile of apology Caleb released Gen and walked to the gate. "Well, I see Evie as a very cute unicorn, but where is Maya? Wow, there are two Thors. Somebody cloned the dog!"

Maya giggled. "It's me!"

"It is you! Look at that. I couldn't tell who was who." Nothing he could have said would have made Maya happier. Evie looked a little jealous that she hadn't come up with the idea, but she was placated when Caleb asked her to turn around so that he could admire the multicolored mane and tail of her unicorn costume. The people at Francine's senior apartments were holding a fall carnival fundraiser this afternoon, and the girls couldn't wait to attend. According to Francine, they could expect all kinds of old-fashioned games like ring toss, cakewalks and fishing for prizes.

"Aren't you gonna wear a costume?" Evie asked Fleur, who was dressed in black yoga pants and a long-sleeved black T-shirt, but with a silk-flower lei around her neck.

"I can't sit in my costume, so I have to wait until we get there."

Gen laughed. "That sounds elaborate. What is this costume?"

"It's a dice. Die. Whatever you call one of them. Mark and I are wearing matching costumes to a party tonight."

"A pair of dice. A great couple's costume. But where does the lei come in?"

Fleur touched the lei and grinned. "Think about it."

"Okay, you're dice. With a lei. A Hawaiian pair of dice. Oh, I get it. Hawaiian Paradise! Very clever!"

"Thanks! The costume contest at the party has a pun category, so we thought we'd give it a try."

"I'd give that idea the prize for sure," Gen told her.

"Don't forget your other big surprise," Vickie reminded Fleur.

"Oh, yeah. Come look!" Fleur herded everyone through the house and into the kitchen, where the biggest pumpkin Gen had ever seen was taking up most of the room on the newspaper-covered kitchen table.

"Oh, wow." Maya stopped and stared.

"It's ginormous!" Evie squealed and ran toward the pumpkin. "Where did you get it?"

"From the Sullivans' farm. They won this year's competition for biggest pumpkin at the Alaska State Fair. The winner weighed sixteen hundred pounds. This one was one of their rejects. It's only eighty pounds."

"Are you gonna make a jack-o'-lantern?"

Caleb patted the pumpkin. "It's pretty tough. I think someone would need power tools to carve this one."

"But we can paint it," Fleur told the girls. "You want to help me later?"

"Yes!" the girls yelled in unison.

"Right now, lunchtime. What would you say we get something from the Now and Forever Farm food truck?" Vickie asked the girls, who enthusiastically agreed, since they loved the fruit and cheese kabobs from there. "Great. Then we can hit the carnival when it opens at one."

Gen started to follow, but Caleb reached for her hand. "I wanted to talk with you about something. How about if we meet them there a little later?"

"Okay, sure." Gen reached into her pocket for her keys. "Vickie, why don't you take my minivan rather than wrestling with the booster seats?"

"Thanks." Vickie accepted the keys and shot Caleb a conspiratorial smile. "See you in a bit."

Fleur looked smug, too, as she shepherded the girls outside, carrying a cardboard box she'd covered with white contact paper with different numbers of black spots on each side. Once they were gone, Gen turned to Caleb, her eyebrows risen. "Why do I get the idea there's a conspiracy going on here?"

"Because you're intelligent and perceptive," Caleb answered without hesitation. He pulled her into his arms for another kiss, this one not so brief. "Not to mention beautiful and loving and—"

"Stop." Gen chuckled. "I can only take so much flattery. What are the three of you planning now?"

He kissed her once more before releasing her. "We were talking about Thanksgiving. I know it's a lot, but we were thinking we could have it here at the farm this year, with all your family and Vickie."

"That would be perfect."

He tilted his head. "What do you think of

also inviting Mallory and her new husband? Would that make things awkward?"

"I love that idea. It would be nice for Fleur to be able to celebrate with both her parents." Mallory and her husband had stayed in the cabin for several days the week before, and Gen knew Fleur had enjoyed the time with her mother.

"Good. I wanted to make sure you didn't have any objections before I said anything to Mallory."

"Not at all. I think it's great you and Mallory are getting along better."

Caleb shrugged. "And all it took was for her to move four thousand miles away."

Gen laughed. "Oh, by the way, I have some good news. Or if not news, at least a possibility. The principal at Fleur's school called yesterday. It seems their counselor is planning to retire at the end of the school year and the principal was feeling me out to see if I'd be interested. I'm not sure how she found out about me, but I do know she and Vickie are friends."

"What did you tell her?"

"I said I would jump at the opportunity. She sent me a link, and I just need to turn in my application to the Mat-Su School District system."

"That's great news!"

She held up a warning hand. "I'm trying not to get ahead of myself. People sometimes change their minds about retirement, or the principal could choose someone else, but—"

"Whatever happens it will work out just the way it's supposed to." Caleb reached for her hand. "Come with me. I want to show you something." He led her to the desk on the other side of the kitchen and opened his laptop. Once he was past the security screen, a page loaded with several glamorous pictures of coral peonies. "New Variety" flashed at the top of the page, and the tagline read, "Meet Genevieve, a new peony destined to become a classic." The rest of the write-up went on to describe all the positive traits that made the variety unique.

Gen clicked on one of the photos to blow it up and then cycled through the rest. "Oh, these are gorgeous pictures." They'd captured all the subtle shading of the flowers as well as the graceful shape of the bush.

Caleb leaned over with his arms around her shoulders. "This catalog is for wholesale nurseries," he explained. "So far sales are strong."

"Of course they are. Who wouldn't want to grow these beauties?" Gen put her hands over Caleb's and hugged them to herself. "I still can't believe you named them after me."

"It's the perfect name. And you're the perfect woman."

She laughed. "I'm far from perfect."

"You're perfect for me. And that's why I wanted your opinion of one other thing about Thanksgiving."

"What's that?"

"Would that be a good time to make a formal announcement?"

"Announcement? What kind of announcement?"

But he had pulled something from his pocket and dropped to one knee beside her chair. "Genevieve Rockwell, will you marry me?"

"Oh!" Her hand flew to her mouth as she took in the sparkling diamond. "What a beautiful ring!"

"It was my mother's. We could reset it if you want something different—"

"No. I couldn't imagine a more perfect ring."

"Does this mean—"

"Yes!" Gen tugged him to his feet and threw her arms around him. "Yes, Caleb DeBoer, I will marry you!"

After a long and thorough kiss, she looked up at him. "You realize this will make us parents of three daughters."

"Three daughters." He nodded, a look of satisfaction on his face. "It's a good start."

"A start?" She raised her eyebrows. "What are you thinking here? Are we talking about expanding the family?"

He grinned. "I wouldn't be opposed to the idea."

Images ran through her head. Caleb driving two hours at the last minute to attend a counselor meeting for his daughter. Caleb carrying Evie after her bicycle fall and so tenderly bandaging her scraped knee. Teasing Maya by pretending he couldn't tell her from the dog and making her smile. Then Gen pictured him in the rocking chair on the porch, looking out across the fields of peonies with a baby in his lap. Their baby. She smiled, too. "It's a definite possibility."

"Let's see if the ring fits." He slid it onto her finger, where it nestled as though it was made for her.

Gen loved the way the round diamond and wide golden band looked on her hand. "It's a perfect fit."

"I got it resized. Fleur sneaked one of your other rings onto a sizer thing Vickie gave her."

"What a wonderful surprise." Gen laughed. "See, sometimes secrets can be good."

"Sometimes. But it's no secret that I love you."

"I love you, too. And I love Fleur, and Vickie, and Thor and this farm…" She rose on her tiptoes and brushed a kiss across his lips. "Because they're all part of who you are." She pulled him closer for another long kiss until a yowl sent Thor scrambling across the kitchen floor to cower behind Caleb. Someone must have let the kittens loose in the house before they left. She chuckled. "Poor Thor. He's going to have to put up with Velvet and Lacey full-time."

"He'll adjust. We all need to learn to face our fears. Speaking of adjustments, if you don't get the counselor job at the school here next fall, how will we handle that?"

Gen thought about it. "We have options. I'll apply in Wasilla and Palmer, too. And if I can only find a job in Anchorage, I suppose we could go on as we have for a while, with me and the girls living in Anchorage and getting together every weekend." She touched his face. "I know that's a sore spot for you. If you really want me to quit—"

"No. You've worked too long and hard to give up your job because of some old insecurity of mine. Besides, there's no need." He looked deep into her eyes. "I trust you, Gen.

One hundred percent. I know you love me. I can feel it, whenever we're together and even when we're not. You take the job that's best for you, and we'll work out the details together."

"Together. I love that." And then the most amazing idea occurred to her. "I know! Let's get married in your experimental garden at the end of next summer when all the Genevieve peonies are in bloom. Wouldn't that be glorious?"

"I can't think of anything more glorious." He kissed her forehead, and then her nose, and just before their lips met again, he whispered, "Other than you."

* * * * *

For more great Alaskan romances from Beth Carpenter and Harlequin Heartwarming, visit www.Harlequin.com today!

COUNTRY LEGACY COLLECTION

Get 4 FREE REWARDS!

We'll send you 2 FREE Books <u>plus</u> 2 FREE Mystery Gifts.

FREE
Value Over
$20

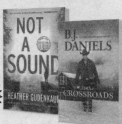

Both the **Romance** and **Suspense** collections feature compelling novels written by many of today's bestselling authors.

YES! Please send me 2 FREE novels from the Essential Romance or Essential Suspense Collection and my 2 FREE gifts (gifts are worth about $10 retail). After receiving them, if I don't wish to receive any more books, I can return the shipping statement marked "cancel." If I don't cancel, I will receive 4 brand-new novels every month and be billed just $7.24 each in the U.S. or $7.49 each in Canada. That's a savings of up to 28% off the cover price. It's quite a bargain! Shipping and handling is just 50¢ per book in the U.S. and $1.25 per book in Canada.* I understand that accepting the 2 free books and gifts places me under no obligation to buy anything. I can always return a shipment and cancel at any time. The free books and gifts are mine to keep no matter what I decide.

Choose one: ☐ **Essential Romance**   ☐ **Essential Suspense**
                  (194/394 MDN GQ6M)   (191/391 MDN GQ6M)

Name (please print)

Address   Apt. #

City   State/Province   Zip/Postal Code

Email: Please check this box ☐ if you would like to receive newsletters and promotional emails from Harlequin Enterprises ULC and its affiliates. You can unsubscribe anytime.

Mail to the Harlequin Reader Service:
IN U.S.A.: P.O. Box 1341, Buffalo, NY 14240-8531
IN CANADA: P.O. Box 603, Fort Erie, Ontario L2A 5X3

Want to try 2 free books from another series? Call 1-800-873-8635 or visit www.ReaderService.com.

Visit
ReaderService.com
Today!

As a valued member of the Harlequin Reader Service, you'll find these benefits and more at ReaderService.com:

- Try 2 free books from any series
- Access risk-free special offers
- View your account history & manage payments
- Browse the latest Bonus Bucks catalog

Don't miss out!

If you want to stay up-to-date on the latest at the Harlequin Reader Service and enjoy more content, make sure you've signed up for our monthly News & Notes email newsletter. Sign up online at ReaderService.com or by calling Customer Service at 1-800-873-8635.

RS20